OATH OF SUBMISSION

A DARK MAFIA ROMANCE

DEVIANT DOMS
BOOK 7

JANE HENRY

Photography by
WANDER AGUIAR

J HENRY PUBLISHING INC

Copyright © 2022 by Jane Henry

All rights reserved.

No part of this book may be reproduced in any form or by any electronic or mechanical means, including information storage and retrieval systems, without written permission from the author, except for the use of brief quotations in a book review.

Cover art by Popkitty Designs

SYNOPSIS

She's left me two choices: ***Take her life or marry her.***

When Marialena Rossi sauntered into my life and destroyed my plans, little did she know what she was getting into. Who I am. The consequences.

She'll take my name.

Bear my children.

Submit.

No matter what, she'll learn two things: ***Vows are unbreakable, and my word is law.***

CHAPTER ONE

Marialena

I finger the sparkling amethyst crystal before I place it in the palm of my hand and hold it to the light. A ray of sunshine hits a facet. It feels as if the crystal glows in my hands. At its very core, the gem is a deep, translucent shade of lavender.

"It's beautiful," someone breathes beside me. "What is it?"

I answer without turning to see who's speaking, I'm so mesmerized by the crystal. "Amethyst. It's a violet-colored quartz. A semi-precious stone, but so powerful."

"Powerful?"

I finally turn and look into the curious eyes of a young, pretty blonde with pale blue eyes, her hair cut into a short but stylish cut. Waif-like and thin, I can see the pale blue veins at her throat. She's a full foot shorter than I am and looks like she probably has to shop in the children's section of the store for her clothes and could maybe use a cheeseburger.

"Yes, powerful," I respond. "It gives protection and security and used to be recognized as a symbol of royalty. Amethyst calms the mind and spirit and protects against nightmares." I shrug. "I keep a large one by my bed to help me sleep."

She gives me a skeptical look. "A *rock* can do that?"

I'm used to the skepticism. I have four testosterone-laden brothers.

I smile and look back at the stone. "Why not?" I ask. "Sodium chloride is a rock, and we all widely accept the beneficial qualities of salt, don't we?"

I don't hear a response. I continue.

"But you don't have to take my word for it." I've long since given up trying to convince people to believe what they can't see with their eyes or touch with their hands. And I don't need others to believe what I do. I know what I believe. I know who I am. Her doubt doesn't have anything to do with me.

She only gives me a thoughtful look and nods. "Thank you," she says softly, but I'm not sure why. I watch as she retreats to the back of the store, glancing nervously over her shoulder and adjusting the strap on her handbag.

I look back at the stone in my palm and breathe in the cleansing air permeated with burning incense. Breathe in peace, exhale stress. *Namaste* is one of my favorite stores in Boston. Just wandering in here seems to make me calmer, more centered. Windchimes softly tinkle above us, hanging from circular hooks in the ceiling. Large glass domes filled with crystals of every shape, size, and color line shelves upon shelves, and some of the less precious stones lay piled in handwoven baskets, glinting in the overhead light. Silken, hand-crafted meditation pillows with satin covers and embroidered details are scattered throughout the store, beckoning customers to rest a while and let inspiration and intuition guide them to their next purchase. And Murry, Namaste's resident goldendoodle, peacefully wags his tail in the corner of the store.

I love it here.

My bodyguard *does not.*

"Hmph," he grunted under his breath when I told him I was heading to Namaste. He was half a second away from rolling his eyes when I scowled at him and frosted my voice.

"You don't have to like it. You don't have to buy anything. Why do you hate that place so much?" Amadeo's one of our most seasoned guards, having been with us since before my father passed away.

He pursed his lips. "I don't hate the place," he said curtly. "Literally, go have a séance or whatever the fuck it is you do in there. It's that the store's design makes it impossible to keep a good eye on you. It's all narrow and dark with only one entryway." He punctuated his critique with a grunt. "Fire hazard if you ask me, especially with all that incense burning."

"Ugh, *hello,* incense is the smoke that comes *after* you blow out the flame. And you people are ridiculous," I protested. "I'm a grown woman who doesn't need *a good eye* on her. When are you going to realize that?" He fixed me with that no-nonsense look I know all too well, like he took lessons from my brothers.

"The day your brother gives the order to lift my instruction to guard you."

I rolled my eyes and scratched my forehead with my middle finger, casually flipping him the bird. "Of *course.* Right. Romeo says *jump* and you ask how high."

Cue another eye roll.

And here we are. I may be Marialena Rossi, mafia princess under the thumb of the Rossi family hierarchy, but if I want to go to Namaste, *I go to Namaste,* and anyone who wants to give me shit about it can kiss my Italian ass.

Luckily for me and unfortunately for Amadeo, I am an expert at losing my bodyguards, much to my big brothers' chagrin. So I watch. And I wait, carefully making my way toward the back of the store.

Maybe it's juvenile, but I am *so done* with the overbearing protective bullshit. I'm over having *bodyguards* and *surveillance* and everyone knowing every text I send and breath I take.

My sister-in-law Elise once fell in *love* with her bodyguard, before she married my brother. I cannot even *imagine*. It would be like kissing one of my brothers. *Ew.*

The second I catch him looking away, I duck behind a velvet curtain meant to give privacy for palm readings.

The scent of incense is nearly cloying behind the curtain, and I swear it's ten degrees hotter in here than in the shop. Maybe they think air conditioning interferes with an accurate reading or something. Considering the fact that it's July in New England, it is not exactly super comfy.

I sit on one of the two fabric-covered stools in here and flap my hands at my armpits so I don't sweat through my thin white peasant top. Should've worn the tank top.

A row of unlit but well-used candles sits on a tiny table between the two stools. Tacked in the center of the table is a bright picture of a full moon, and on the wall right near the entrance there's a poster of an open palm, drawn like a map. I know the image well. I've studied palmistry for years.

A horizontal line at the top, near the base of the fingers. *Heart line.* Right below it, curving more downward. *Head line.* The vertical line through the center of the palm. *Fate line.* And my favorite, the curved line that traces the muscle below the thumb. *Life line.*

I hear the jingle of the shop door opening, and the general buzz of conversation in the front come to a halt. I hold my breath. I've been born and raised in the Rossi family, and I know all too well the signs that someone either important or dangerous has entered a room.

"Can I help you?" someone asks, their tone guarded and concerned.

"Blonde woman." The voice is curt and deep, husky and unnerving as if the speaker hasn't had the need to speak in a very long while but when he does, he speaks as little as necessary. "Small. Blue eyes. Pink dress. She's hiding in here. You seen her?"

"No, sir, I'm sorry, I haven't."

Hiding in here? She was just wandering around shopping like a normal person a minute ago.

I listen for more people entering the store. I tuck my feet further up on the stool and hold my breath. I close my eyes so I can concentrate.

The voice continues. "Amadeo. Fancy meeting you here." Someone knows my bodyguard.

This is not good.

This is not good.

Amadeo must be frantic looking for me. I can't help but feel a little twinge of smugness at that. *Good.* Let him sweat it. Serves him right, like he's the smothering *boss* of me.

Who would enter the store who knows Amadeo?

I look around the small enclosure frantically, as if there's some magical way to transport to safety, but I don't see a way out. This is only a small, cramped hole of a place where people come to have secrets revealed and the fog of the future lifted. It isn't meant to be a hiding place.

As footsteps draw nearer, something catches my eye. In my haste, I've pushed aside a worn rug that's likely meant to cover the center of the floor. And right beneath the curve of the little throw rug, I glimpse the golden edge of a handle that almost looks like a doorknob.

A handle?

Why is there a handle in the floor?

My mama tells stories of how when I was a child, I would hide in the large family room of our home aptly dubbed The Castle, for a glimpse of Santa Claus, the Easter Bunny, or the Tooth Fairy. I knew I was supposed to be in bed. I knew I wasn't supposed to be downstairs after bedtime, and that I risked punishment. My father punished us all harshly, and often without much provocation, but I learned to grin and bear it like the rest of my siblings.

They say curiosity killed the cat. Me? I'd rather be dead and know who's behind the damn curtain already.

I was never afraid of getting caught. I was afraid of being conned.

I hear the jingle of beaded curtains being moved, and the clang of glass jars filled with candles being pushed aside.

"Sir, you can't—" She comes to an abrupt halt. I wonder why. As a woman born and raised in the mafia, I can hazard a guess.

Whoever "sir" is has just proven he *can.*

I have no time to waste. That little golden handle might be my ticket out of here. I imagine it's an exit to a hiding place, or a storage compartment. I have to move quickly.

My heart beats frantically as I reach for the handle. I lift it. I stifle a little squeal of delight when the handle quickly gives way and the entire panel rises on a hinge. It *is* a door.

But as quickly as I uncover it, I stifle a gasp and cover my mouth with my hand.

I'm not alone. Beneath the floor, crouched and hiding, the little blonde pixie with wide, terrified eyes holds a finger to her lips. Her eyes plead silently with me.

And then I know. Those heavy footsteps and that deep voice came to carry her away. She wasn't meant to be followed and found.

I know what I have to do.

I stare into her pleading eyes and nod, a promise that I'll protect her, or, at the very least, *hide* her, as footsteps draw so near to me I feel the vibration of each heavy footfall landing. I silently put the trapdoor back down, tug the rug back over it fully, and sit back on my perch. I grab a worn copy of *Palmistry Through the Ages* just as the heavy curtain's pushed aside.

I knew they were opening that damn curtain.

But there is no *they*.

There's only him. One person. And given the air of authority that surrounds him, I'm confident he doesn't need backup.

If I thought this little room was small before, I know better now. It becomes a nook instead of a room as this man's entire presence fills every inch. His hulking frame looms in front of me. So tall he hides every filament of light behind him. Black-brown hair cut shorter on the sides and longer on top. A scruffy beard covers a strong jaw and sturdy chin. I watch as a flare of recognition lights his eyes—he knows me?—but just as quickly, the look disappears and I wonder if I've imagined it, as his dark eyebrows slant in a frown.

I quickly glance at his clothes. Nice, well-made, probably custom work. But it isn't the cut of his pants or the way his white polo reveals cut, bulging biceps and shoulders too large to fit in here comfortably that catch my attention. It isn't the faint fragrance of cologne that makes me want to sniff his neck and moan, or the commanding air of authority. No.

It's those... *eyes.* I've never seen eyes so blue. They remind me of the blueness of the hot springs in Tuscany, deep cerulean eyes almost too pretty for a man. Almost. The stern, ruthless cruelty embedded in those eyes erases anything that even smacks of femininity. No. He's all male, every inch of him, and my body doesn't miss the memo.

I swallow, finding it hard to breathe. I'm glad I'm sitting down. He catches me in that gaze. I lose the ability to speak. I open my mouth, but nothing comes out.

His eyes flick from me to the palmistry chart and the book in my hand. I hope it's obvious I'm an employee, prepared to read some palms, not a mafia princess hiding from her bodyguard and nearly sitting on the head of the nameless woman I'm protecting, the very same one he's looking for.

I finally find my voice.

"Why, hello there," I say pleasantly, leveling the full wattage of my powers of flirtation at him. "Are you my two o'clock?" I'm stunned at how nonchalant I sound, but Marialena Rossi's been here a time or two. You don't have to *be* nonchalant. You just need to fake it. Thankfully he can't hear the frantic beating of my heart or feel the dampness of my palms.

He glances at his watch. "It's three twenty," he says suspiciously. "And I'm never late."

Fuck.

I smile and I really, *really* hope it's the dazzling one.

"Oh, right. I get so lost in my head sometimes I don't pay attention to the time. Time *is* so capricious, isn't it? My three thirty, then?"

I pretend like I'm going to rise from my chair and offer the other for him to sit on. Maybe if I'm casual about getting up off this chair he won't even suspect I'm hiding a full *human* beneath these floorboards.

"No." He shakes his head. "I'm looking for a woman."

I settle back on the chair and give him a coy smile. "Are you, then? Just any woman, or do you have a type in mind?" I wave my hand suggestively as if to say, *yoohoo, woman here.*

His eyes narrow dangerously. Calculating. *Heated.* I stifle a gasp as an erotic pulse of need shoots between my legs when his look grows stern.

Mamma mia.

Why, why, *why* is it always the bad ones that spark my fire? *Why?*

When the corner of his lips quirks up, showing a flash of white, I know he isn't amused. It's the look of a predator baring his teeth.

"Looking for a blonde who came in here. Smallish woman."

Play along. *Play along.* I imagine my heart races in time with hers. Is there enough air under there? Oh, God, what if she's suffocating? But no, if that's a storage room…

My voice thankfully doesn't wobble. "Oh, the one with a little pixie cut?"

"Yes. Have you seen her?"

The best way to lie to someone is to give them a few threads of truth.

"Yes, we were admiring the amethyst before I came in here. Just a brief conversation." I sigh as if sad, as if I wish I could give him better news, and try to ignore the rapid beating of my heart. Was he watching us? Did he see her talking to me? Does he know she's beneath this floor, hidden? "But I'm so sorry, I didn't see where she went."

Without a word, he turns to leave. Maybe he bought it, then.

Please, go. Go, go, go!

Against every good sense that I have, I continue to play my part. "Leaving so soon, sir? I'm happy to give you a reading."

And I'm not fully lying this time. Though I want him to go, I imagine the feel of his heavy, masculine palm in mine. I'd feast my eyes on the tendons in his forearms, the corded muscles that I could imagine wrapped around me, while I—

But no, it's only part of the innocent act.

"Maybe some other time," he lies, as the curtain falls heavily behind him and he leaves. Good. I should be glad he's left. I can breathe more easily now that he isn't taking up all the air in here. Why do I stare at the swinging velvet with a vague feeling of disappointment?

I shake my head and stand. I'm unsure of the air quality in the little hidden passageway. What if she's smothering to death in there? My hand itches to yank up the little carpet, but I can't risk opening the trapdoor quite yet. I need to be sure he's gone.

After I count a full sixty seconds silently, I pull aside the curtain and look to see if he's really gone. Instead, I catch Amadeo's furious gaze. If looks could kill... Thankfully, I see no other customers.

I hold up a finger to tell Amadeo I need just one more minute, but of course he doesn't care about *that*. Ugh, no respect. He marches straight toward me and backs me into the small enclosure.

"Oh, there you are," I begin, but he ignores me and instead grabs my wrist and begins to yank me as if to physically drag me out of the store.

"Let me go," I hiss, fruitlessly trying to pull away from him. When he doesn't budge, I try to step on his foot. "Let me go or I'll tell on you to Romeo!" My oldest brother doesn't like any man to put his hands on me, which is decidedly in my favor right about now.

"Oh, good," Amadeo says. "How convenient. That's exactly who I'm going to."

I successfully stomp on his foot. He hisses out a breath and releases my wrists long enough that I'm able to run back into the little room.

"They don't pay me enough for this. They *do not* pay me enough for this!" Amadeo grunts behind me.

"I'll tell Romeo to give you a raise," I mutter as I open the door. It's then that I realize it isn't a storage room, but a *ladder* she's standing on.

"You okay?" I ask her.

She nods, her eyes wide and terrified, and whispers two words that are impossible for me to ignore. "Help me!"

CHAPTER TWO

Marialena

Romeo pinches the bridge of his nose, closes his eyes, and exhales.

"Amadeo, you're getting a raise," he says. I nod in agreement. Yes, it sounds quite fair for Amadeo to get a raise even if he is a jerk. "Dario will be in Tuscany," Romeo says thoughtfully, almost to himself. Dario, an inductee into The Family and newly married, has been assigned to a job in Tuscany. He and his wife leave the next day.

Wait. Why does he mention that? Is he thinking of sending me away? *Again?*

Romeo opens his eyes and shakes his head. He's been looking older in recent years with hair graying at the temples, lines around his mouth, and eyes that remind me a little bit of my father. He's nothing like my father though. Some call him harsh, yes, and he's no pushover, that's for sure. But he leads our family with honesty and loyalty and has never used any of my father's bullying tactics.

"Marialena," Romeo says on a sigh. He beckons for me to draw closer. I sit in the chair and fold my hands on my knees. I do feel badly that I've caused Romeo any grief. I didn't *mean* to.

"Romeo," I begin, but he holds up a hand to stop me. My brother may love me, but he is, at the end of the day, still the leader of the most feared mob family in all of New England. Maybe even the US, especially since we've joined forces with our cousins, the Montavios, and solidified our bond through marriage when cousin Vivia married Dario, a Rossi not related by blood.

I sigh and wait for the lecture. I know what he'll say before he does. I know this so well I could recite it. He'll pull out the same words my father used to say, and my mother and my other brothers still say as well.

Your own good

Protection

Dangerous enemies

Blah, blah, blah.

I try to look repentant, but I'm still back in Namaste. I see myself handing the little blonde whose name I never got all the cash I had as Amadeo reluctantly but in no uncertain terms explained the ladder led to a secret night club which I was, under *no circumstances,* ever to enter without express permission from Romeo. Didn't stop blondie, though. It was really her only escape.

I hope she made it. I hope blue eyes didn't know more than he let on.

There's a knock at the door and a voice I recognize. "It's me."

Mario, the youngest Rossi brother and my sworn ally in everything.

"Come in."

I exhale a sigh of relief when I see him. "Thank goodness," I say. "I need an ally here!"

Mario's jovial eyes dance at me. "What'd you do now, Lena?" He tugs a lock of my hair affectionately. "Heard you got yourself in trouble and flirted with the club entrance?"

Romeo grunts. Apparently, he prefers we don't talk about *the club.*

"Hardly! I saved a poor woman running from a man who was going to hurt her, and these two are acting like I just tight-roped across a den of lions," I say with a pout. I can't help it. Mario has always given me what I wanted, the only one who really *listens* to me.

"There's more, boss," Amadeo says.

"There is!" I say, like a fractious child. "He grabbed my wrist!"

Romeo lifts a brow. "He has permission to physically restrain you if you don't do what he says and your life is in danger."

I snort. "My *life* wasn't in danger! I was in the *crystal shop*. I—"

"Salvatore Capo," Amadeo interrupts me.

The entire atmosphere of the room changes.

Romeo's demeanor shifts on a dime. He goes from concerned older brother to calculating Don in seconds. His voice chills me. "What about him?"

"He came into the shop, boss. He talked to her. She lied to him when she hid the girl."

Romeo's eyes narrow to slits as he turns to me.

Mario groans. "No, Lena..."

"Correction, little sister," Romeo hisses. "Your life *was* in danger. What were you thinking? Salvatore *Capo*, of all the fucking men you could've crossed! Do you have any idea who you're playing with?"

When Mario looks at me, I don't see the camaraderie I hope for, but fear and sadness. "Marialena," he says softly. Reproachfully. My belly churns.

"*What?*" My heart beats so fast I feel nauseous. I knew the man I saw was dangerous and powerful, but I had no idea who he was. What has he done to inspire fear in the most fearless men I know?

I've never heard the name, but my brothers' reactions tell me everything.

"Salvatore Capo was released from jail a month ago after an eight-year stint for assault, battery, and murder. The person he murdered was his betrothed. Her crime? She cheated on him."

I blink. I swallow. I try to speak, but my voice is a whisper. "How can anyone only serve eight years for that?" I ask. I shove my hands onto my lap to hide the trembling.

"Don't be so naïve. Any other man would've served life, you know that." There is no death penalty in Massachusetts. Romeo shakes his head, dismissing the question, and I understand why. I'm a Rossi. I understand how this works. With enough power and money, everything's negotiable, including jail time.

"Well, I didn't really... *do* anything."

"*Enough.*" Now Romeo *does* sound like my father, and my own temper rises.

"Way to act like our father," I say through clenched teeth. "Shutting me down and not letting me speak. You—"

"*You* have no idea who you're dealing with," Romeo says, his voice rising. "You have no idea the danger you're in." He raises a finger to make a point, and his hand trembles with anger as he lifts his phone and presses a button. His voice is tight when he orders, "Call a full meeting of the entire inner sanctum in my office. I want those overseas on video. Ten minutes. I'm calling a state of emergency."

State of emergency?

Well, shit.

A vein pulses in Romeo's temple, his cheeks flushed. "I want your side of the story. The whole truth. You tell me everything." He turns to Amadeo. "And you. We'll discuss your punishment for letting her out of your sight after you tell me your side of the story. You should've *razed the fucking city* to find her rather than let her within a fucking *mile* of Capo." He curses and fumes under his breath. "Too old for this bullshit. You hid when you were a child, Marialena, why haven't you gotten the fucking memo that you're a full-grown adult yet?" I wince at the anger in his tone.

Amadeo pales but nods. I didn't mean for him to get in *trouble*. Punishment in our family at Romeo's decree could mean anything from a beating to excommunication to a brutal, vicious death. I feel sick to my stomach and a little dizzy.

He's called everyone here.

I've messed up before, but I think this time… I think this time I may have gone too far.

"She was scared," I whisper.

Romeo scoffs. "Scared? A nameless woman you've never met asks for your help and you give up *everything* to help her? You know who should be scared?" Romeo fumes. "*You.* You have no idea what Capo's capable of. No idea what he could do. If he–" He stops himself mid-sentence. "No." He takes a deep breath. "Let's hear the story."

I had no idea, I think to myself, but a small voice in the back of my head reminds me that I did, I had a suspicion that he was someone to be feared. He knew Amadeo. Every warning bell in my mind went off and still, I *had* to just throw caution to the wind, as if somewhere in the back of my mind I knew that I'd land on my feet like a cat.

There's nothing for it now but the truth. I tell him everything in a rush of words, wishing I could take it back, wishing I could stop the room from spinning as member after member of our family enters Romeo's office stationed in the war room at the back of The Castle.

"Then he left," I finish.

Romeo nods and turns to Amadeo. "Your side."

To his credit, he tells things exactly as they happened and thankfully doesn't demonize me any further.

When we've both told our stories, we look up to see all the members of the inner sanctum— my brothers Mario, Tavi and Orlando, Mario's wife Gloria, my sister Rosa's husband Santo, and my cousin Sergio—standing around us in a semi-circle.

"Marialena's in grave danger," Romeo begins.

Gloria's eyes narrow as he tells them what happened. "He didn't know the trapdoor in the palm reading room led to the sex club? Everyone knows that."

Mario winces. "Uh, not everyone, babe."

Alright, so that's something I didn't need to know about my brother and his wife.

"Especially not someone who's spent the last eight years in jail," Tavi reminds her.

"Right."

"We're wasting time," Romeo says, shaking his head. "We need to find a safe place for Marialena. He recognized Amadeo, so he likely recognized her."

That flare of recognition in his eyes. Yeah, he knew who I was alright. *Dammit.*

I squirm.

"Marialena?" Romeo says warningly.

"Yeah, I think he knew who I was."

Romeo curses under his breath. "We can't send her to Tuscany this time. We don't have enough manpower to protect her."

"Safe house X?" Gloria says, holding Romeo's gaze. I don't even know what that means, but she hasn't given a location of the safe house, so it's either new or highly confidential.

Romeo frowns. He doesn't like that idea. "That would work as a temporary solution, but we need something more long-lasting. Capo's type hold grudges for years."

Years? Shit.

"If he realizes Marialena had anything to do with hiding the woman from him..." His voice trails off. "Gloria, I want you to go and see if you can find anything at all that hints at a potential marriage for Capo. See if we can at least identify the woman Marialena hid."

I'm still stuck on *years*.

Gloria nods and pulls out her phone, as the others continue to talk about further solutions. Their voices meld into a stream of gibberish as the reality of what I've done hits me.

I'm not safe anymore. Even my brothers—the strong, powerful men I love and trust—can't protect me now.

I've never felt so alone in my life.

I let them hash out my future and tell myself I'll do whatever they say. My heedless actions have caused enough problems as it is. And then I hear the one word that makes me come back to full attention.

"The only safe choice is probably marriage," Tavi says with a grimace.

Marriage.

Marriage!

Marriage?

I'm the only single Rossi woman left, and I've known for a while—we all have—that my marriageability and virginity make me a really, *really* hot bargaining chip. The very thought makes me sick to my stomach. I've never even really given myself permission to think too much about it, because if I did, I'd want to leave. And I love it here. I love my Nonna and Mama, my brothers and sister, my nieces and nephews and those who've married into this family. I don't want to leave them, and a part of me hoped my family was secure enough, especially after solidifying ties with our cousins, that he wouldn't *need* to marry me off.

Marriage.

My sister was married young to a man who cheated on her. My brothers have broken the mold by being faithful to their wives, but none of us are fools. We know that a typical mobster only marries for convenience. Infidelity is their bread and butter. My father and his brothers all had mistresses, and Tavi's wife, my sister-in-law Elise, has told me horror stories of the loveless marriages she witnessed in her own family.

Marriage.

The chances of me marrying anyone who would be faithful to me… who would really *love* me… are between slim and none. I'd be better off planning the life of a spinster, which doesn't really sound half bad to me…

"It might be the only way," Romeo says, stroking his chin.

He turns to Tavi. "Ottavio, I want you and Orlando to pull in all the resources you can find and compile a list of eligible men we might consider for her to marry."

"Hello!" I finally speak up, my momentary meekness forgotten. "You're talking as if I'm not right here."

"We don't have time, Lena," Mario says earnestly. "You're in mortal danger, sister."

Mortal danger? My brother doesn't use such terms lightly. He's not prone to dramatics or exaggeration. If anything, he's the one most likely to brush things off.

My stomach roils with nerves.

Mortal danger?

Outside the window of Romeo's office, I hear the sound of cars approaching the newly procured security gates out front. My stomach lurches.

Could be anyone. Delivery, my sister Rosa or Mama returning from an errand, one of the nannies come to watch one of the children.

Romeo jumps to his feet and looks out the window, then curses under his breath as every guard we have stands at attention at the gate. I peer over Romeo's shoulder to see not one, but three heavy black SUVs lined up at the gate just as Romeo's phone chimes.

This is not good.

The sense of foreboding grows in my belly. Mario closes his eyes and mutters under his breath. Orlando swears to himself in Italian. Gloria meets my eyes across the room, frantic and wide.

And I know before they tell me.

It's him. He's come. I've hardly processed what's happened and he's already shown up at my doorstep.

Romeo puts the phone on speaker.

"Salvatore Capo asks for an audience, boss," the guard says.

No.

Already? Did he follow us here? Maybe stopped for a cup of coffee to give us time to sweat it out? God!

Romeo's lips thin. He draws in a shaky breath, then releases it. "He may enter with the occupants of his car alone. The others wait outside the gate."

There's a momentary pause, and then more muffled voices. Romeo looks at me before he takes the phone off speaker and puts it up to his ear. My brother pales when the voice on the other end speaks again.

I've… never seen Romeo so pale. It feels as if the sun stopped shining, or the moon has gone away. As if something in my world is off-kilter.

"Yes," he says in a defeated tone. "Then they may come, too."

He hangs up the phone. "Capo's here. All of you to the Great Hall." He reaches for my hand. I take it, his much larger, rougher hand engulfing mine. I haven't held his hand in years.

A lump rises in my throat when he whispers to me, "I'll do everything I can. I promise. Please know I'll do everything I can."

I don't really know what he's talking about. I don't know what he means. But I've never been so afraid in my life. Something tells me Romeo's best this time won't be good enough.

CHAPTER THREE

Salvatore

I pass the gates at the Rossi family castle, impressed with the striking view of the time-worn home against the blue-green backdrop of Cape Anne. I've never been here before, but we all know about it. Passed on to the Rossis from family, The Castle is a point of pride. To this day, most of them take at least temporary residence here. Some live in Tuscany, some in Boston, and others are scattered throughout various places in New England.

I know because I've watched them. I've waited. I've bided my time.

Marialena makes her primary residence here, and that's what matters.

Marialena.

Her name means "star of the sea." Apt, then, that she lives in a castle by the sea's edge.

A woman as stunning as the name she bears. She doesn't know it yet, but she's mine. She's set this battle in motion, and now I've come to capture my spoils of war.

Petite and vivacious, the woman begs to be tamed and vanquished. *Mastered.* Her thick, wavy, dark brown hair hangs to her waist like a modern-day Italian Rapunzel, waiting for her prince to come. I imagine wrapping that hair around my fist, the silky strands like a harness I'll hold to capture her attention. I've thought more than once about those blue-gray eyes, the Grecian nose, and the whimsical chin she holds proudly with an air of defiance.

I'll enjoy breaking that defiant attitude of hers. Showing her that mafia princesses don't deserve to be spoiled.

I've done my homework. I know she's graduated college but has only dabbled in various jobs since then. Whether that's her choosing or her brothers', time will tell. She's slim and fit, well-dressed and fashionable, and makes up for her tiny frame by wearing death-defying heels. She wears Chanel and spends more on clothing than most people make in a year.

My sources tell me she also smokes weed with Mario, takes her coffee—and lots of it—black, carries a flask, and she's also an excellent shot. That doesn't matter, though. She won't be allowed to hold a gun. There won't be a need, and I won't give her a chance to turn it on *me*.

She might think about it.

She may not be who I would've chosen for a wife, if I'm honest. I imagined myself with someone more influential, or at the very least someone more docile. But she made this bed, and I don't have the time or the interest in shopping around. I know my next move, and once I do, I never hesitate to make it.

Ever.

No one makes enemies of the Rossi family, especially since they've united with the Montavios, but I know exactly how to play this. I'm not afraid of Romeo Rossi. Some say he's the most powerful Don in all of New England.

Works for me.

I don't live in New England.

He can keep his domain and I'll keep his sister.

Romeo Rossi and his band of brothers can rule these states all day long. My home's far south of here, and as long as we respect one another's boundaries, we'll get along just fine.

"Park here." My observation tells me the security gate by the Rossi home is newly installed, and when

I go to corroborate this, I find it to be true. Before I went to the big house, the Rossis were known for having ruthless Rottweilers and no security gate, one of the few families that didn't find it necessary. Interesting. I wonder what precipitated the change. I'd guess it had something to do with the extended family being added every year—wives and husbands and grandkids. The more the vulnerable and innocent among them, the more they'd need to up their protection.

I never enter a place unless I know as much about what I'm going into ahead of time as possible.

I exit the car and observe everything. Blooming roses on vines by the front door, their bloodred, velvety leaves reminiscent of the Rossi family symbol that each wear on their forearm. Rhododendrons stand, sturdy and well-maintained, in a border around the walkway that leads to the main entrance.

Something on the ground catches my attention before I get to the doorway. Frowning, I bend to investigate. A shiny golden moon, as delicate as spun glass, hangs on a thin golden chain. I pick it up and slide it into my pocket. Finders keepers.

I wonder if it's hers. Looks like the kind of shit she'd be into.

My bodyguards flank me on either side, armed and ready, though any mob worth their salt will demand they check their weapons at the door. Still, I don't like going into a confrontation without a well-armed guard. Romeo probably won't give me shit, but his mother…

The door opens before I ring the bell. None other than Romeo Rossi himself answers the door. His poker face betrays nothing.

"Capo," he says with a nod. "What'd you do to get outta the big house early, brother?" Ah, so we're playing that angle. His handshake is firm, a warning and a promise. "Heard you got sentenced to life."

I shrug and follow him into the house when he beckons for me to enter.

"My uncle knows people."

He grunts in response as we enter the hall. "Good to know people on the inside."

I don't see his other men, but I feel them nearby, armed and ready. I'm not here to fight, but if someone wants to attack me first, they're fair game. I've got three men with me. We're outnumbered, but my other men are nearby. Whenever two mob leaders are together, no matter how friendly they are, it's always a matter of two predators circling each other. There are no real friends in this war.

"We'll go to the reception room. Can I get you a drink?"

"Espresso, please." It's been a long day, and I know if anyone's gonna give me a good cup of espresso, it's the Rossis. I came with my guards and have my inner circle a phone call away, so I trust Rossi not to pull any poison bullshit on me. It's not his style anyway.

Our footsteps click on the gleaming floor. I wonder if he'll still want to offer me espresso after I tell him why I'm here. I'm ready, no matter what.

I quickly take in every detail. Main reception's circular, with a matching circular staircase to the right, and to the left, a lobby. It's magnificent and regal, impeccably clean, and well-appointed.

Romeo nods to a small side table. "Check your weapons, brother."

It's a reasonable request, and I was prepared for it. I take out three guns and a knife and slide them onto the table. Romeo raises an eyebrow. I wink at him as I take the final gun out of the hidden harness at the small of my back. He doesn't trust me, though, and nods to one of his guards to pat me down.

"Got enough of the frisking in jail, you guys feeling frisky?" No one cracks a smile.

I wonder if he'll still give me the pat-down when I'm his brother-in-law.

Beyond the lobby and reception area there's a coat room and another stairway, then the entrance to the Great Hall. Hung with flags and enrobed in stately stones, it's one of my favorite parts about the house.

I've only been here once, and it was a while ago, but I remember every detail.

"You guys still have the wine wall?"

Romeo nods. Reserved. He knows, then. I wonder what he'll try to bargain with. "We do. You're welcome to take some home."

To toast my wedding to your sister? Don't mind if I do.

"Thank you." I'll be taking more than a bottle of wine home.

In my peripheral vision, I note two armed guards in the corners of the room we're entering. Romeo himself is packing a weapon, and when I step through the doorway, four men in suits rise to meet me, all armed, all ready—Ottavio, Orlando, Santo, and Mario. It's been years, but I don't forget names.

I nod and smile at them. They don't return my smile. "Gentlemen."

"What brings you here, Capo?" Mario asks. The youngest of the Rossi brothers, he's usually the most genial, known more for his skills with women and cars than with weapons or cunning, but I've heard recently he's newly married so maybe his capers with the female breed have come to a halt. Maybe not.

"I hear congratulations are in order," I tell him, as I take a seat on a vacant sofa across from them and the door opens. I stand back up when Tosca Rossi enters bearing a tray of espresso cups. She nearly topples on her heels when she sees me, but quickly schools her features.

"If it isn't Salvatore Capo," she says, her voice cold as ice, belying the smile she's plastered on her face. I once knifed someone who'd betrayed me over brunch with the Rossis. She didn't even flinch, but also didn't hesitate to send me the bill for the carpet I'd stained with my betrayer's blood. I paid it, naturally, though it gave me a chuckle. Tosca Rossi's made of stern stuff. I'm curious how much her daughter's like her.

I sit back down and take the espresso with a smile and a nod. "Thank you."

She doesn't respond but sits opposite me, ignoring Romeo's frown of disapproval.

"Mama," Romeo says in a low voice.

"Why is he here?" she asks Romeo, though her eyes are on me. She lowers her voice. *"Porta pericolo, figliolo."*

"I'm honored, Tosca, that a woman like you who survived marriage to Narcisso Rossi and raised the most notorious made men in New England finds *me* dangerous." I sip the espresso. "It's delicious."

Her eyes narrow on me. Did she forget I speak Italian, too?

Romeo stands and places his hand on Tosca's elbow. He speaks in a hushed tone. Though she clenches her jaw and shakes her head, she allows him to lead her to the exit. She'll be back.

When Romeo returns, he stands across from me with his arms folded. "Capo."

I nod and place my espresso cup back on the tray beside me.

Here we go. I wanna crack my knuckles and smoke a cigar.

"Earlier today, I had an errand in town. I trust your guard filled you in?"

A muscle clenches in his jaw. "He did."

"Your sister Marialena was present as well. Did he tell you that?"

A barely perceptible nod.

"I was betrothed to Castellano's youngest daughter, Erica. We were to wed last night. She escaped, and my sources found her hiding in Boston. I tracked her to Namaste, and nearly caught her. You see, Rossi, marrying Erica Castellano would've been an incredibly beneficial move for my family. However, that did not happen."

The Rossi men fall silent. Watching. Listening. Waiting.

"And who do you think helped orchestrate her escape, Romeo?"

He pinches the bridge of his nose. "Go on."

"Marialena helped her escape. She exited by way of a club I didn't know existed until after she'd left."

"Did you catch her?" he asks sharply. He knows the consequences for an arranged marriage going sour. He knows the repercussions for interference in a planned joining of two Families.

"Not before she took her own life." My voice is emotionless. I didn't care about the woman. I'd never met her before.

Orlando curses. "And how do you know Marialena aided her?"

"I knew who she was when I realized your guard, Amadeo, was in the store. I knew he wouldn't have been there alone. I managed to persuade management to give me their security footage." I keep my anger in check. I don't like when my plans are thwarted, and that little brat knew exactly what she was doing. I also don't like when people lie to me.

Romeo nods, his face paling. "What do you want, Capo? How much did the deal cost you?"

"Seven million."

"Jesus," Ottavio mutters. "We can write you a check."

I turn to him sharply. "I don't want a check. I came to New England to obtain a wife. You know as well as I do the money was only icing on the cake. The point was to join the Capo and Castellano families, to form alliances." I sip my espresso. It's already cooling, but pleasantly bitter and sharp. "I will not go home without one, and I'm due to arrive home tomorrow." I wait, feeling the eyes of every man in the room on me. "Her life is mine, Romeo. You know that. I'm within my rights to take her life for interfering, and any recourse against me would start a war." I feel my anger rise. "And I don't take kindly to people lying to me."

"Who's lied to you, brother?" Romeo asks quietly.

"Marialena." Saying her name feels like a summons. I want to see her. I want her to own what she did.

No one responds. No one blinks.

"But I decided I don't want to kill her." I shake my head. "Your sister's beautiful, and my research tells me she's single and eligible." I smile as I deliver the final blow. "If I take her home tonight, none of you will be harmed. I'll even waive the promise of a dowry." It's a step I do not need to take but will, to keep a modicum of peace. I don't need the money.

"You want to take her to marry her," Romeo says, his voice hoarse. "I'll pay you more than—"

"I don't want the money, Romeo. I want your sister."

A door swings open. Marialena, wide-eyed, a little stunned, but as beautiful as I remember her, stands in the doorway. Her brothers tense and Mario half-rises from his chair, as if she was safe before she entered. They know better than that, but I can't blame their instincts.

Rosa, the eldest sister, stands beside her with a possessive grip on her arm, as if her small hand on her sister will prevent me from taking her away. Their loyalty's almost cute.

Rosa shakes her head. "We heard you," she whispered. "Marialena didn't know that woman was betrothed to you. She didn't know who you were."

"Go upstairs, Rosa." Santo, her husband, is on his feet. He knows interference won't be tolerated. But I have no need of punishing more than one Rossi woman tonight.

I shake my head. "That doesn't matter. What's done is done."

"I can't marry you," Marialena whispers, then, more vehemently, "I *won't*."

I don't respond to her but look to Romeo. He knows refusing me brings war. Blood. Devastation. Death.

Romeo Rossi's a man of honor, well-respected among his peers. Will he falter now?

He swallows and turns back to Marialena. "You have to. You've left us no choice." He hangs his head, defeated. "Rosa, help her pack a bag."

Tosca enters the room holding a tray of wine. It seems she's ready for more than espresso and needs an excuse to come back in here.

I can tell by the look on her face she hasn't heard the news yet.

"Mama," Romeo says, his voice still husky. "Help Marialena pack. She'll be going home with Capo tonight."

"What?"

Romeo's voice rises, betraying his emotion. "She's marrying Capo. She leaves tonight. Say your goodbyes." He looks to his sisters, his tone sharp. "I told you to go pack. *Go!*"

The tray of wineglasses falls to the floor, shattering them. No one flinches as crimson red wine splatters over the walls, the carpet, and Tosca's clothes.

"No," she whispers. "Romeo—"

He snaps, "You know the rules as well as I do." His voice has taken on the edge of a leader as he quickly loses his patience. "Go! Help her pack." He waves his hands at the girls. "Go, all of you! There is no getting out of this. There is no arguing. Don't make this any harder than it has to be." His voice shakes as he levels his angry gaze at Marialena. "I told you it would come to this eventually. I told you to stay safe, to stay out of things, but you couldn't leave well enough alone. And now, you've left me with no choice."

He frowns. *"Go.* And call someone to clean this up, Tavi," Romeo says, a bit gentler.

Tosca lifts her head. I see the tears shining in her eyes, but they don't move me. The Rossis may have disarmed me when I entered, but I'm prepared to fight if anyone interferes.

"Mama," Marialena says, her face pale. She doesn't look at me but at Tosca, begging. "Don't let them, Mama. You can't." Then she turns to her brothers. "Mario!"

Rosa tugs her hand and speaks to her in low tones, urging her to leave the room.

But Tosca's had enough.

"You," she begins, her voice laced with venom. Tosca Rossi may play nice from time to time, but it's impossible for anyone to survive marriage to Narcisso Rossi without a spine of steel. *"No.* I don't care who you are. I don't care what claim you think you have on my daughter. I've seen what my Rosa has gone through, and it will be over my dead body that you take Marialena from here."

Over her dead body. Hmm.

I look at her thoughtfully. Stroke my chin. Flick my eyes to Romeo, who's clenched his fist and taken a step closer to her. I'll let the Don handle his own. Still watching, I take another sip of espresso and watch as Romeo speaks to her in Italian, words I don't catch, but she shakes her head.

"You're no better than your father!" she screeches. "You—"

I stand, prepared for her to attack me. Italian women can go from screeching to physical violence in the blink of an eye.

But now the Rossi men have had enough. Orlando, the largest of all of them, reaches her first with a sigh and looks as if he's going to hug her but actually restrains her in his big arms. She fights and smacks at him, but he only shakes his head. "Fighting won't help," he says with an air of resignation. I blink in surprise when she ducks, kicks him hard on the shin, and the next moment lunges at me.

I'm ready, though. I duck her blow and quickly block a second as Tavi joins Orlando and they reach us just as I lift her up and restrain her with her back to my front, her arms tucked by her sides.

"Maybe," I say to her as she kicks and screams and curses at me, "you should've thought of this when you were training your daughter. Now you've left the job to me, haven't you?"

Tavi's eyes blaze at me but he takes his mother from me. Between him and Orlando, they wrestle her to the door. She sobs and pleads, half in Italian, half in English. "Let me say goodbye! Let me help her pack! Please," she begs. Her voice cracks. *"Lei è la mia bambina!"*

Romeo remains stoic. Marialena and Rosa are gone, likely unwilling to witness their mother's breakdown. The door closes behind Tosca and her sons with finality.

I sit back down and finish the last cold dregs of my espresso.

CHAPTER FOUR

Marialena

I think I'm in a state of shock. I'm not sure what that looks like, but I don't *feel* anything. My body is numb, like I've taken an ice bath and every cell has been neutralized. No, no, that's not it. I'm not numb. My heart feels as if it's breaking, I do feel that. It's my reactions that are numbed, because I don't want to make anything worse than I already have.

I heard my mother screaming. I heard her crying. I heard her tell Romeo that I'm her baby. I don't know if I'll ever forget the pleading in her words, the way her voice cracked, or the way they dragged her away. My brothers don't ever manhandle my mother, but they physically dragged her out of the room as if they feared Capo's retaliation at any moment. Rosa hustled me out of the room before I had to witness it all, but I heard it.

And now I stand in my room. Rosa is pulling out luggage. She's yelled for Elise, her friend and Tavi's wife, but she doesn't call for Vittoria, Romeo's wife. She probably knows that Vittoria will find out what happened sooner or later, and I doubt that she wants to involve her now. Vittoria may not forgive Romeo.

I stare at an empty suitcase. How many times have I delicately packed my clothes, shoes, and toiletries in preparation for a trip to Tuscany, or France? Every time I layered my clothes and shoes and toiletries in the bag, it was with a sense of anticipation, not the sense of dread I'm feeling now that's numbed me from the inside out.

Elise stands in the doorway. And when I see the look on her face—sad, but resigned, detached but determined—I know why Rosa called her here. Elise was raised in the mob like us. She, too, has known what it was like to be married to a man who didn't love you. She will not break down and cry.

I expected Rosa to ask her to help me pack, but she doesn't. "Have you heard?" Rosa asks Elise. Elise stands stock-still, her hand at her throat.

"I heard a little."

"Marialena accidentally helped a woman who was betrothed to one of the mob's most dangerous to escape."

"*No.* What are the consequences?" she whispers. Her voice wavers. "Is he..." He has the right to kill me. If he decided to execute me, I couldn't stop him.

"I have to marry him," I say, trying to be brave, but my voice breaks at the very end. I wring my hands and pace the floor, trying to wrap my brain around leaving my family... The Castle... My sisters, my brothers, my nieces, my nephews. "I don't even know where he lives."

As if that matters. Prison is prison whether it's in Siberia or Hawaii.

Elise blows out a breath. "Who is it?"

"Salvatore Capo." Elise flinches as if someone slapped her.

She speaks in a whisper. "Capo?"

I wonder if I'm the only one that sees the irony in the fact that my new husband's last name means Captain. Leader. Head. *Chief.*

"Oh my God," Elise whispers. "He's..." She shakes her head and doesn't complete the sentence. Dread builds inside me at her reaction. Elise was raised among brutal men and is horrified to think of me going with Capo? What does she know? She won't tell me, not if she thinks I can't prevent this from happening.

She turns back to me. "What did he say he will do?"

I force out a mirthless laugh. "Besides treat me the way he says my mother should have? *Train me?* Oh, not much."

Another flinch. My brother Ottavio was no angel when it came to the two of them marrying, but I turned a blind eye to that. He's my brother, and it's hard for me to think of him fulfilling any other role. I chose ignorance instead.

"I'm sorry," she says, and she really is. I can tell just by the look on her face. "Marialena, I am so sorry."

I am, too.

I'm talking to a woman who fled the country with a man she loved so that she could escape my brother. So she wouldn't be forced into the exact same thing I am being forced into.

On impulse, she crosses the room and gathers me up into her arms in a fierce, sisterly hug, while Rosa haphazardly tosses shoes, dresses, bras, everything, into suitcases. None of it matters much, what I take. They're only things, as meaningless as the passing tide that comes and goes. It won't take much for me to replenish my supply of clothing if I need to. And I don't know if I want to take them with me anyway. What if they just remind me of home?

Elise finally lets me go. She smells a little like baby powder. I wonder if she's put her children to bed for the night. She has a nanny, but like most women in my family, insists on mothering her own children as often as she can, the nanny reserved for the times she has to travel.

She whispers in my ear, "Be brave, sister. I hate this for you. I hate that this family and mine are bound by these crazy rules and expectations, and we have no choice. It's wrong, we all know it's wrong, but we also know that we're not going to change it." Her voice catches. "I hope that he's good to you. I hope that he's faithful. You must tell us how he treats you. If he mistreats you…"

Her voice trails off. We know the truth. She's only placating me. It won't matter if I tell her he mistreats me. As much as I appreciate her concern, how stupid does she think I am? I saw the way my mother was treated by my father. I've known for a long time that my brothers are faithful to their own wives, but that my cousins haven't always been. Infidelity's a part of life among our kind, and that's only one of the many ways he could hurt me.

"Will I get to say goodbye to Mama?" I wonder out loud.

My voice sounds small like I'm a child, and it's no surprise to me because I feel exactly like a child who just wants her mama.

Rosa shakes her head. "I doubt it," she says sadly. "I'm sorry, Marialena. I can't imagine Romeo would allow her to. She caused… a scene downstairs." Rosa looks away. "It's for your own good." She flinches when she says that. She's been on the receiving end of that pat line for so long, she knows how it grates. "What I mean is… Romeo can't risk inciting Capo's anger. He's a dangerous man, he could hurt Mama. If she yelled at him again, or, God forbid, struck him…"

I have to be brave. My foolhardy ways have come to haunt me. It's my fault my family's in this situation.

I can't risk anybody else being hurt because of me. My only choice is to move forward bravely.

"Maybe he won't be as bad as people say he is," I say, trying to be ever the optimist. Rosa and Elise share a glance that I don't quite understand, and Elise nods her head.

"Maybe," she whispers. "But it doesn't matter what the rules say, Marialena. If he truly does hurt you… If he really is mean to you…" She shakes her head, draws in a breath. But when she speaks again, her voice is pure steel. She looks into my eyes and takes one of my hands in both of hers. "I don't care what the rules are. If he hurts you, he dies. You call me. I still have connections. I still know people."

Elise and Rosa may be women in the mob, which we all know gives them less power than their husbands, but they are not pushovers. Both of them have keen skills, massive quantities of money saved, and connections all over the world. I swallow the lump in my throat and nod. God, I hope I don't have to take her up on that. Still, it's a small consolation.

"Thank you," I say, my voice shaking. "I love you. I'll miss you, and—"

"Marialena! Are you girls almost done?" Romeo yells from the foot of the stairs. Romeo might pretend that this doesn't disturb him, that he's being pragmatic and detached, but I know better. My older brother loves me, and this is killing him. I hate that I've put him in this position. I hate that so many decisions are out of my hands. I hate that anyone is hurting because of me.

I'll make the most of it. I've never met a man I couldn't charm, and maybe… just maybe… there's hope with my new husband.

Rosa cracks the door and shouts, "Yes, we're coming down now."

"Maybe he'll let me come home for holidays," I say hollowly. It seems like a big ask, and I doubt that he'll really be okay with that anyway. I don't think he'll let me come home at all. "Does anybody know where he lives?"

Elise nods. "He's in Tampa, Florida," she says. "One of the biggest crime rings north of Mexico." She shakes her head.

Tampa. Tampa in July? It'll be so damn *hot*. Am I actually going to experience hell on earth?

I sigh and turn to Rosa, trying with everything I have to put a smile I don't feel on my face. I feel like a mannequin. "Did you pack a bathing suit?" I ask her as Rosa puts her hand on my shoulder.

"I did," she says. "Maybe you'll really like the home."

I can make the most of this… maybe it's a nice house. Maybe it's got a beach view. Maybe he likes to work all day and only come home to his wife when he— my cheeks flush.

No, I won't think of that now.

I don't respond because we both know the old saying. A home isn't where I live, home is where the people I love live. Home is where my heart is. I don't care if he lives in the most magnificent mansion anyone has ever seen, it won't be home and we both know it.

"You told me this so many times," I say to Rosa. "You told me to stop. You told me to mind my own business. You told me that I would get in trouble. But I didn't wanna listen." My voice cracks.

I swipe angrily at the tears that fall down my cheeks. Rosa sighs.

"I never wanted to stop you from being who you are. I didn't want to stop you from having to make choices that will be out of your control. But you still have a choice, Marialena. You can make this work. Observe everything you can." She pauses and when she speaks again, her voice wavers but holds conviction. "You are a *Rossi* woman. And there isn't one of us that isn't strong and resilient, and *you are no different*. I don't know anything about the circumstances you're going into, but I can tell you that I'm pretty confident it will not be easy. I don't... *think*... he's a monster. There's something about him that's... human. But he definitely isn't someone who knows you or loves you. He'll probably take care of your most basic needs, and that's all you need. You make the most of it." Her voice trembles. "You bring that beautiful, vibrant, positive heart of yours with you and you make the most of this. You stay strong when it's hard. And you call me every damn day. Stay *strong*. And maybe, just maybe..." She falters. Maybe she doesn't want to give me false hope.

I force a smile. For her sake. "I will do my best." I flash a grin, even as my heart shatters. "Who can resist this smile?"

I know who. That ruthless monster downstairs, that's who.

I've never seen my brothers quake in fear of another man. But Romeo did. Romeo Rossi doesn't usually show fear.

Romeo shouts again from downstairs, more impatient now. "It's time, girls. Now!"

Elise opens the door completely, and I stifle a scream. It isn't just Romeo waiting at the foot of the stairs, but my future husband.

Earlier today, I thought he looked hot. Now he just looks terrifying. Tall, muscled, but it's that danger in his eyes that gets me every time. That knowledge that he's someone who has seen terrible things. Who has done terrible things. He's a man who fears no one and expects obedience.

And now he's going to be my husband.

"Maybe our babies will have those eyes," I mutter under my breath, trying to break the tension. "Small consolation, eh?" It works. Rosa breaks into a watery grin, and Elise smiles.

"I was terrified when I was engaged to Tavi," she says. "You girls might think he's a good guy, but I didn't know him. And he wasn't very nice to me at first. He was very hard on me, actually. But we got through. We made our way. We fell in love." She draws in a breath and lets it out slowly. "It wasn't easy, I won't lie. We've had our share of struggles like anybody else, and some of them were things that I didn't even know how we would overcome. But here we are." She shakes her head. "I don't know that your brothers are different. I really don't. But that doesn't mean we can't hope."

Romeo glares, warning us silently not to try Capo's patience.

I don't wanna talk anymore. They mean well, but with every second that passes I feel more nauseated.

"Let's go," I say. My family will have a much better time of this if I don't kick and scream the whole way. I won't do that to them. I can't.

So I hold my head up high. I hold one of the bags that my sister has packed for me, and I walk down the stairs to meet my future husband.

"Can I have time to say goodbye?" I direct my question to Salvatore and not Romeo. I wonder if I imagine Romeo flinching when I defer to my future husband's authority instead of his.

He shakes his head. "No. I'll allow you to come back and visit under my supervision. It's a short flight and I have frequent work that calls me here." My heart blooms with hope, just a little. "But tonight, I have to get back for a meeting. Say goodbye to Romeo, then we leave."

He glances at his watch as if to underscore the whole "we're on a timeline" thing.

"The cars are waiting out front," Romeo says hoarsely. I don't see any of my other brothers. I imagine them restraining and consoling my heartsick mother. Sometimes, it's good not to know.

Romeo leans in to kiss my cheek and whisper in my ear, "Do your best, sweetheart. Be the amazing person you are, and he can't help but fall for you. But if he hurts you... If anyone hurts you..."

"You'll be the first person I call," I say, though it brings me so little consolation.

I can only call him if I can get to a phone. If I'm still alive.

CHAPTER FIVE

SALVATORE

Italian women like a dramatic entrance and they like a dramatic exit. Italian men are a breed all their own. I ought to know. We have our own love affair with drama. But the point is, I know how these things go. I know how quickly this could become a drama fest. So I stop it before it starts.

Her goodbyes are brief. I place my hand on her forearm to secure her. It's the first time I've touched her. I note the softness of her skin, the way she doesn't resist but allows me to lead her.

And when she holds her head up gracefully, I fight a wild desire to kiss her beautiful, haughty face. To teach her who she belongs to now. To make a hard and fast claim right here and now declaring exactly who the fuck she belongs to.

But I won't claim her until we're married. That much I can honor.

I get a phone call as we approach the car and quickly answer it. I've wasted enough time as it is, and I've got shit to do. I spent more time at the Rossi house than I had planned, but I'm walking away with the spoils of war I came for, so it was worth it.

As I take the phone call, I watch her. I don't miss the way her chin trembles. The way she swallows hard when she gives one last backward glance at The Castle, or the way her knees knock against each other. I have my men take all of the luggage that she has and put it in the back of the car. It isn't much. I wonder if we'll arrive home one day to a shipment of all the shit she's ever owned sitting on the doorstep.

On instinct, I open the door for her. I gesture for her to take a seat, then slide in the back beside her. I have work to do, so my men will drive us to the airport where we'll catch our private jet home.

I finish the call quickly. We ride in silence for long minutes before she gives me a haughty little lift of her chin—is that a sneer? I hope it is. I can't fucking wait to make her behave herself. She tosses her pretty head and asks, "I want to know if I'm allowed to have a cell phone."

"Depends," I say to her. "Nearly everything that you're allowed or disallowed will depend on your behavior." It's the truth. "If you follow my rules and expectations, you'll have free rein of the house we'll live in together. You'll have access to the internet and your cell phone. You will go nowhere without a large guard on you, a minimum of three men on property and six off and none of those bullshit clowns your brother hired." Her shoulders tense, lips thinning. My Italian princess doesn't like it when I criticize her brother. "You'll be allowed to socialize and to shop, and in some cases, I'll even expect you to. You'll attend any function with me at my request, and during holidays and when I travel, you'll be my companion."

She has a very specific role to fill, and I'll train her immediately in the ways I expect. It doesn't have to be all rules and drudgery.

"How I behave..." she says, as if mulling this all over. "So I'm your companion. Your little trophy wife. What exactly does that mean?"

Ah, now we're getting somewhere.

"We'll discuss all of this after you take your vows to me."

"After?" she says. "That makes no sense. Why wouldn't you discuss any of this *before* we take the vows?"

I choose my words carefully and hold her gaze when I speak to her. "I'm tired and I have work to do, and what I expect of you won't impact whether or not you take your vows."

She cannot escape from this, we both know that. But I won't have her defiance and anger at the altar. We'll make this as cut-and-dried as possible.

Time to test the spoiled little girl's temperament. Let's see if her training is as lacking as I suspect.

"Hand me your phone." I put my palm out to her.

She eyes it angrily, and a few beats pass before she complies. I wonder if she'll defy me already, or force my hand. If she's been raised by the Rossis, she'll know what's expected of her. She'll know her place. I'm confident I'll have to teach her a lesson or two, but time will tell if she's a quick study.

"Do you live with any of your siblings?" The question takes me off guard, but considering where she came from, I suppose it's no surprise.

I shake my head. "I have two sisters, and don't get along with them. Both sisters are married, and I haven't seen either of them since their weddings."

Her eyes widen at that. "They were never allowed to come back? How could you exile them like that?"

I move closer to her and shake my head. "Lesson one, Marialena. Never make assumptions. Yes, they would've been welcomed back with open arms to visit. They had no interest."

My sisters rejoiced when they were able to leave the house. One married into another Italian family, another to an American family on the West Coast. I don't know if they're happy.

Happiness is overrated.

"No interest? Is your family that cruel?"

She has no idea.

"I guess you'll see for yourself soon enough."

It surprises me that people like the Rossis are as close as they appear to be. It's definitely not something you see very often in our line of work. I wonder if that's served them well, though. With a close-knit family like theirs, forming allegiances to anyone else can be detrimental. I'll have to force mine.

Winning her over is going to be a long, hard battle, but a woman won the right way is worth her weight in gold.

But we're nowhere near ready for that.

I need to know more about who she is before I know what my plan of attack will be. "Do you live anywhere besides The Castle?"

"Apparently now in Tampa," she says with a mirthless laugh. "And yes, I know that's not what you mean, but it's the truth. I've lived in Tuscany with my family, but other than that only at The Castle. It's the only home I've ever really, truly known."

I don't miss the way she swipes away tears on her cheeks, or the way her voice shakes. It doesn't bother me. But I note it, just the same.

She turns and looks out the window. We're only minutes away from the airport at this juncture.

"When do we get married?"

"Tomorrow night."

I watch her shoulders stiffen in my peripheral vision while I check my email on my phone. I hit *Call* to my cousin Cristiano.

"You don't waste time, do you?" she asks.

I shake my head just before he answers. "Never."

"Hey, cuz." He always sounds more friendly than he is, like a smiling viper. "Rumors I'm hearing true?"

"Tell me what they are, and I'll tell you if they're true."

"Now where's the fun in that?" He chuckles to himself. "I heard you scored a pretty Italian princess from the *Rossi* family."

"You heard right."

"How'd you manage to do that?"

I scowl and look out the window. The less I say the better. "She fucked up a business arrangement. I retaliated."

He chuckles softly to himself. "Retaliated by scoring a Rossi woman. Only you, you fuckin' genius asshole." He sounds friendly, familiar, like he's pleased with me, but I know him well enough to hear the underlying jealousy.

"I want the wedding tomorrow."

"Beach house?"

"Of course."

I roll my eyes and look over at Marialena.

I wonder if she's a virgin.

I'll know soon enough.

"Who do I invite?"

I stretch my shoulders and flex my neck. I need a good lifting session, soon, and a good night's sleep.

Who to invite?

I'm making an announcement of huge proportions. We're joining two families together on the East Coast. My family hasn't made a strategic move like this in decades.

It's time.

"Invite everyone."

She tenses but doesn't speak, doesn't move.

"On it. Father Esperanza?"

"Yes."

"He'll be there. Food?"

I give him a litany of family favorites, then cover the mouthpiece and ask Marialena, "You have any food or cake preferences?" I can at least throw her a bone.

She gives me a sardonic smirk, her lips pursed and eyebrows raised as if to say, *"really?"*

"I'll take that as a no," I say in a low voice. "But we'll talk about how you address me."

The smirk leaks from her face. She looks back out the window.

"Can my family supply the wine?" she asks, not looking at me. I wonder why that matters to her.

"No."

Another stiffening of the shoulders. No one supplies food or drinks to my family functions except me.

She doesn't reply.

"I'll consider allowing them to come to the ceremony."

"Fine," she says, then tacks on with a sarcastic flair, *"Sir.* Or do you prefer *Your Highness?"*

Ah, so we've gotten there already. Didn't take her long.

Cristiano chuckles on the line. I disconnect the call, slide the phone into my pocket, and reach for her wrist. I spread my knees, and without warning, tug her fully over my lap.

"Hey!" she protests, her eyes wide with alarm. "Hey, this is not fair. Don't you *dare!*"

Too late. I've already dared, my palm already stinging from the first smack of my palm across her ass. I give her six searing swats without pausing for her to catch a breath, then unceremoniously dump her back beside me as we pull into the terminal.

Her cheeks are flushed, her hair askew. Before she can speak, I reach for her chin and hold it firmly. "Apologize, or we do that again and the next time will be your bare ass over my knee."

I watch as her eyes smolder with anger and pent-up frustration.

"I'm sorry," she says quietly. Eying me, she moves further away as if to distance herself from me.

"Don't you dare. Get over here."

Slowly, she moves back closer to me. I take her wrist and pin it to my side as we cruise to a stop.

I don't waste my breath lecturing her. Marialena was raised Rossi and knows from her brothers what's expected of her.

It's a good start. Now she'll learn from *me* what's expected.

Outside the tinted window, I see our jet waiting. I get out first, then reach my hand to her. She looks as if she'd rather grab a python but takes it when I narrow my eyes at her. Hanging her head, she obeys, likely only meek because of the brief punishment she earned.

Still, I don't give her a chance. I don't know who's watching us, but I want her and any onlooker to know that I'm literally carrying this woman home as my prize.

So as soon as she gets out of the car, I yank her over to me. She stumbles and gasps when I dip, lift her up, and toss her over my shoulder.

"What are you—how—why—*Salvatore*!"

Ah. It's the first time she's called me by name. I love the way she pronounces it without the American plainness, the roll of the *r* like a good girl who knows her Italian upbringing.

Salva-TOR-ay.

I stand and steady myself with her over my shoulder.

"Put me down," she says softly, in a pleading voice.

"No."

"I don't want to be—"

With her conveniently over my shoulder, it's an easy matter to crack my palm against her ass to silence her. She's instantly subdued. Hell, yeah. I like *that*.

"I didn't ask you what you wanted," I tell her as we march toward the open door of our waiting plane. "I told you what you can expect. I have a statement to make, and I'll make that right here, right now." I squeeze her ass as a reminder that she belongs to me now, and when we get to the tarmac, I slide her down, her body pressed up against mine.

I wrap my fingers around her neck and yank her to me. When her mouth falls open in protest, I kiss her. Hard and punishing, my lips pry hers open as my tongue invades her mouth. She tastes like wine and berries, her lips so soft I groan into her mouth. Her hands fly up to push me away, but her efforts are fruitless. I easily deflect her protest and guide her hands back to her sides.

I kiss her until she submits. Until her knees go weak and she slumps against me.

I kiss her until she kisses me back.

I pull back and hold her gaze, her jaw still tight in my grip.

"I hate you," she whispers, but her words bely the heat and hunger in her eyes.

"That's a good start, then. I don't care if you hate me or not. You'll learn what I expect and learn to make my expectations your priority. Right now? I care about making a statement." I give her a patronizing smack to the ass that makes her instantly seethe at me, her body rigid against mine. I pour sarcasm and condescension into my tone. "You did good, babe. That'll do."

I release her. When she stumbles, I grab her arm and yank her back over to me, standing upright.

"You get that picture?" I ask my bodyguard.

"Yes, sir."

"Post it."

"Where, sir?"

"Everywhere."

CHAPTER SIX

Marialena

My mama always told me that it didn't matter what happened, who hurt me, who was watching. The most important thing to remember is to never bow my head or look afraid. She told me that I would always be a target, and she would do everything in her power to make sure I didn't end up with a husband like hers.

I wonder if that's why she's as upset as she is, if she feels she failed me. But when she said "everything within her power," she wasn't lying.

What was she going to do? Offer herself to Salvatore instead? My brothers likely offered money or favors, but that wasn't what he wanted.

I don't yet know if Salvatore's like my father, though I do know this. He's nothing like my brothers.

But I was raised by Tosca Rossi. My mother prepared me for many things, and I remember her advice now. I can almost hear her voice in my head.

Shoulders straight. Chin up. Rossi women do not flinch or hide. Never be ashamed of who you are. Never let anyone beat you down.

I am not ashamed of who I am, and I will never give him the satisfaction of besting me. Just because Salvatore's biological makeup makes him a little stronger than I am doesn't *change* who I am.

In this one particular circumstance, he has more power than I do. But I've known for a very long time how little control I actually have when it comes to mob dynamics. I've learned from my sister, my brothers' wives, and my mother, though. A woman has a lot more power than some people give her credit for, and I will not forget that.

I learned how to stare my father in the eye when he hit me, making him face what he was doing. I did not cower. I did not protect myself or beg for his mercy.

And Salvatore won't get weakness from me either.

For now, I observe everything I can. Observation is the key to knowledge. Fools don't notice details when their world is swept out from underneath them, and my mama didn't raise a fool.

I look away from him and try to forget the way my blood heated when I was overpowered. I hate that my body responded without my consent, but I console myself when I remember conversations with my sister. I'm not a teenager anymore, and I've talked at length to my sister and sisters-in-law. I've especially watched Rosa and Santo. I see how he is with her. My sister's the most independent, hard-ass woman I know, but she's... different with Santo. He's the one exception for her. She said some women—most especially strong women—*like* being overpowered or dominated, that we can't help our body's intrinsic response.

Guess she was right.

I just didn't really know what that would feel like.

She warned me that one day I might experience the same, given who I was and my place in our family. Makes sense. My brothers associate only with powerful men.

Rosa told me I might not be able to control the way I responded. She told me that many women don't want to admit that they *like* being overpowered and ravished by a raw, primal male who claims her as his.

Isn't that part of it, though? That he's... staking a claim on me.

Rosa said it isn't every man. It isn't every woman. But she wanted me not to be surprised if I had less control over my reaction than I hoped.

And she was right. The funny thing about reactions and emotions is that sometimes we have so little control over any of them. And sometimes, our emotions contradict themselves.

I want to slap his face at the very same time that I want him to kiss me again. I want to kick him between his legs and make him scream in agony for daring to pull me over his lap, and at the same time I have to admit... I want him to do it again. Slower. More deliberately...

I want to run away, to skip the prison he's bringing me to, while at the very same time I'm curious and hopeful. I knew there would never be autonomy when it came to my future, and a part of me wonders if he's really that bad?

He's so arrogant it makes my blood boil. What could I possibly see in a man like him? I can't love him, and I never will. He can't love me. We'll be together as husband and wife, but like most marriages in the mob, it's only a farce. I'm assuming a role in name only, and I've known this would be my lot in life for a very, very long time.

But when you've been raised the way I have... When you've seen what I have... You start to understand that often things aren't what they seem.

Not all bad men are *all* bad. Not all good men are *all* good. Humans are a wild, unpredictable concoction of complexities. And something tells me that Salvatore is no exception.

My mama always said one day my optimism would make a fool of me, and here we are.

I observe my surroundings. I watch in particular how everybody else addresses him. I'm not quite sure yet what his role is, if he's the Don, the one in charge, or maybe an heir to the throne. There's no way he's just a captain. No... Romeo wouldn't have given in to his demands unless he was a man of exceptional power and rank.

Don, then, I would guess. He's at least someone powerful.

So I observe. I take note.

Among the dozen or so men here on the plane with us, I sense fear. When you've grown up the way I did, you develop a sixth sense. You learn to recognize fear. There's a certain scent in the air, a vibrating silence of collective breaths held at once.

There's one that stands apart from the others who doesn't seem to fear Salvatore, though. But I don't gather confidence from the guy, only ineptitude and ignorance. I feel as if I stumbled into a boot camp with a new client, where everybody knows the steps to the dance except one.

The blond guy in the white suit doesn't hide from Salvatore. He's clearly amused by Salvatore's treatment of me, which makes him no friend of mine. But while the other men are intent on following Salvatore's orders, this one seems intent on…. well, *me*.

Intriguing.

Did Romeo send him? No… I don't recognize him. And that's not Romeo's style.

"Pretty little Italian princess probably hasn't been treated by a real man before," he says in a low voice in my ear. I wonder if he's trying not to be overheard by my future husband, or by the other man beside him, or if he just wants to make an idle threat or bully me.

Bold move.

I don't respond to him at first. I'm a little bemused. There's not a single man who works for my brother who would ever try to be disrespectful to me without suffering great consequences. Part of me wonders how different Salvatore's family is from mine.

It also doesn't mean I have to put up with it, I'm just not sure what the rules here are yet. At first, I ignore him. But he keeps it up. He's standing too close to me, he's whispering things in my ear about what a spoiled brat I am.

I glance over at Salvatore, who's intent on the phone, having a deep conversation. His eyebrows are a slash above his eyes as he spits Italian curses into the phone. Excellent.

"Miss Rossi, please sit beside Mr. Capo," a gentleman to my left says.

Not Miss Rossi for much longer.

I nod and go to sit. Before I do, the guy next to me starts in again. I don't know if things are just different here or he really just has a death wish.

"Your brothers think they're the hottest things on the coast, don't they?" Ah. So this is about my brothers. Excellent.

I look to see if my almost-husband is noticing, more out of curiosity than anything, but nothing yet. I can feel the tension of the other men near me. I see the way they look. I decide I don't have anything to say to him, even as he's getting under my skin.

I miss my brothers already. Will my new husband treat me badly?

Salvatore is still busy on the phone, his back to me and the man next to me who continues to taunt me. "Go ahead," he sneers. "Have a seat. Let's see how you like things in Tampa. It's hot as hell, which you should be familiar with."

Still, I ignore him. I sit beside Salvatore and buckle my seat belt.

"Little Rossi bitch," blondie says under his breath.

Is this a test? Did Salvatore put him up to this?

I don't expect him to actually touch me, so when he reaches for me, I don't block him or move to stop him as his fingers wrap around my arm. It only lasts a fraction of a second.

The second he touches me he's yanked back. Salvatore has him by the back of the neck, suspended several feet off the floor. I turn away and buckle my seat belt. Nothing to see here folks. I turn back with a casual glance as Salvatore shakes the blond.

The guy croaks out, "He said he wanted me here as backup."

In one swift motion, Salvatore throws him bodily against the wall of the cabin. I've been here before. I don't even flinch when the guy's body cracks against the wall and crumples to the floor. I don't react in any way, though I feel a little smug this guy is getting what's coming to him.

A smart man would probably realize that he's crossed the line. But maybe this guy is missing a couple of brain cells because he doesn't become subdued, or question whether or not he's going to be killed in the next minute. Instead, he scrambles to his feet, his face red with fury.

The other men watch, ready, waiting for instruction from Salvatore. But one, a tall, lithe ginger, stands right next to me.

"You okay?" he asks.

I nod. "Of course."

If Salvatore is like my brothers, then those who work for him will learn who I am and how to respect me. It's important that I show them I am not easily intimidated. "I'm fine. Someone seems to have overstepped, hmm?"

I try to keep a stoic face, but when Salvatore grabs the man by a fistful of his hair and yanks him around, I feel it.

I won't let myself look away.

I watch as my almost-husband beats the shit out of the guy that touched me. A vicious right hook that breaks bone, a splatter of blood across the airplane window. No one moves or even makes a sound as Salvatore punishes him severely.

"You think I didn't hear your fucking bullshit when I was on the phone? Who the fuck are you and how did you get here?"

"Cristiano hired me," the guy says.

"He told you to bully my betrothed? Did he?"

Salvatore yanks him to his feet only to knock him down again. And again. And again.

"Who the fuck do you think you are, talking to my future wife like that? If we were home, I'd cut off your fucking fingers for daring to touch her. You don't ever fucking touch what's mine. You don't talk to her. You do not even fucking *look* at her."

Everything he says with a calm, cool collectedness I'm familiar with.

The guy's face is unrecognizable, his clothes shredded, and his face a bloody mess of bone, flesh, and blood. Still, I force myself to look.

Salvatore shoves him to his knees. I didn't notice when he drew his weapon, but now he cocks it and points it to the guy's temple. Blondie starts begging for his life, crying.

My heart beats so wildly I can't stand it, but I keep my face impassive. This is what a woman does in the face of cruelty in my family. This is what a woman does in the face of cruelty in *his*.

He could kill him. He might just be threatening him. In any event, I will not look away.

"You're dismissed from my company. You ever come within fifty yards of my future wife again, I will cut off your balls before I put my gun to your temple and shred your brains. Do you understand me?"

The other guy cries and pleads like a child. His mouth is a swollen, bloody mess, but he still manages to eke out, "Yes, sir." He spits blood onto the floor.

Salvatore knocks the butt of the gun against his temple and mercifully puts the man out cold. None of his men move, but I can tell that every one of them is waiting for a command.

Salvatore bends down, grabs the guy by the arm and drags him. Blood and spittle fall to the floor of the plane. I still don't flinch.

Salvatore looks over his left shoulder and makes eye contact with a tall, burly guy about ten years older than him. "Throw him from the motherfucking plane."

He hands him to the older man, who holds him like a sack of rotten potatoes. Another guy opens the plane door. I watch as the brutalized man falls to the ground with a sickening thud.

The door shuts. Salvatore shrugs and scowls at his hands. One of his men scrambles to get him something to clean them with.

The ignition of the plane starts.

Salvatore stretches, cracks his neck, and walks over to me. He crouches in front of me, miraculously now devoid of blood or lacerations after delivering that beating.

"You did good, *bella mia*. No one will ever speak to you that way."

Yeah, I get it. I've heard it all before.

Still, I swallow a lump in my throat because a part of me can't dare to hope that he means any of this.

Crouched in front of me, he brings his hand to my face. Ah, yes, so apparently his hand didn't remain unscathed. I don't flinch when he touches me. I just stare into the blue depths of his eyes, the most beautiful part of him.

"You watched and didn't react. You've been raised properly. You're a brave girl."

Is this guy mentally ill or something? He thinks he can be mean to me one second and sweet the next and I'm supposed to fall for the sweet guy routine?

I don't think so.

He brushes his thumb against my chin. The skin is calloused and hard, like him, but his touch is gentle, almost as if he needs to remind himself of why he had to be so brutal.

"I'll find out why he was here. I'm sorry that happened."

Every man on this plane is watching me. How I react is crucial. I hold my head high like my mama taught me. I hold his gaze and give a little nod, as if accepting his apology though it's slightly beneath me.

"I wondered if you'd allow your hired man to speak to your future wife that way," I say truthfully. "Thank you."

Do I truly believe he did the right thing? Did he truly believe *I* did?

It's debatable.

We're on the verge of establishing a relationship here that will make or break me. I need to do whatever's in my best interest. And, I suppose... so does he.

Salvatore jerks his head to the redhead. "How much training did that fucking asshole have?"

To my surprise, the guy chuckles. "Not enough, sir."

Salvatore smiles. It's his signature predatory smile that doesn't reach his eyes, designed to approve of this man's words but not actually show any humor. "You got that fucking right."

His gaze falls to the floor, and the humor fades. He snaps his fingers. "Clean her fucking shoes."

I look down to see my shoes splattered with blood. Well if that's not a goddamn nuisance. I extend my feet and purse my lips as his men scramble for something to clean my shoes with.

"Careful," I chide. "I like my Louboutins."

"You hear her?" Salvatore growls. "Be careful."

Someone quickly cleans my shoes while Salvatore settles in beside me. I inspect the job and nod approvingly. Shoes clean and not damaged.

Salvatore stands and shrugs out of the suit jacket he puts on the back of a seat. Then he sits back down and buckles up. "Are you hungry, Marialena?"

I nod. "That's one thing about me," I tell him. "I'm sorry to say, that like apparently every other member of the female of the species, my appetite never wanes. Death? Disaster? A bloody beatdown? Being ripped from my family home and taken to another? Nope, I'm still starving." I give a self-deprecating sigh and look out the window, but he seems amused. I'm not lying.

"Good girl. I hope your appetite extends to… many things."

He did not just say that. Why yes, he did.

Lovely.

I bite the inside of my cheek to stop myself from blushing, but it doesn't work.

Salvatore orders food from one of the men, who I guess might be the flight attendant for this trip. "Do you have any preferences?"

I shake my head. "I like everything."

"Everything," he repeats disbelievingly. "Sushi?" I nod my head.

"Oysters?" Another nod.

"Avocadoes? Black olives? Beet salad?"

"I literally like everything. I've never met a food I didn't like. What about you?" I ask. I doubt that I'll have anything to do with his food preparation, but I guess it's probably helpful to know what my future husband likes to eat.

"I like Italian food with ingredients I trust and food I cook myself. I like most foods but hate processed shit."

"So no gas station burritos for you. Shame. They have a certain *piquancy*."

I swear he almost smiles. Almost.

Not that I care. I'm not trying to make him smile.

I don't say anything else as he orders us food, but I do feel a little surprised that he has this spread on the plane. Antipasto, tossed salad, small bowls of Italian wedding soup, followed by little slices of filet mignon, roasted potatoes, and grilled asparagus.

"This is pretty impressive for plane food."

"I am a very particular guy when it comes to food."

Now that I can deal with. I love good food.

"My brothers don't just love good food. They love *any* kind of food. It isn't a holiday in my house until a fistfight breaks out over the last cannoli."

He doesn't respond. I hate when that happens. You tell someone something and it's just… crickets.

Still, I'm starving, and the food is delicious, so instead of small talk I work on eating. I nearly lick my plate clean.

"Good girl," he says approvingly, though he's not looking at me but at his phone. "I like."

I'm not really sure what he likes about me eating a lot of food. But whatever. Fine with me.

"Continue your good behavior, I may even let you have dessert."

Is he joking? Or does he really mean that the dessert is a reward that I earn?

We'll see about that.

I don't know exactly how much control he's going to wish he had over me. I don't really know how much control he's going to insist he has over me.

But I've got a say in this, too. I'll just bide my time.

"I definitely like dessert," I say. "One might say it's my favorite part of a meal."

"Let me guess. You never met a dessert you didn't like, either," he says. This time I get an actual smile. Brief, like the slightest flash of sun when clouds part only to be covered by the next burst of clouds, but it's there.

"Bingo."

"In Florida, we're famous for our key lime pie. Have you ever had it?"

I shake my head. "Hmm. No, we usually eat Italian desserts. My Nonna..." I pause, because to my surprise my throat begins to close. I feel tears prick my eyes, but I will not give him the satisfaction of my tears. If he notices my delay, he doesn't say anything. I quickly recover.

"Nonna makes the best desserts. It's her specialty. Torta Caprese, panna cotta, tiramisu. And I love my brothers' cannoli." My voice does catch at the end. I miss them already. I look away so he doesn't see my eyes welling with tears.

Thankfully, he isn't looking at me at all.

"So if there's no food you don't like," he says, "do you have any favorites?"

"Of course."

"Well, let's hear them."

"Steak grilled on an open grill outdoors, topped with caramelized onions and loads of mushrooms. Particularly delicious if the mushrooms have been marinated first. Stuffed manicotti, homemade pizza made on a wood-burning stove. My mama's ravioli, the one she makes with spinach and ricotta."

"And wine?"

My voice is a whisper now. Still, he doesn't look at me. I answer truthfully.

"I like any wine from my family's vineyard."

It's true. Red, white. Sparkling, sweet, dry. If it was made in a Rossi vineyard in Tuscany, I will drink it.

"Anything comparable in the common market for us plebians?" If he's being sarcastic, it doesn't show.

I shrug. "Maybe. I've never had a reason to ask, though, because we've always just had my family's wine. It would be almost sacrilegious to drink anything else." I sigh. Not *almost*. "You like to cook your own food. We like to drink our own wine."

His phone rings again. This time, instead of ignoring me, he makes a brief apology before he answers it.

I can tell before the conversation has lasted longer than ten seconds that this time he has his cousin… Cristiano?... on the line.

"Ah, cousin. So when I give you a motherfucking instruction to hire someone, you follow protocol. You don't send him on a plane untrained, do you? Oh, really? Did you teach him anything about what my expectations were? Because that little asshole seemed to think he was running the ship here. He not only disrespected Marialena, he had the nerve to put his *hands* on her. Yes, really."

I can actually hear the gasp of surprise from the other end of the line.

"You bet your ass I did. I want him gone. I want all of his belongings off my property before I get home. If I see a trace of him, I'm coming after you. And you and I will have a long talk later about what I expect in a new hire."

When he hangs up, he looks at me. I wonder if he's waiting for a reaction. Horror? Surprise?

"You don't seem bothered by any of this. You don't seem ruffled at all."

"Any of what?" I ask him honestly. I'm curious what he means.

"You were bullied by one of my men. I beat the shit out of him and threw his ass off the plane. My staff cleaned blood off your fucking shoes. I'd think the average woman would at least be ruffled—"

"You didn't choose an average woman, Salvatore," I say with a sigh and a forward thrust of my chin. "I'm a Rossi. You'll have to try a lot harder to shock me."

A slow smile spreads across his face. I shiver.

"I'll keep that in mind."

CHAPTER SEVEN

SALVATORE

I don't make decisions for emotional reasons or any other bullshit like that. I've been born and bred to use nothing but cold reasoning.

Marialena Rossi, with that winsome way of hers, will *not* change that. She will be my bride, and I'll take care of her as my role dictates.

But she will not be someone I fall in love with. She will not be someone who makes the decisions around here, and she sure as hell won't lead me around by my dick.

I've seen it happen all too often, men turning into fucking pussies over a woman. They become untrustworthy. Vulnerable. Weak. And a man in my position can't afford any of that shit.

When she holds her head up, with that proud little chin thrust, to announce that she's a Rossi, she's adorable. But that's all it is… adorable. No more, no less. She has a lot to learn yet, and what she's learned as a Rossi isn't the end of the fuckin' line around here.

I hand her the phone back, and she takes it with a wary look.

"You can use it for now, under my supervision."

I want to see what she does.

Within minutes, she's connected to the Wi-Fi we have onboard, scrolling through her messages and social media. The job I have means I can't afford to be without the internet, so I've invested in a high-speed internet connection everywhere.

"How long is the flight typically?" she asks.

"The flight down is about two and a half hours. Coming back to Boston will take closer to three because of wind currents. Have you ever flown this way before?"

She shakes her head. "Never. Only to Italy, and that's it."

I watch her frown as she scrolls through her phone. "What's this little blue bar at the top of my screen?"

No reason to hide it. "It means I'm mirroring your phone on mine."

I note the slight tension in her shoulders. "Oh, how quaint. You decided to monitor your future wife like I'm an untrustworthy teenager." She barely restrains herself from rolling her eyes.

I give her a warning look. If she disrespects me, most especially in front of my men, she'll feel my palm across her ass right here. She should know better than that, unless Rossi fucked up and spoiled her. Something tells me she wouldn't like being dressed down in front of my men. Marialena might be cute, but she can be prickly.

I might have my work cut out for me. Excellent.

"So sorry," she says. "Of course it's your job to protect yourself. And to make sure that I don't do anything *dangerous*." She whispers *dangerous* like it's a loaded weapon, with mock horror in her tone.

Alright, enough of that. "Watch it, woman."

She huffs at me but closes her mouth.

I don't dignify that with a response but open my email and get to work.

I ignore her for a little while, let her play on her phone, and about twenty minutes later casually open the app that lets me see what she's been up to.

The first few searches are social media, but the last few are pretty interesting.

How to murder your husband in his sleep.

How to poison your controlling husband.

How to be married to a mafia man and never have sex with him.

How to survive oppression.

How to overturn the patriarchy.

Adorable.

Clever little thing.

"I'd say the whole pillow over the face thing would be most effective, if your husband was dumb enough not to have security nearby. Poisoning is impossible, I'm way too careful with my food, but I suppose you could slip something into my drink if you were clever enough and could get your hands on something toxic, but again… security. And the only way to be married to a mafia man and not have sex with him would be to get your own private jet and flee to another country. What is *oppression*? Hmm. I doubt my expectations are all that different from your brothers'. But I suppose we'll find out."

"I wasn't married to my brothers," she spits out.

"Too true. I'm going to text you a few more things I want you to look up during your free time, since you're so invested in this search history."

She eyes me warily while I text.

How to learn how to defer to my husband's authority in a traditional marriage.

How to learn to take a vow of submission to my husband

What if I like being dominated in bed?

What if I like it when my husband spanks me for being naughty?

Her jaw predictably unhinges. "Are you seriously that full of yourself?"

"If we weren't on a plane right now, I would definitely consider that a disrespectful attitude, one that you'd get punished for. In fact…" I scratch my chin thoughtfully. "I'm starting to not care about the fact that we're on a plane. Maybe I should make a demonstration of you in front of my men."

"So that's how you can control things? Squelch anyone who bullies around you because you leave all the bullying to yourself," she says. "Makes perfect sense."

"I thought you were a Rossi. I thought you'd be familiar."

She clenches her jaw but does not respond.

We don't talk for long minutes. I continue to work. Out of the corner of my eye I see her head bobbing as if she's fallen asleep. It's late, it's comfortable in here, and the quiet hum of the engine lulls one to sleep. I casually watch her.

Her phone falls into her lap. The tension around her shoulders eases. She no longer clenches her hands. I suspect Marialena would hate to know that as she sleeps her head falls to my shoulder.

I keep working, but this time I let myself enjoy the feel of her leaning on me when she sleeps. The quiet fluttering of her breath.

I gesture for staff to bring me a blanket. It tends to be cold in here, and she sits right beneath the draft. Wouldn't do to bring home the woman I'm going to marry only to find out that she's sick.

I take the blanket, quietly unfold it, and drape it over her without waking her.

She sleeps until we land. When she wakes, she lifts her head off my shoulder as if to deny she allowed herself to be so vulnerable.

I watch as she blinks, disoriented like a child, then looks out the window as we prepare to land. Though the sun has set hours ago, the coast is lit with bright white lights, illuminating the palm trees and white sand.

I wonder if she'll like it.

But I'm waiting for the next show of defiance. I'm waiting for her to try to escape, undermine me, or attempt to get away. She's not here of her own volition, so I'm waiting for the other shoe to drop.

"Did you put a blanket on me?"

"Yes. It's cold."

I finish the last email, shut off my phone, and slide it into my pocket.

She picks up hers and sends a couple of texts. I watch her text after we touch down.

Landed. I'm here. I'm fine.

I can either walk with her, or I can carry her inside because she's tired and she's my bride and I want to make a statement. I reach for her, lift her up, and she does not protest. I exit the plane with her still in my arms.

Turns out Cristiano is lucky I'm holding her when I get off this plane, so my hands are occupied.

"New bride?"

The dick.

"No, I decided the flight attendant looked tired. Yeah, asshole, she's the one I'm marrying tomorrow. Show her the respect she deserves and ensure everyone else does the same." I will not have anyone fucking up like earlier.

Cristiano is the very picture of apology. "Say no more. It's my fault, and I'm sorry."

"We'll talk about this later," I tell him. We sure as fuck will.

"Your mother's home."

Fuck. I wonder if I imagine the note of smugness in his tone.

I stifle a groan. I do not want to have to deal with her tonight or any other fucking night.

My nearly senile uncle's the head of our mob, but not for long. We all know he's prepared to abdicate his authority to me once I'm married, one of the reasons why getting married is a top priority for me.

"Who else is home?"

Cristiano gives me a litany of names. Most of my top-notch staff is on. That'll help.

I'm tired. She's exhausted. We have a big day ahead tomorrow, and the last thing I want to deal with is my goddamn mother. But I know if I don't, tomorrow will be much worse.

Marialena doesn't need to, though. Not tonight.

She hasn't said a word. She's still in my arms, and it looks as if she's going to fall asleep again at any moment. I slide her down and arrange her in front of me.

I suppose it's time to start the formal introductions.

"Cristiano, meet Marialena. Marialena, Cristiano." He's ever the gentleman as he takes her hand and shakes it. I'm guessing she's savvy enough to see straight through the act.

"Pleased to meet you," he lies. Cristiano despises women and considers them his to use then discard as he wishes.

"Pleased to meet you," she repeats back at him. Also a lie.

We enter the waiting car while my men gather up our luggage. Cristiano joins us and fills us in on what happened during my brief absence. I've been gone for four days, and a lot has occurred in that time. I had wondered if I'd feel rusty after getting out of jail, but it feels as natural to me as riding a bike.

During a lull in the conversation, Marialena speaks up. "I looked up your home on the plane," she says quietly.

"I know."

Her jaw clenches, but she doesn't say much else at first.

"It's huge. How many people live there?"

"It depends on the day. My sisters are all gone. My mother frequently visits, but also spends time in Italy. Sometimes it's just me and staff."

"That sounds lovely."

An introvert, then, or does she just prefer a simpler life?

"It isn't."

I idly wonder if that's a lie. Or have I just never really given it much thought? Is it lonely? I like when I don't have a lot of people in my space. I like not having to entertain or put on an act.

"Do you have any pets?"

"Fish."

She takes this in and mulls it over. "Are there any beaches nearby? Are they public?"

"Some, yes, but you won't be using public beaches. The house is on a private beach. You can walk from the master suite down the dock to the beach. Not alone, of course, but you know."

"I do. Do you like the beach?"

"Yeah, but it's not like I ever take time to enjoy it." I look out the window and don't see anything else. "I'm a busy man."

"I can see that."

"You taking any time off for the honeymoon?" Cristiano asks. Marialena flushes madly. I wink at her, and her mouth drops open. I will fuck her, and often. And she'll *like* it.

"No."

This is a business arrangement, not a joyride, and the sooner she realizes that the better.

She looks away, but doesn't respond other than to ask, "Have you told your mother that?" What is that supposed to mean?

"Why would I tell my mother?"

"Italian mothers have a way of assuming that certain things will go a certain way. She could be planning the biggest soirée Tampa's ever seen."

"You'll see soon enough. Don't pay attention to her. She has no authority over you."

She's been warned.

Her lips tip downward in a frown, but she lets it go.

Cristiano shifts beside me. "I'm sorry about Brahm. I fucked that one up."

"We'll talk about this privately."

He winces and doesn't respond. He knows what the consequences are, and no matter what I decide, I'm confident he's earned them.

The drive to my home from the airport is about thirty minutes. I take advantage of the entire time to finish my work. My visit to the Rossis cut into the workday, and I never like to start the day behind.

I watch Marialena from the corner of my eye. I have a very short time with her to teach her, but I expect her to be ready before we have a public display between the two of us. I'll have to use my time wisely.

I don't want to test her obedience in front of my cousin. The sadistic motherfucker will get a hard-on if I dominate her in front of him. Then I'd have to kill him. Inconvenient to deal with the day before a wedding.

But she doesn't do much except look out the window. "Is it usually this hot here even at night?"

Cristiano laughs. "It's about twenty degrees colder right now than it was earlier in the day, only because we had a torrential thunderstorm before you guys arrived. You'll be happy to know it'll be one hundred ten on your wedding day. I hope you don't like makeup because it will just melt right off your pretty face."

I definitely hate him. If my mother didn't make him work for me, I would've excommunicated him a long time ago. But now, I'm obligated to let the asshole in my company because he's family and that's how we do shit here.

Marialena looks at him as if he is a large beetle stuck to a card with a pin. Disgusting, and worthy of not much besides vague observation.

"Thank you," she says, voice dripping with sarcasm. "I'm not much of a makeup person. You?" I don't want to like her, but she's already getting to me. Anyone that can handle my asshole cousin with the grace she does is worthy of a modicum of respect.

"Seriously. Are you unfamiliar with the Florida climate?"

"Of course I know it's hot. You're literally residing on the Gulf of Mexico. So no, I'm not *ignorant* about Florida and its climate, but I've never been here before and it's surprisingly hot for someone like me. And do you frequently insert yourself into other people's conversations? Or is that just a privilege you reserved for me?"

Oh, good girl.

Cristiano looks at me, and I watch his eyes. "I can see you haven't trained the girl yet."

"I've given her no expectations to treat you with respect. Looks to me like you're the one who hasn't been trained yet."

Marialena snorts.

I sit back in my seat and cross my arms on my chest. "She'll learn to obey me. She won't have to listen to you, nor anyone in my family. No one who works for me. Just. Me. And for your information, she has my full permission to give you shit back when you give it to her. In fact," I say thoughtfully, stroking my chin. "She has my permission to give you shit with no provocation."

Cristiano stares at me. At first, I wonder if he's going to have one of his little temper tantrums, but instead we both start when he laughs out loud. It's a chilling laugh, and neither of us are amused.

Fuck Cristiano. I look to Marialena instead.

I have no doubt she has many questions, and I'll answer those questions as the days go by. I don't expect love from our relationship, but a marriage devoid of outright antagonism might be nice.

I wouldn't know. I've never seen one.

"Update me on your deal with Columbia."

When I left, Cristiano had been reaching out to one of the newest mobs in the country.

"What do you have to do with Columbia?" Marialena asks curiously.

"The better question is, what do *you* have to do with any of this?" Cristiano says.

"Cristiano." She flinches at the tone of my voice. I wait until he looks at me. "Stay out of this. I already had to beat the shit out of somebody tonight. I'm tired. Don't make me fuck you up."

I won't hide shit from my wife. Not business stuff anyway. "Here, in the Gulf of Mexico, we have easy access to their trade. It's in my family's best interest to make friends with the Colombians. We all know that some of them tried to interfere with your family. The men who threatened the Rossis were dealt with, but those from Columbia interested in American trade were a much greater number. It was my family that gave the Rossi family intel on the Colombian crew. If your family hadn't prevented them from getting a foothold in Boston, they would've been solidified a long time ago."

I don't know every detail about what happened with Jose's group and the Rossis, but I know they were trying to prevent the marriage between a Montavio and a Rossi, as well as trying to get established in New England.

I don't give a shit about any of that. But clearly, she does.

Cristiano stares at me, likely surprised I told her this much.

She's intelligent and experienced. I'd be a fool not to.

I suspect she'll have a lot more questions for me as the days go by. I have plenty for her, too.

"How much were you allowed to know about the business your brothers did?"

"Not much," she says. "Most I ever learned was when I was stationed in Tuscany, because it's difficult to be ignorant of anything in such close quarters. My brothers didn't much care what I knew, they cared about keeping me safe." Or so they said.

Her voice catches at the end. "So even though they would tell me things when I asked, I was always kept at a distance intentionally."

"Then it'll come as no surprise to you it will be similar here. You can ask questions, I won't hide anything from you, but most business dealings will be private."

She nods.

We're silent for the rest of the ride home. A few times I catch Cristiano looking at her, but she doesn't wilt under his stare, and he finally looks away.

At first, she yawns as we pull up to the house, but her eyes widen when she sees the estate lit up with a spotlight.

I don't know why I care if she likes it here. But there is something wistful in her eyes that makes me hope she does.

"Bed," I order. "We've got a big day tomorrow, and I'm tired. So Cristiano, I want you in my office at seven a.m. Don't be late." I frown at the front door. "And if my mother's anywhere near here, get rid of her. I want sleep, not a confrontation."

Marialena looks at me. I wonder if she knows I'm not the one I'm trying to keep away from my mother.

"Get some sleep tonight," I tell her. "Tour tomorrow."

She likely only obeys me because she's tired, but I'm thankful we don't have another battle.

I lead her inside, show her to the room she'll stay in tonight. I wonder if I imagine she looks disappointed. I'd expect nothing but relief.

I turn away and, leaving her with a female member of staff to tend to her needs, head to my last business meeting of the night.

CHAPTER EIGHT

MARIALENA

I dream that Salvatore comes and claims me in The Castle dining room. Orlando smashes the wine wall, and smacks Salvatore across the back of the head with a nice bottle of pinot grigio. Mama lights a cigarette, which should tell me this is a dream because Mama never smokes in the house, but it seems appropriately nonchalant.

"Why the pinot, son? You know that's my favorite. Next time you need a makeshift weapon, go for the chardonnay."

I wake up and blink, coming to before I remember where I am. I half smile to myself at the memory. I miss my mama. I miss my brothers. None of them are perfect, and my family is seriously fucked up, but they're *my* family.

He said something about them being allowed to come today. I'm not sure who will be allowed or who can make it, but I'll hold onto that.

I barely remember the night before. I was vaguely aware of a majestic house, white columns and pillars and the depths of the deep blue sea in the background. I remember him assigning me a member of staff to get situated, an older woman with graying hair and a plump figure. I remember her turning down the bed and handing me a soft nightgown to change into. I remember wiping my face with a makeup wipe, brushing my teeth, then climbing into the large bed alone. I remember thinking it was the last night I'd sleep alone, but I was too tired to care. I spread my arms and legs and sprawled out anyway, to make the most of it.

I remember him leaving me, and I questioned nothing because I was asleep before the door shut behind him.

He didn't touch me. But I'm not surprised, because today is our wedding day, and the ironic thing about men like him is that they have a surprising code of ethics. The same guy that would brutally beat a priest, his own brother, or pull a knife or gun on an enemy as easily as he would pour a cup of coffee, will not touch his future wife before she's taken vows.

They typically demand a virgin in their wedding beds but have no scruples about their own purity. The very idea is laughable. He would fuck up anyone in his company who questions his authority, or who betrays him. But loyalty also demands he lay down his life for his brothers.

It's a brutal but predictable juxtaposition of power and control.

I suspect Salvatore's family is different from mine in some ways, though. He said as much when he described his sisters' eagerness to be married. My sister and I went kicking and screaming, almost literally. At least Rosa did for her first marriage. But he says his family was glad to leave. That doesn't make me too excited to meet my future in-laws.

He's mentioned his mother but hasn't said anything about his father. If his father was the Don, no matter the hour, I would've expected him to meet us at the door last night, but he didn't. Maybe he's traveling.

There are a lot of maybes.

I blink and look around the expansive room. I grew up in both The Castle on Boston's North Shore in New England, a bona fide castle with turrets and a courtyard and an actual swimming pool indoors, as well as my family's sprawling estate in Tuscany. When I was a child, my parents would allow tourists and news agencies to tour The Castle. It's opulent, worth millions, and our residence in Tuscany is the same. Over time, they demanded more privacy, but our main family home is still a bit of a legend.

But from what little I've seen in person and online, I can already tell this place is… different.

There's more space, for one. I've never seen cathedral ceilings in a bedroom, but these vaulted ceilings reach to the heavens. At the very center of the ceiling above me hangs a glittering chandelier. Doorways are elegantly arched, the woodwork is painted a vivid white. Most everything is a shade of white, from the bedding to the walls to the Berber carpet under my feet, though lavender satin accents —the drapes, throw pillows, and a tufted ottoman in front of a weathered vanity—lend pops of color that make the room less sterile and decidedly feminine.

Unlike The Castle with its floors upon floors, this home appears to only have two floors.

It's wider, though. The ceilings are higher. And oh my God, when I look out one of the windows….

Palm trees, their large, broad leaves sagging toward the ground, border the estate. A vibrant red brick walkway leads to the main entrance guarded by a heavy black wrought iron fence I don't remember seeing in person the night before. The house itself is painted white, but various roofs, decks, and balconies contrast in reddish brown brick.

It's hard to imagine the ocean I saw outside The Castle windows is the same one I see here, or is it? No… we're on the West Coast of Florida, on the Gulf of Mexico, and my family's home is on the

Atlantic Ocean. Although they flow into one another, the cold waters of northern New England and its rocky shores don't look anything like this gentle lap of waves onto white sand. The beach is also dotted with palm trees. Ironically, it looks as if we're actually living in paradise itself.

This bed I'm in has to be some kind of extra-large king. I can't even imagine where he would get sheets this big. I lay on my back and stretch my arms and legs as far as they will go. I bet I could fit my sister and friends here quite comfortably for a sleepover. I close my eyes.

I miss you. I miss you all.

While everyone else married off and started families of their own, I didn't. I stayed home. I stayed with Mama. I held down holiday traditions and kept things together and didn't *leave.*

Until now.

I have a job to do. A job I've known about for decades. It was only a matter of time.

I roll to the left, noting a sitting area with two lavender armchairs facing another window with the drapes still drawn. I rise, pad over the carpeted floor to them, and pull the drapes open.

I gasp. When he said we were on the water, he meant *on the water.* Online pictures didn't prepare me for *this.*

From the bed, I could see the ocean out one small open window. But here, there's a balcony so close to the water I can smell the salty air. I open the balcony door and step outside.

I'm hit with a wave of heat that shocks me. It's rarely, if ever, this warm this early at home. I could sit on this balcony and sunbathe in a matter of seconds. To the right, however, the large balcony extends to where it's shaded. Lounge chairs beckon from beneath a shaded roof.

I take a seat on a sunny lounge chair and stare at the ocean in front of me. I remember it's a private beach, which would explain why there isn't a sailboat or swimmer in sight. I can see them in the distance, though. Something below the balcony catches my eye, so I stand and look over the stone wall.

Wow.

A crystal-clear almond-shaped pool bubbles below. Slabs of stone wall the pool in, and bright, tropical plants and flowers nestle amongst palm trees along the border. Slatted lounge chairs dot the perimeter. No one's there either, though.

There's supposed to be a wedding... *our wedding...* here today. Where will it be, I wonder? Something tells me I've only seen a fraction of what this home has to offer.

I want to see all of it. If I'm supposed to be uprooted from my family and forced to marry Salvatore, I can at least take some comfort in living in the lap of luxury here.

I stare out at the open expanse of ocean and hear birds cawing from the water. I look out to see a waterbird I've never seen before sailing over the open sea, when a knock comes at the door.

I look down at myself, still barefoot, wearing nothing but the nightgown from the night before.

"Hello? Who is it?"

"Your future mother-in-law, dearest. Open the door, please. Are you decent?"

Salvatore's mother. The way he seemed on edge when he found out she was here gives me pause. Does he know she's come here? Will he be angry? Still, it would be rude not to answer.

I quickly go to the door. "I'm so sorry, I'm still in my nightgown."

"Oh, I don't mind about that," her voice coos. "Open, please."

With a trembling hand, I open the door.

A petite, frail-looking woman with eyes much darker than Salvatore's stands holding a platter of food. She's dressed impeccably in a fitted navy skirt and jacket, her hair pinned back in a merciless bun.

"Oh, my," she says quietly, then arranges her features in a smile that looks not unlike Salvatore's predatory grin. "Well, are you just going to stand there, or may I come in?"

Charming. I feel awkward and uncomfortable, and I wonder again if my future husband approves of her visit. Still, I quickly move to the side and gesture for her to come in as if I actually live here.

"Please, come in."

"Thank you."

My own mother is no saint. She had to learn survival skills married to my father with his vicious, tyrannical ways. She taught us to be resilient and strong. But even my mother has a trace of warmth in her. Natural maternal instincts. It's a well-known fact in my family that if any of the babies have trouble falling asleep, Mama's the one who will rock the fussiest baby until they're drifting off to Lalaland.

Salvatore's mother is carved from ice. If I had a baby, I wouldn't want her to come anywhere near it. I'd be afraid she'd freeze it to death with her nearness.

"Agnesia Capo," she says, extending a well-manicured hand to me, her nails painted bloodred. "Pleased to meet you."

Why would she lie about such a thing? I can tell she doesn't mean a word. What does she have against me or my family?

"Marialena Rossi," I finally say awkwardly, taking her hand because it seems that's what she expects of me.

"I know. Have you eaten?"

I look down at the platter of food she's brought and my stomach rumbles. I haven't eaten since the plane, hours ago.

Little paper cups with egg bites topped with melted cheese, mini cinnamon rolls with thick vanilla icing, and a large fruit salad with melon and cantaloupe cut into the shape of flowers are piled on the platter. There's a silver pot of what smells like cappuccino and a small pitcher of cream, as well as a semi-circle of flaky pastries and a jar of peach preserves beside a crock of butter. One little juice cup and a small, covered pitcher of orange juice sits beside the cappuccino.

"Oh my," I say, my mouth watering. "I could eat this whole platter."

She frowns slightly. "Well, I wouldn't do *that*," she says with a laugh that chills me. "You do have a dress to fit into later."

I feel my cheeks flush slightly. "Do I? No one measured me for a dress." I've always had a hearty appetite, and I'm not going to let a little bird-like woman shame me out of it. Salvatore actually seemed pleased that I like to eat. The Rossi family likes their food.

"Your mother was kind enough to give us your measurements and size," she says, pulling out one of the chairs by the little table near the balcony. "Eat up, dear, you won't have much time until this evening."

"Oh?" Something tells me she doesn't really mean the *eat up* part, but I'm starving and it looks delicious, so I fill a plate. I ignore the way she eyes me. I eat one of the egg bites, followed by a pastry, before I swallow it down with a small cup of juice and continue our conversation.

"This is delicious. My compliments to your kitchen staff."

"Oh, didn't he tell you? Salvatore prepares all the food he eats himself."

"For everyone?"

"No, most of us aren't as paranoid as he is, but he insisted on preparing your food himself."

Wow. When did he have time? I eye the platter a bit differently, knowing my future husband made my food.

"That's… nice of him."

"It has nothing to do with being nice," she says with a toss of her head, as if I've insulted him. She looks over my shoulder at the ocean behind me. "My son is anything but nice. He wouldn't waste his time on such frivolities as finding a wife to wed, only to have to do the whole process over again if she's poisoned. Not to mention the fact he'd have to avenge your death, which would be frightfully inconvenient."

"Frightfully inconvenient indeed," I repeat to myself from between clenched teeth.

She eyes me disdainfully when I take another pastry, but I'm nowhere near done, and if she says I won't have time to eat later, I'm eating now. I take a few bites of fruit first.

"Wow, that's the most delicious berry I've ever had." The slightly tart, sweet fruit nearly bursts in my mouth. Unlike the berries we get up north, these are pink all the way through, perfectly ripe. "Won't you have something to eat with me?" I ask sweetly, knowing full well she's likely already eaten dry toast and a broiled grapefruit with black coffee or something.

"No, no, I don't eat breakfast."

A beat passes where neither of us speaks again. Just to piss her off, I take the rest of the pastries and slide them onto my plate. Her eyebrows go up but she remains silent until she can't take it anymore.

"Has anyone shown you the home gym yet?"

"I've not seen much beyond these walls. I'd love to get a tour of the rest of the house." I ignore the hidden insinuation that I need to work off these calories. "And I prefer to run outside."

She snorts. "My dear, no one runs outside in Florida."

"No one?" I ask her incredulously. "But it's so much nicer running outside than in."

"Have you been outside yet?"

She has a point.

"I'll have to go much earlier in the morning, then," I murmur to myself.

"I'm sure Salvatore would prefer you run inside on the treadmill, safe within the confines of our workout room."

"I'll see what it is that Salvatore prefers," I murmur, not bothering to hide the steel in my voice while still speaking in a pleasant tone.

When she doesn't get under my feathers that way, she tries another tactic. She begins to stare at my face with another look of disapproval.

"Everything okay?" I ask, as I slip another berry into my mouth.

Another frigid frown. I wonder if she smiled, actually *smiled*, what would happen. Would her face crack? The idea amuses me, but I quickly school my face so she doesn't see the amusement.

"Darling, what *is* your skincare routine? You've all sorts of little red splotches on your cheeks that won't do at all for the ceremony tonight."

Ah, so now we're criticizing my complexion. There is absolutely nothing wrong with my complexion.

"I—just woke up," I say slowly. "I'm sure I still have some pink splotches from sleep."

"No," she says with concern. "It looks a lot more like rosacea. Tell me you have a daily SPF routine, please."

Instead of answering, I eat another egg bite deliberately, chewing it in front of her, before I smear a liberal amount of jam on a scone. "I've always had a perfect complexion. I suppose I take it for granted, but I have no qualms about my skincare routine."

I do. I absolutely do have qualms about my routine, but she doesn't need to know that, and who asked her? Rosa would likely give me a smug *I told you so* look. She's been going on about proper skincare for years.

"Well," I backtrack sheepishly. "I use… makeup remover wipes… I do a mask once in a while." Literally, like when I spend the night at Rosa's.

She grimaces. "I'll make an appointment with my facialist. Unfortunately, we won't be able to do anything about that today, since a treatment may cause more temporary redness, and that wouldn't do at all."

My God. Who has a *facialist?*

"We'll get you on a good routine. Fortunately, you have small pores and good genes, and it doesn't appear you've done irreparable damage."

"That *is* fortunate," I say, wondering if she can hear the sarcasm in my tone.

She eyes me thoughtfully. "Good bone structure," she murmurs. "Has anyone ever told you that?"

"I… am not quite sure anyone's ever mentioned my bone structure. But thank you."

She stands and walks to the balcony window, her back to me. I breathe more freely, as if being near her had stolen my breath.

"I have delicate bones. It comes from being thin and small," she says, as if she's somehow… the opposite of me? "But I didn't bear children well. My hips couldn't stand the pressure of a child, despite my efforts to remain fit and thin. My first baby broke his clavicle upon delivery, which was quite dramatic. After that, I chose nothing but C-sections." She turns to me and eyes my plate before she looks at my eyes again. "But your hips are perfect for child-bearing."

I manage to swallow my mouthful of cappuccino without choking.

"Excellent. I suppose the size of my hips and solid bone structure will be a decided point of delight for my future husband."

I ignore the way her eyes widen and her cheeks color.

"He's mentioned the demands and needs of a dominant male, and it seems sturdy hips—"

She puts her hand out as if to stop me. "Oh, dear, there's no need—

"Oh, but there *is*," I continue, pushing to my feet. "Just so you know how seriously I take my vows to your son. *All* of them. And the only way for me to *bear* those children my hips will gladly support is to—"

"I—I get the point," she says with another really pathetic attempt at a smile. She ought to practice in front of a mirror. It might crack, but it would be better than scaring little children away when she's let out of the dungeon. When she sees me reach for the last scone, she walks over to the tray and quickly sweeps it up.

"So glad you've enjoyed your breakfast. Staff will be up in about half an hour to begin preparations. You should shower, though don't wash your hair yet, since the hair stylist will be here momentarily and may need to treat your hair before styling." She leans in, scrutinizing my *hairline*. "No gray yet, I see."

If she sticks around long enough, I'm going to sprout gray right under her very eyes.

"Not yet," I say with a smile. "Though my mother was fully gray by thirty, so it is likely to happen at any minute. Ooh, fingers crossed," I say with mock enthusiasm. I pull that one out just for fun. My mother wasn't gray until she was well into her late fifties.

I watch her eyes widen. She's questioning whether or not marrying a capricious Rossi like me is worth their family's trouble, I'm sure.

I suppose we'll have to see about that.

I drum my fingers on the table and look thoughtfully out at the wide-open sea. "I wonder if I have time for a quick dip before we begin preparations? Salt water is *so* good for the skin and this morning's horoscope reminded me to make sure I'm earthing as often as I can. Are you familiar with earthing? Some people call it grounding." I go to the window and wriggle my toes in the carpet.

"I like to go barefoot and connect with nature at least daily, because it brings stress relief and prevents so many illnesses. I suppose it might even stave off gray hair…"

The door shuts behind me with an audible *click.*

I smile to myself and pour another cappuccino.

CHAPTER NINE

SALVATORE

"You shine up nice."

Cristiano approves. Like I fucking care.

I stifle a yawn while I fasten my cuff links and cast a casual glance at myself in the mirror.

It's my job to shine up when in the public eye, so I do. I dress nicely, I keep myself well-groomed, I do everything I can to be the photogenic pretty boy for the Capo family's legion of paparazzi.

The weight lifting isn't for show, though. It helps to be prepared.

I shrug. I want to get this over with so I can move on to the work I need to do. The work I'm *eager* to do. Namely, teaching my new wife what's expected of her. Showing her off when we travel or I have business to tend to. Coming home to the bed she's warmed at night.

I'm not, shall we say, disappointed that this turn of events means Marialena Rossi takes my last name.

"You do, you look good." Cristiano pulls a flask out of his pocket and takes a long swig.

I don't return the compliment. It's rare that any human resembling a pit bull shines up nice. "You'd better be fucking sober for this," I tell him.

"I am. Jesus, relax, will ya? Of course I'm sober." He stifles a belch. I roll my eyes as the door opens and my mother enters.

"Why did you move up the wedding?"

"Because I want to." I owe her no explanation. I want this over with so I can move on to bigger and better things. "It's not like people have had fuckin' *save the date* postcards on their fridges. They can either make it, or not." I've already checked that Romeo Rossi could get here in time. It matters that he's here to witness our vows. It matters that word gets out that I'm married and to whom.

"She's insane, son," my mother hisses out. "You picked a goddamn *insane woman* to marry, did you? Of all the—"

But I've already heard enough. I slap my palm up into the air to signal for her to *stop*. Her gripe with the Rossis isn't mine.

"Your opinion isn't welcome here. I'm marrying her for reasons I have no interest in sharing with you. But soon," I glance at my watch, "in ten minutes, to be exact, we will take our vows to each other. And you will not, under any circumstance, say anything against my wife. Am I clear?"

As of last week, I should've been the acting Don of the Capo family. As of today, I am.

She'll defer to my authority whether she likes it or not. It isn't my fault she hasn't accepted our roles yet, but she will. I know exactly how she behaves, and she won't pull her bullshit on me.

I watch as the color drains from her face and she pulls one of her lips into her mouth. I don't feel bad for her. It might be impossible for anyone to feel sympathy for a woman who punished me, her only son, when I was eight years old by putting my favorite dog down and pulling me out of bed so I could watch one of my uncles bleed out on the kitchen floor.

"This is your life, Salvatore," she said. *"Watch."*

The dog incident was because I "should've known" enough to tattle on my uncle when he knocked up our housekeeper.

Fun times.

Many take it for granted that an acting Don is a brutal sadist. I'm not sure I've ever met one that isn't. His wife, however, is a crap shoot. "Salvatore," she whispers, her fingers at her neck. "You can't—you don't mean—"

It's rare to see my mother at a loss for words.

"Can't what? Pull rank? I can. I don't mean what? To forbid you to disrespect my wife? I can and will."

"What do you see in her?" she demands, her eyes narrowed like a raptor's. "She's got wide hips, vapid eyes, and—"

Then I realize what I should've realized the minute she came in here. I turn my gaze to my mother and advance on her.

"Did you go to see her? Without my permission?" I've learned to keep my anger simmering just below the surface. I've seen men like my uncle be incapable of keeping their tempers under control and decided long ago that a man in control of his temper was a much better leader than one who wasn't. No one respects a man who flies off the goddamn handle.

My mother's eyes widen.

"I brought her breakfast. The breakfast you made!"

"The breakfast I instructed my staff to bring her with my permission," I correct. My mother backpedals until she sits in a chair.

"I wanted to see her."

"You wanted your way."

She opens her mouth as if to say something, then slams it shut with a sigh.

"I don't know why you picked this woman. Have you ever even *heard* of *earthing?*"

I shake my head. "No. What does that have to do with anything?"

"She said she likes to *earth* every day. Like take her shoes off and become one with nature." She wrinkles her nose in disgust. "She's insane!"

I want to slap her. I keep my hands in fists by my sides.

I don't even know Marialena, yet I feel the need to protect her from this woman. And I won't allow a show of disrespect.

"Wanting to be some green, earthy-crunchy palm reader has nothing to do with insanity. And even if she was insane, that has nothing to do with you."

"Nothing to do with me?" Her voice rises an octave, and I know what happens next. I don't fucking care about her tantrums, though. She continues, "As if I have nothing to say for my grandchildren?"

I turn and give her an incredulous look. "Excuse me?"

"What if I don't want a crazy woman bearing and raising my grandchildren?"

I need a full minute to compose myself this time. I breathe in deeply through my nose and exhale through my mouth and my mother takes the opportunity to spout more bullshit.

"She's unpredictable. Does she even have any manners?"

As if she should talk about manners. "She was raised properly by Tosca Rossi. She's been taught what's expected of her by her large, extended family. So yes, she knows manners." And I fully plan on teaching her the ones she hasn't learned yet.

"Good. I'd hate for her to embarrass you in front of anyone."

I clench my jaw.

"What do you even know about her?" she persists.

I've had hardly any sleep, and whatever patience I had has long since fled. I have no interest in perpetuating this conversation.

"Get her out of here," I growl at Cristiano. *"Now."*

My mother blinks in surprise. "You order my removal as if I'm some stray animal!"

I ignore her protests. "If you come to the wedding and step one *eyelash* out of line, I'll have you escorted to a private jet and taken to Italy. I won't have you in this house anywhere near her showing disrespect. You're not welcome here anymore. Attend the wedding, as you're expected, then plan to leave before the sun rises."

She opens her mouth, then clamps it shut.

Cristiano offers her his flask. "Shot of whiskey, Aunt Agnesia?"

She curls up her nose in disgust and turns to the door. Cristiano takes her by the elbow, but she slaps his hand and shoves him away. He only chuckles.

I nod to my guard by the door. "Six men on her. If she comes within ten feet of Marialena, have her forcibly removed. Any guard that loses sight of her faces prompt punishment and dismissal from *me*."

My men nod with a chorus of *yessirs*.

Another knock at the door.

I'm in no mood to talk to anyone but today I don't have that luxury. I'm starting to second-guess my choice not to take a honeymoon.

I turn to see Giuseppe, one of the younger men on my staff who's more like our secretary than anything. His beard is still scant, his eyes still hopeful and not yet fully jaded like the rest of us. He wants to strike it rich without getting his hands dirty, but he'll learn soon enough. He's eager to please, quick to do my bidding, and that's what matters right now. "Find me a place to go."

"Go, sir?" he asks.

I finish fastening my cuff links and head to the door. "With my wife."

"A honeymoon, sir?"

I speak through clenched teeth. Too many eyes watch us here. I need her alone, at least for a little while.

"Yes. Don't disclose the location to anyone but me. I want someplace with a white sand beach not far from here, but far enough away that I won't have unwelcome visitors shitting on my parade. You got me? Good food." I'll have it vetted. "Privacy. Maybe a boardwalk where my new wife can buy whatever she wants. Gucci or whatever the fuck." I smirk. "*Crystals* and shit."

"On it, sir."

The other men watch in stony silence. I cast them a quick glance. They're all dressed impeccably, prepared to be my groomsmen. "We ready?"

"Flowers, sir," someone mutters. A wide-eyed florist with a box of bloodred rosebud boutonnieres stands in the doorway.

I jerk my head for him to come in. "Let's get this over with. I take vows in minutes. This should've already been done."

"He got held up," Giuseppe's brother Federico mutters. Federico's been a member of my company for much longer, and he's the reason why his younger brother's been recruited.

"Why?" I snap, standing in front of the shaking florist. I scowl. "Get your shit together. Unless you plan on stealing from me or touching my new wife, you got shit to be shaking about, you get me? Pin the fucking flowers on and be done with it."

"Yessir," he mutters.

Federico smirks. "Guard at the door thought the pearl-covered pins were a weapon."

I pull one of the pins out of the box and roll my eyes. "I'd pick my teeth with one of these for Christ's sake."

"Saw someone take out an eye with one, once," one of the guys mutters.

"When, fucking prom night?"

Cristiano slips back into the room.

The men all laugh, but I can't help but wonder if we've taken things too far. Too much caution so now my men are fucking worried about pearl-headed pins?

I don't often feel nervous, and I'm not even sure the adrenaline that surges through my veins is what one would even call nerves. I'm about to take vows to Marialena. My decision to marry her is one no one can change or even impact in any way.

And this decision will be life changing.

I envy the men that know for years who their wives will be. I even envy those who marry for love, not because of the position they put themselves in—it's one reason I'd never choose to marry for love myself—but because there's at least a semblance of autonomy with such a marriage.

This is a forced circumstance due to situations beyond our control. I suppose there's a certain refuge or even weakness in granting choices to someone else. And even though I orchestrated the marriage part of our arrangement, I consider it even now a mercy.

I want to take these vows.

I want to claim her, mark her, and make her mine.

I want everyone to know that precocious, stunning woman bears my last name and took vows of submission and obedience to me.

I want to serve as Don with a mafia princess at my side.

"Ready, bro?" Cristiano asks from the doorway.

"In a minute. Everyone but Cristiano take your positions."

I don't miss the way his eyes grow apprehensive when I detain him. He knows I haven't forgotten his infraction against me.

The door clicks shut behind the last guard. Cristiano shifts nervously on his feet.

"Come here."

Slowly, like a child about to be scolded, he drags his feet to me. When he's only a few feet away, I reach my hand to his face. He flinches.

"Listen to me," I say in a low, warning voice. "The only reason I haven't fucked you up yet is for the sake of pictures. Memories. So we have those framed prints on the mantle to show what a big fucking happy family we all are."

His watery eyes widen, but he licks his lips and nods just the same.

"Got it."

"But if you fuck this up—if you touch my wife, or even talk to her, if you overstep your position or who you are—you'll answer to me, pictures be damned. You get me?"

He nods. "Of course. You're the boss," he replies, unable to hide the disdain and jealousy in his voice. Ahhh. So now we're getting somewhere.

I nod, because I am. "I'll deal with you later."

Another nod. I give what others might think is an affectionate slap to his cheek before we part, but it stings my palm and leaves an angry pink mark on his cheek. "Remember what I've said."

With a nod, he turns from me and discreetly rubs his cheek. "You ready?"

"I'm ready. Let's go."

This home that I inherited is on the austere side of things to say the least. Cathedral ceilings inside, with living rooms that feature balconies overlooking the Gulf of Mexico, we have almost double the average water frontage as the average luxury home here with two hundred feet of private beach. It's kind of showy. That's the point.

I didn't want a beach wedding, though. Sand gets fucking everywhere, and it's so hot under the direct sunlight this time of year it's like walking through hell. So instead, we've set it up so that the vows and following reception will be outdoors near the pool. We have covered verandas, paved patios, and seating galore. My plan is to host the celebration under full coverage from our security cameras, and staff and guests wilting under the heat can cool off indoors or in the pool.

I look out the plate glass windows. Tables are set up, decorated with white tablecloths, green vines, and boughs of white flowers. The elegant strings of a violin play in the background, and the soft murmurs of staff serving hors d'oeuvres blend with the music.

We put on a good show when we want to. That's what this is all about, I tell myself. *Show.* There's no love lost between me and my future wife and never will be. The best I can hope for is that we can tolerate each other. Hot sex might season the deal.

One of my men opens the double doors that lead to the paved patio in the back. To my far right, I see a cluster of women dressed in elegant dresses, a flash of white behind them. Marialena's there, then, with her staff.

The women are at ease, talking and laughing freely, like old friends. How has she done that already? She only came here last night and passed out as soon as her head hit the pillow.

I hear Marialena's voice, then a peal of laughter from one of the younger women of her staff.

"Shh," one of them hushes her. "It's a somber time!"

This makes them all lapse into laughter. Someone whispers something to Marialena, and her delicate laugh joins theirs.

Of course. She's here for less than twenty-four hours, and she's already managed to beguile my staff.

I feel my own lips turn down in a scowl. They'd better fucking respect her.

Cristiano walks ahead of me, and one of the staff catches his eye. As if someone shut the lights out, their faces sober. No one laughs any more. They stand stock-still as if expecting me to berate them for poor behavior or to make an example of one of them for not taking their roles seriously.

Someone claps me on the back, but by the time I turn around, they're gone. This is why I fucking hate crowds.

"Let's get this started," I mutter to Cristiano.

"We're doing the best we can," he responds. "But we have to wait—"

I snap my fingers to Giuseppe. "Yeah, boss?"

"I want to get this over with. *Now.*"

"You got it." He speaks into a walkie-talkie, gestures ahead of himself, then turns and smiles to me before he raises his hand, and a trumpet begins to play.

People go to their seats. The crowd hushes.

Mama walks ahead of me, takes Cristiano's arm, then marches down the aisle toward her seat.

My turn.

Cell phones flash as people take pictures of me and Giuseppe walking down the aisle. I hear the murmur of voices. I don't look at anyone or make eye contact. I hate ceremonial bullshit and want this over with.

I take my place up front as the music shifts. This will be a short wedding ceremony, albeit a Catholic one to appease my family and tradition but without a full mass with all the bells and whistles. Still, I want out of here, and fast. I want my ring on her finger. I want her to take vows, and I want to be done with this whole affair so I can move on and we can get all these people the fuck off my property.

"You look *amazing*." I blink in surprise to see my eldest sister Techla standing right near Mama up front. I didn't think either of my sisters would be able to make it.

"Hey," I say warmly, reaching for her. I give her a big hug, as the music changes. "How have you been?"

"I'm good," she says with a shrug. "Glad to see you're finally tying the knot. Whoever picked out your clothes for today did an awesome job. Your shirt matches your eyes."

I shrug. I seriously don't care.

"Good," I say. "Thanks."

She laughs, as the crowd gets to their feet.

"Good luck," she whispers.

I turn. The crowd parts, and I watch as my future wife heads toward me.

The throng of people dissipates, their chatter dying as the haunting lilt of a violin wafts through the humid air around us. All eyes focus near the house when a billow of white precedes my bride.

My breath leaves me when I see her.

I barely know the woman. I definitely don't love her. But damn if I don't feel speechless at the sight of the woman about to take vows to me walking down the aisle toward me, hanging on for dear life to Romeo Rossi's proffered elbow. Romeo looks the part of experienced and respectable Don as well as eldest brother. He wears a well-made charcoal gray suit. His jaw's clean-shaven, his blue eyes staring at mine unblinkingly.

He says something in a whisper to her and she smiles, lighting up her whole face. I hear gasps around us as my guests see her. She's lovelier than any model that's ever graced the cover of a bridal magazine.

Swathed in lace, satin, and tulle, she wears head-to-toe white, little satin pumps peeking out from beneath the lengthy hem of her dress. Her hair hangs about her face in delicate waves and curls, at once fetching and whimsical. The dark curls around her temples enhance her dancing eyes, eyes too vivid and full of laughter to ever be sober too long. Her full pouty lips curl upward as if she's amused by everything. If fairy tales came true, I'd believe that Marialena stepped out of the pages of one and came to grace us with her presence.

The music plays on as she walks to me, people snapping so many pictures the flashes are nearly blinding for a moment. In my peripheral vision I see the flash of a camera from behind a bush. A snap of my fingers, and one of my men quickly tends to that. Goddamn paparazzi on my damn *property.* That'll cost them.

Even wearing heels Marialena's a full head shorter than Romeo, but what she doesn't have in stature she makes up for in personality. She doesn't need to say a word to win the hearts of every damn person here. There's just something… charismatic about her I can't compete with. She's undeniably mesmerizing, with nearly hypnotic twinkling eyes that make people want to fall at her feet and worship her.

I'll have to keep a close eye on her. There's something so attractive about her I fear that my staff will choose her above me. And if the two of us come to cross swords, that could be a problem.

But they will love her. They will adore her.

When Romeo and Marialena meet me, she needs to crane her neck to look up at me. I don't miss the way she swallows hard or the way she stumbles a bit and Romeo has to steady her. I definitely don't miss her little smile, or the hopeful look in her eyes that tells me she wants to know I'm pleased with her.

"You look very handsome, almost husband," she whispers. Romeo's eyes widen and he barely stifles a little grimace.

I ignore him. I don't know what he's told her about me, but she's taking her chances.

Almost husband.

"Thank you," I say in a whisper, bowing my head. "As do you, almost wife. You look gorgeous."

Apparently all that was missing to make her look like an angel was a faint flush of color across her cheeks. Now, she's perfection.

"Say *thank you,*" Romeo reminds her.

"Thank you," she says in a barely audible whisper. Romeo nods, his stoic face carved from stone as he faces me. If he has an emotional reaction to this moment, he hides it well.

I reach for her arm. He doesn't let her go.

"It's time, Rossi," I say in a low voice.

Still, he won't release her, as if she's glued to him and some invisible force of nature keeps her attached to him.

I sense Cristiano stiffen behind me.

"Rossi."

Marialena gently extricates her arm from Romeo's, leans over and kisses his cheek. Bending his cheek to hers, he closes his eyes and whispers something in her ear that makes her face go soft and her eyes water, before he releases her hands and turns to me.

"Take good care of her," he says in a husky whisper. "Promise me, Capo. You'll take good care of her. I'll remind you it's part of our contract."

I take her arm as he lets her go, and nod. "I will," is all I tell him. It's all he gets from me. Taking care of people I'm sworn to protect is the only thing that keeps me from being a totally unforgivable asshole.

The priest behind me clears his throat just as the unmistakable sound of a gun goes off.

CHAPTER TEN

Marialena

If we were a normal couple, or if this was a normal wedding, I suppose there would be screaming, running, fainting. But we aren't normal people, and this isn't a normal wedding.

So when a gunshot blasts on my wedding day just as Romeo hands me off to Salvatore, the two men devoted to my protection spring into action. Salvatore shoves me to the ground as Romeo reaches for me, but Salvatore's already got me in his grip and Romeo's a fraction of a second too late. I lift my skirts and take out the small pistol I have in a thigh holster. Thanks to my brothers, I can shoot as well as any man here, and my low vantage point will come in handy.

I half expect my almost husband to growl at me and tell me to put it away, but he doesn't. He takes one look at me and gives me a proud smirk. "Cover my back," he orders, his own weapon poised. His guard rushes to find the source of the shot.

No one's fallen to the ground. No one's bleeding. There's no evidence that anyone here at the wedding has been shot. I glance quickly at the priest, who's pale but otherwise unharmed. I'm disappointed to see Salvatore's mother also unscathed.

A few murmurs go up from the crowd. "Sit, all of you," Salvatore barks, his voice like a sledgehammer. The entire crowd, every man, woman, and child, does what he says and hardly breathes, as if the entire group of them fears Salvatore's wrath more than being shot.

Interesting.

"Scan the front entrance. Secure the gate." I watch as he barks out orders and speaks into a mouthpiece. Men in suits run to obey, guns drawn. Still, everyone else sits, all eyes on Salvatore.

"You see anything by the ocean front?" he mutters. It takes me a second to realize he's talking to me. From where I am, I can see several boats just beyond the waterfront, but nothing out of place. "No, I don't think that—no, wait. There are two men on a sailboat maybe ten yards from shore.

They're in some kind of a fight. I wonder if one pulled a gun on the other."

"For fuck's sake," he growls, turning to look at the ocean. "What the fuck kind of vision do you have?"

"Perfect," I mutter. He gets grumpy over the oddest things.

I hazard a glance up at my scowling brother who isn't amused there's shenanigans at my wedding.

"I've got a team at the beach," he says. "I can have them investigate."

"Do it," Salvatore agrees.

Romeo pulls out his phone and issues a few short commands in Italian. Wordlessly, Salvatore reaches for my hand and lifts me to my feet. "Sit and put your gun away." He pulls over a vacant white chair and yanks me onto it.

I mutter under my breath but don't make eye contact with him. Why does *he* get to keep his gun out? I freeze when he leans down toward me, one hand on the back of my seat. The scent of his cologne wafts over me. I'm struck by the way his body moves with fluid grace, the stark blue of his eyes that pierce straight through me, the masculine scent of him that's fucking erotic.

"I know you're an excellent shot," he says quietly. "And I trust you know when and how to make the call to shoot. But I don't need everyone here to know that about you. Sometimes, a wild-card shooter comes in very, very handy."

"Are you flattering me?" I mutter.

"Is it working?"

I note the heat in my chest and the way I'm oddly pleased he wants to keep me as a wild card. "Yes."

A swift curling of his lips tells me he's pleased before he turns away again.

I do what he says and casually slide my gun back into the holster. I like the familiar cold heft of it against my naked skin.

Ten minutes later, his men have given the all clear, and Romeo's guard have indeed ferreted out the men near the shoreline. Ironically, the Rossi crowd manages to get local authorities involved and returns to the ceremony in record time. By the time they do, staff is pouring out glasses of wine in disposable stemware, as if we're starting the reception early.

Don't mind if I do. I take a glass of champagne in each hand.

Salvatore clears his throat. "Let's have a wedding." I down both glasses of wine and hand them to a nearby server.

My feet feel wobbly, my head a bit fuzzy, as I take my place at the altar with him. It passes in a blur, a jumble of prayers and well wishes and vows I've heard before. I say my part and he says his, though I stumble a bit over the *love, honor, and obey* part. Whereas modern weddings have struck the archaic language from their vows, my family and his still maintain them as a necessity.

I won't love him. It's silly to even take that vow. And that promise to honor and obey, which I knew was coming thanks to witnessing my sister and brothers' weddings, is a huge pill to swallow.

The crowd erupts into cheers when Salvatore takes my hand and makes a fist, raising our joined hands like a victorious boxer. Romeo kisses my cheek, then walks away. Seeing his retreat pings my heart, as if he's turning me away from the Rossi family.

I stare at the crowd in front of us. I look to see the rest of my family, but only Romeo has come, for reasons I don't understand. Maybe it was less risky.

I look at the faces of his family and guests. I don't know them, but I already know they aren't *my* family. They aren't the Rossis.

No one is.

I hear a startling *chuf chuf* in the air above us and quickly look up. Everyone does, as a helicopter circles above us. When I look at Salvatore, however, he's not surprised. He only takes me by the elbow and walks away from the crowd.

"Uh. What's up with that?" I ask him. "News footage? Someone getting a ride somewhere?"

"Changed my mind on the honeymoon," he mutters, as his mother rises from her seat and marches over in front of us to block our way. Her pale skin seems paler than ever, though bright splotches of red unnaturally dot her cheeks. Girlfriend needs a makeup artist.

"You can't mean this, Salvatore," she says in a tone that implies *he will not.*

But I just watched this man command several hundred people to sit, and I just watched several hundred people obey him like well-trained dogs. I believe whatever it is he wants to do, he can, and he will.

Honeymoon. He said honeymoon. He wants us away from the crowd. My cheeks flush pink when I think of the implications...

"I've about had it with the *can'ts* and *shouldn'ts*," he mutters. "My wife and I are taking a short honeymoon. The location will be closely guarded and we'll return in a week. You will not hinder us. No one will." He looks over at me. "You look pouty, Marialena."

"I wanted that cake," I say with a frown. "It's chocolate. And those finger sandwiches are my favorite."

When I see the note of disgust on his mother's face, I put a little whine behind my complaint. "They had little wedges of *cheesecake*, Salvatore. Mini appetizers and those twice-baked potatoes slathered in butter and cheese. Mmmm." My stomach actually growls. "And did I see chicken alfredo? Crusty bread with whipped butter? *Tiramisu*?" I sigh.

His mother doesn't even try to hide her disapproval. Fine with me. I'll eat her food, too.

"Fill up a plate of food for my wife," Salvatore orders someone to our right. "Everything. A generous amount."

My wife. The very words terrify me.

"Wait, what about you?" I ask.

"There's plenty of good food where I'm bringing you."

"We're leaving now? I haven't packed yet!"

"It's been done already."

Of course it has. He's planned this all out.

"Why did you change your mind on the honeymoon?" I ask.

His mother cocks a brow at him and crosses her arms over her chest. "Why, indeed?"

"On second thought, don't answer," I say when I think about his possible response. He only clenches his jaw and holds me closer to him, marching me toward the waiting helicopter.

Cheers erupt around us. A tight circle of guards waits for us as we climb aboard. I feel a bit shell-shocked and bewildered as I look out at the mass of nameless faces before us. In the distance, the flash of red and white indicates police are dealing with the brawl on the shore, as if they couldn't care less that Tampa's most wanted are wining and dining only yards away from them.

In the midst of the chaotic swarm of faces, I catch a pair of eyes I know so well. Romeo holds a glass of champagne in one hand, his other hand tucked into his pocket.

As the door to the helicopter closes, he raises his glass and winks at me. I wink back and mouth, *I love you.*

I close my eyes against a wave of emotion. My moment of sadness is fleeting, though, as my husband wraps his hands around my waist and drags me over to him. He sits heavily in one of the two seats in the back, the pilot sitting up front.

I knew the interior of a helicopter was tiny, but this is something else. *I'm on his lap.* We've barely touched before now. He's kissed me, but other than that, he's hardly touched me, and now… now I'm his. Through this strange, fast-paced, shocking turn of events… *I'm his.* His wife. And he's already made it clear he expects me to fulfill my vows to him, not the least of which is sharing his bed.

It very well might be the *most* important thing to him.

"Hungry, Marialena?" he asks in my ear. The heavy warmth of his large hand spans my belly as his fingers splay, and he holds me closer.

"I'm pretty much *always* hungry," I say on a sigh. It's true, though. "It's the Italian in me."

"Good. Let's get you fed."

I'm waiting for the monster to show his fangs, but so far all I've gotten is this somewhat grumpy, definitely violent, but very hot, kinda handsy Italian stallion dressed in a tux.

But Romeo doesn't exaggerate, and he definitely doesn't lie. He was—*is*—scared of Salvatore. And I know my brother would have good reason.

I wait for him to slide me off his lap onto my seat, though riding in a helicopter is nothing like riding in a private jet or airplane. There are no stewardesses, no flight attendants, no galley kitchen where someone may prepare food. The door to the helicopter is still open, however. Salvatore snaps his fingers, and four uniformed members of the waitstaff bring platters of food, the good stuff from the wedding.

He lifts a thick pair of earmuffs and slides them over my ears. Interesting. They're not unlike the ones I wear for target practice.

I adjust them, and the loud *chop* of the helicopter blades quiets.

"Testing," I say, my eyes on him. "Can you hear me?" I can hear my own voice, though distantly.

He nods. "I can still hear you, it's just muffled."

They stand beside me with the food. I look at Salvatore questioningly. What now? Someone unfolds a little tray and makes a plate of food.

"Eat," he commands. He brings his hands to my hips and anchors them there. I look curiously from the trays of food to him, then back again.

"With my fingers?"

A curt nod.

"Is this another test?" I ask.

He doesn't respond, but I swear there's a flash of impatience in his eyes. There's a monster in this closet, and someone's just cracked the door open. I'm not sure yet what summons the monster, but I do know that disobedience is *probably* pretty effective.

My stomach rumbles. "You cooked this?" I ask.

A muscle twitches in his jaw. "Are you stalling?" His grip on my hips tightens.

I shake my head. "No." But it's a lie. I'm definitely stalling. I'm not sure what his endgame is here, but I've never fed myself with my fingers while sitting on a hot, dangerous guy's lap *on a helicopter,* and I've just realized that in order for me to eat, I'll have to lean over him. Press my body closer. And that very well might be exactly what he wants.

My instinct warns me not to stall anymore, not to ask any more questions. My rumbling belly likes this plan.

So I reach for the food. My breasts mash up against his chest as I lean over, my body flush against his. I reach for a bacon-wrapped scallop, thankfully stacked on a little frilled toothpick, and slide it into my mouth. An explosion of sweet yet salty bacon and scallops cooked to perfection explodes in my mouth. "Mmmm," I mutter. "Oh, God."

Tingles of sensation skim over my breast. I gasp. His thumb gently traces the hardened bud of my nipple beneath the thin layer of fabric that divides us.

Well, then.

I stay leaned over and take a little toothpick with a fried ravioli, its edge dipped in bright red marinara. I close my eyes and slide it into my mouth. Crispy with a slight tang, filled generously with well-seasoned ricotta. My eyes flutter closed and I make a husky sound of approval somewhere between a moan and a sigh.

He fingers my other breast.

I hold my breath.

Next, a golden twice-baked potato, stuffed to overflowing with bacon and cheese-laced mashed potatoes. This one takes several bites, enough for him to hold both breasts in his hands while he fingers my nipples. I swallow and chew while my body grows warm and pliant against his. If this is how he plans on garnering my submission, I think I'll make it.

A slice of crusty bread slathered in whipped butter is next. By the time I lick the last crumb, he's lifted my skirt and worked his way past my lace thong. I'm vaguely aware of the pilot in front of us, his men outside the door, the loud noise of the helicopter blades overhead, but it all somehow fades to my periphery.

"Where's the alfredo?" I ask on a smile, as I lay my head on his chest and his rough thumb finds the slit between my thighs.

"Thought that might be hard to eat with your fingers," he whispers, his voice a near growl. "And you need to have a bit of an appetite left for our honeymoon. I don't want you totally sated, now, do I?"

I don't respond, because *totally sated* sounds pretty damn nice.

Then the next moment, he's sliding me off his lap onto the seat beside him. I stifle a whimper. It's a test, I know it is, just like much of what he'll do to me over the next few days. A man like Salvatore will want to prove to me that he's in charge, will want to test my obedience and allegiance to him. They're all the same, so I'm not surprised.

Not that it makes it easy. But at least I'm not going into this with any expectation of an egalitarian marriage. I know why I'm here. I know what's expected of me. And the eternal optimist in me hopes that I find my joy again, that I find my place apart from my family and everyone I love.

I swallow the lump in my throat.

"I promise you," he says, straightening beside me. "There's more where that came from if you behave yourself."

Oh, right. He thinks I'm still pouting over him not touching me anymore. A little full of ourselves, are we?

I bite my lip and look out the window. "Good," I say, almost pouting but not quite. "That ravioli, though…"

That earns me an almost-chuckle and light swat to my leg. I sigh. Let him wonder why.

I change the subject and try to get an answer again. "So I thought you didn't want a honeymoon. What changed? Where are we going?"

I half expect him to say, "you'll see," but he actually humors me.

"Private island south of here. That's all I can say for now, because no one but my closest guard will know the location. As far as why I changed my mind, I decided we needed a little time to get to know each other without the prying eyes of every fuckin' person in my family or yours nearby."

In other words, his damn mother. Good.

Wait, did he say mine, too?"

"My family is in Boston." All but Romeo, anyway.

His brows rise but he doesn't respond. What's that all about?

Aren't they?

I look out the window at the crowd below.

"Buckle up."

I look down for the belt, but apparently I'm too slow, because he reaches across me and grabs the buckle from my fingers to snap it in place. I guess someone else might be offended or feel like he's treating me like a child, but I don't. My brothers do shit like this all the time, this over-protective thing, so I'm used to it.

I learned a long time ago it's far better to reserve your energy to fight the more important things. If you fight everything, you become the boy who cried wolf.

I expected with my belly full of food and the rhythmic chopping of the helicopter blades I'd be sleepy and ready for a nap, but I'm energized. Excited. I've always loved adventures, and even though this was not one I'd have ever chosen on my own, I can't help but wonder what happens next.

"Some people say life is a hardship," I say softly. "*I say life is an adventure.*"

Salvatore doesn't respond at first, and I half wonder if I should've kept my mouth shut.

"Why's that?" he finally asks me. "What's the difference?"

"Because you don't know what's coming around every turn. But if you view things as an adventure, it's more exciting and less... well, terrifying."

"And if you think of life as a hardship, you'd think it terrifying?"

I nod, my response barely audible. "Oh, definitely. I bet if you think about it, you know people that feel that way, too."

I don't look to see his reaction, but feel him stiffen beside me. "Are there things in your life you've found terrifying?"

I snort. "Of course. Most people find my brothers terrifying, and while I wouldn't go that far, I've definitely seen them do terrifying *things*. And my father..." My voice trails off as I give an involuntary shudder. "He was absolutely awful. Ruthless and narcissistic. Everything revolved around him, and I mean *everything*. Dinnertimes, our vacations, his plans and wishes for our family. My mother's response to things and how she showed up at public events. He seemed to think that if he only came down hard enough on all of us, his life would be perfect."

Salvatore grunts but doesn't otherwise respond. "Did he hit you?"

I nod. "Of course. He had a vicious backhand and wasn't afraid to use it."

I try to decipher his responding grunt but can't.

"So your father was terrifying. Understandable."

"What was yours like?"

"I don't remember much. He died when I was younger, but I know from what I've heard and the few memories I do have, he was no cakewalk."

I look over at him, to try to catch his eyes, but he's intent on his phone. Still, I can ask him.

"When did your father die?"

He doesn't look up from his phone or show any reaction at all. "A long time ago."

"I'm sorry."

"Don't be. The only reason I'm acting Don of our group is because he died and I'm second-in-command after my uncle. Or, *was*."

"Oh?"

"His brother, my uncle, became acting Don until I took a wife. Archaic mob laws trump all."

God, don't I know it.

So *that's* why he was so eager to get married. Must've been an age restriction or time limit. Interesting. And I had to go and somehow fuck that all up by hiding a girl I didn't even know. Now here I am.

I'm waiting for the other shoe to drop.

Yesterday, I saw him beat the shit out of one of his men, then toss him off the plane as if he didn't matter, as if he didn't count at all. I guess some women would've been terrified of him, but it's not much different from anything else I've seen my brothers do.

And I love my brothers.

Maybe... just maybe... I can grow to love Salvatore.

Then a stark realization hits me. Out here, he's no different from any of the men I grew up with.

But what will he be like when we're... alone?

When we're in bed?

I look out the window and squirm uncomfortably at the thought.

As if reading my mind, he interrupts my pondering with a bold question.

"Are you a virgin, Marialena?"

My cheeks flush. I could pretend I don't hear him with the muffs on, but he'll ask it again sooner or later.

"Can't hear you," I say, looking out the window. I jump when his grip on my knee tightens.

"You'll look at me when I'm speaking to you."

My pulse quickens. Now that we're married, is he going to go all psycho on me?

I look up at him like the obedient little wife I'm not. "What was that?" I say. I'm going with feigning deafness here.

"I asked if you were a virgin."

I swallow and nod. "Of course."

Another squeeze of my thigh. "You're not right out of college. You're old enough that it might have happened sooner or later. Are you telling me the truth?"

He'll find out for himself soon enough. I close my eyes briefly before I open them again and nod. "I'm telling you the truth. It's one thing that's non-negotiable in my family. I was once sexually assaulted, but it didn't go far."

"And your brothers took care of that?"

I look away. I can still see Romeo's broken hand, dripping with blood when he took his turn beating the guy who assaulted me, some dumb college student at a frat party. But it was Orlando, our group heavy and the largest one of all, who was the one who made him bleed, who castrated him and hung him from the Zakim bridge. It took me all summer to forgive them, but not for beating and murdering the man. I was grounded to the house all summer for ditching my guard and attending the party to begin with and I wasn't too happy about that.

"Oh, yeah," I say with forced nonchalance. "For sure they did."

"He still breathing?"

The tightening of his mouth and grip on my thigh warn me in this he's like my brothers as well. He wants a name, and he'll hunt that name down.

"Of course not."

"Good."

I'm under no delusion he really cares about me. Someone touched what now belongs to him, and his code of ethics demands retribution on some level if the perpetrator's still at large.

It's the way things are in my family, too.

I tilt my head and look at him. "Are *you* still a virgin?" I ask. I know it's a brazen question, borderline insolent. I know I risk being punished by being bold and impertinent. I can almost hear Romeo's groan, but the truth is, I could write a literal novel on the double standards in mob life and sometimes I get a little ornery about it.

"Careful, sweetheart." Fear pricks my consciousness when he bares his teeth in a smile without a hint of warmth. "You overstep."

Eh, I kinda hope he's not a virgin. Might be nice being married to a guy who knows his way in a bedroom. I wouldn't know. And I don't care if there were others before me. We both know this is a business transaction. The sex and orgasms are just the benefits. The free wine and dessert with a business dinner.

Love how he pulls out the *sweetheart* when he goes all wolfish and growly on me or he pulls out the condescension.

I turn away and look out the window. Perhaps I can distract myself so I don't say something stupid again.

Nothing but bright blue waves below us. I imagine the helicopter blades coming to a sudden halt. I imagine the helicopter nosediving into the idyllic waves below.

I imagine drowning, succumbing to the relentless pull of the undertow and tide.

I imagine finally being free.

CHAPTER ELEVEN

Salvatore

I didn't want to come on this honeymoon, because the endless list of tasks and work I have to do as Don stretch out before me, as countless as the sand on the shore. But as the helicopter begins its descent to the private island where we'll briefly honeymoon, I'm glad I made this call.

Privacy is unheard of, even with a family much smaller than hers. I've spent years in prison with no conjugal visits, and the few hookups I've had since I've been home have barely scratched the surface.

I want to taste her, ravage her, devour her. I want to drink so deeply I drown in her scent, in her moans when I grant her pleasure and ecstasy. I want to glut myself on everything Marialena. I pride myself on knowing how to please a woman, and fully intend on working every angle I can to ensure she obeys me.

So when the helicopter touches down, I'm already hard. I want to tear off the remnants of her bridal gown right here, slide her onto my lap, and impale her with my cock. I want to force her to her knees and pry her mouth apart and slide my shaft between her lips. I want to see her gag on my cock. I want to feel the warmth of her mouth wrapped around me. I want to come and watch her swallow.

"Are you alright?" she asks curiously. "You look... preoccupied."

I'm mentally undressing and fucking her, so damn right I'm preoccupied.

I nod and jerk my head to the water's edge, where a small private ferry waits to take us to the island. "Takin' a ferry to the island."

"Which island?"

"No more questions."

Though she clamps her mouth shut, I don't miss the way her eyes briefly flash at me.

"You've got a problem with that?"

Wide, innocent eyes meet mine. "Of course not, husband. I hear and obey, as we've already established. I took vows, and I meant them. Whatever gave you the impression otherwise?"

I narrow my eyes at her. "Hmm. Not sure. Could it be the attitude? I came here to fuck you, but maybe a good, hard spanking is the foreplay we need first."

I take her by the elbow to escort her to the ferry. I expect she'll behave herself now, at least for a little while, but I'm mistaken. Either she wants to call my bluff, or a part of her wants that spanking.

"Who knew getting fucked or spanked was part of our *arrangement*," she mutters sarcastically.

"*You* knew, sweetheart," I say pleasantly, as we take our seats on the ferry.

"So you'll punish me like I'm a child?" she asks, her cheeks flushed but her eyes dancing. Kinky little hellion.

I cluck my tongue and shake my head. "You heard me."

"I'm your wife," she responds.

"Well aware."

The same woman who nearly clapped her hands at cheesecake and had her entire staff wrapped around her finger in minutes pouts, actually *pouts,* on the way home, complete with arms wrapped over her chest and her lower lip sticking out.

"Pouting won't be allowed either."

She only glowers at me.

Well, if this isn't damn convenient. I knew I needed to train her, train her well, and train her fast, but she's making it a lot easier for me than I expected.

"Really, now," I say to her thoughtfully as the ferry begins the fairly quick jaunt to our private island. "There's no way your brothers put up with behavior like *this*."

"I have no idea what you're talking about."

"Well. We could ask Romeo ourselves, now, couldn't we?" I say thoughtfully, pulling out my phone. That gets her attention.

"Salvatore," she says, sobering. "You wouldn't!"

I narrow my eyes at her. "Just what I thought then. You're more afraid of a call to your brother than you are of my belt across your ass. We'll have to fix that."

That will change, and quickly.

I ignore her wide-eyed look of panic.

My dick lengthens. Fuck it, I need this ferry to move faster.

"Come here, Marialena." I sit on one of the plush seats and gesture for her to come to me.

"And if I don't, will you spank me?" she challenges.

"Yes."

Though she rolls her eyes, her cheeks heat with a pink flush, and she flounces over to me. As soon as she's within arm's reach, I yank her down onto my knee.

"Now, what is it," I say almost thoughtfully as I spin her around to look at me. "Do you want to know if I really mean it? Or is it possible you want a spanking? Maybe both."

I lay my hands across the small of her back and drag her closer to me.

"What do you..." her voice grows husky. "What if it's neither?"

"Liar," I snap. "You want something, and you think the only way to get it is manipulation. That's bullshit. If you want a spanking, you ask for one and don't even think about manipulating me."

The look of outrage on her face is damn near amusing. "Who in their right mind would *ask* for a spanking?"

I shake my head. "Now I know you really *are* a virgin."

"Salvatore!"

I drag her closer to me and reach my hand to the back of her neck. I yank her mouth to mine. Our lips clash, and her hands come flying to my shoulders. At first she pushes, as if to stop me, but when I lick her tongue and her eyes begin to close, she moans. I explore her mouth but keep my grip firm and move one of my hands from the back of her neck to the front. I give her a none-too-gentle squeeze, inhaling her gasp of air.

She tries to yank her head away, but I hold her to me. The sun could rise and set, and the moon could go from waxing to waning and I wouldn't notice the time pass if only I were kissing her. Someone could set off fireworks, a tornado could sweep the state, she could steal my wallet and empty its contents and I wouldn't even be aware. It's an erotic intimacy I wasn't prepared for, a sudden sexual charge between us that damn near puts my hair on end.

Jesus.

Her hands slide up my body, my sides, my shoulders, before she stabs her fingers into my hair as if to hold herself there. I love the feel of her fingers on my scalp as her tongue presses against mine. I love the sound of her soft, erotic moans as my hands find her ass.

I pull my mouth off hers, and it feels fucking *wrong.* Holding her neck against my palm, I whisper in her ear. I'm watching for her signs, waiting for a cue. "You took vows to honor and obey. Those meant something to me."

She nods, breathless.

"If you ever sass me in public again, I don't care who's nearby or where we are, I will take you across my knee, strip you, and spank your naked ass until you beg me to stop. Am I clear?"

She closes her eyes and nods, but it's the quick way she responds that really gets my attention.

"If you weren't so new to this, you'd have earned a punishment tonight. But just because we're new doesn't mean I'll take it easy on you. I'm sure your brothers would never deal with you the way I will, but I know you were kept on a tight leash with them. So I know part of this is a test for me. And believe me, I am up for the challenge."

"Is that what you do?" she breathes. "Someone disobeys you and you punish them?"

"Sweetheart," I whisper in her ear. "You're the only one who'll ever receive this brand of punishment." I bring my hand to her hip and gently stroke my thumb along her thigh. "I'll never raise my fist to you or exile you. I would never shoot you or break your bones. But I will spank you, deny you what you want, tie you up, and make sure I have your undivided attention. I will hold you on the edge of orgasm until you feel as if you'll self-combust. I will force your legs apart and fuck you until the only name on your lips is mine. Until your body tingles at the sound of my name and heats at the sound of my voice."

"You're scaring me," she says, but she doesn't look scared. She looks… aroused.

"You have nothing to be afraid of, if you remember to do what I say."

"So many rules," she whispers.

"Really, only one."

She sighs and thrusts her chin out. "Obey." I don't miss the dripping condescension or the rapid beating of her heart I feel when I gently grasp her wrist. Marialena both loves and hates this.

I nod. The ferry begins to slow, the hum dying down. We're almost there.

Good. I have work to do that only involves her.

I like that her knowledge of mob life overlaps with mine at least in part. We're not the same as the Rossis—their family is larger, more tight-knit, and Romeo gives them more freedom than I do mine—but the general principles are close enough there's none of the sticker shock for her I'd get from another woman. An unexpected perk.

I hold her gaze with mine. "Kiss me."

She knows I expect compliance, and I know she wants to push her luck with me. Her legs straddling mine, my cock strains for relief as she bites her lip and watches me.

One beat passes. Then two.

The weight of her hands rests on my shoulders as she leans in. The flutter of her breath on my cheek makes my dick ache, straining for release. I relish her lingering scent of wildflowers and lavender. Her fingers tighten around my collar, as if holding me to her.

Her mouth drops to mine. Tentatively, her lips move across mine in exploration. At first, I don't kiss her back. I want to see how she responds, see how she kisses.

Her kiss is as gentle as a summer rain, warm and familiar. I open my mouth and let her in further, while I gently ease my fingers through her hair. When I give her hair a quick, hard tug, her mouth parts in a silent gasp and I deepen the kiss. I hold her hostage in my grip, her body pressed to my cock, her lips welded to mine, no slack in my grip in her hair.

I let her go. Her gaze on mine is a little startled. She wipes the back of her hand across her mouth as if she's just had a snack.

"That probably isn't the safest way to ride a ferry," she whispers.

"It's fine. Ferries move at the pace of a turtle." I'd have known if it was time to sit apart and buckle up.

Another tentative nod, before she asks, "How'd I do?"

"How do you think you did?" I can't help but release my grip on her hair and run my fingers through the lustrous length. Again, I run my fingers through her hair from the scalp to the bottom, until her eyes nearly close and she lets out a little moan. Mmm. I like that, too.

Her lips tip upward. Goddamn, it'd be easier to master this woman if she wasn't so damn cute. "Actually, I think I did an excellent job." She opens her eyes.

"What makes you think that?"

"I've successfully turned my frog back into a prince."

"Prince? If you think I'm a prince, I've been too lenient on you."

A casual shrug of her shoulder. "To another woman? Maybe. To me, you'll do."

"Brash, for a girl on the cusp of getting her ass spanked." I can already feel her squirming over my knee, can already feel the sting in my palm while I punish her, her ass warming to the touch every time my heavy palm falls.

"Now I'm on the cusp," she says thoughtfully. "Oh, dear. I'm quaking in my boots."

Is that a challenge?

"You're lucky we're almost at the hotel."

"Oooh, a hotel. I haven't stayed at a hotel in years." I help her slide off my lap. I miss the warmth and weight of her there and stifle a sigh as she sits beside me. "I've always *loved* hotels."

Of course she has. Is there anything she doesn't love? I'm struck with the irony. I have vowed to never love a woman—not a mistress or a lover or my wife—and yet I've managed to end up with a woman who loves everything there is to love.

"Good to know."

"Do you travel often?" she asks, that adorable pucker between her brows telling me she's curious.

I stifle a sigh. "More often than I'd like." I don't give her any more details. Not now.

"Will I travel with you?"

"Absolutely." I wouldn't have it any other way. It's one of her most important jobs. Other guys like me have trophy wives they leave at home, little showpieces to bear their children or wear their rings.

I don't want her in name only.

The ferry pulls into dock at our private spot. Late afternoon's still bright and sunny in Florida, concealing none of the island wrapped in white sand that stretches out before us. "Oh. My. *God.*"

"What is it?"

"This... you said private island. This is something out of a fairy tale." I look around, trying to see what she does—a large, sprawling, luxury hotel underneath the lowered heads of palm trees. Vibrant tropical flowers lining the border, and a well-worn trail to the beach. Beyond the spread of white sand, blue-green water as far as the eye can see.

She gasps and covers her mouth. I try to see what she's gasping at this time.

"Those are *dolphins*," she hisses in a stage whisper, as if she talks any louder they'll vanish away in smoke. "Actual dolphins!"

"They are. They're common this time of day in waters this warm."

I blink in surprise when she smacks my arm. "You're *kidding* me."

"Totally serious," I tell her, taking her hand. "And don't smack me again."

She nods eagerly. I wonder if she even heard me.

"Can I, like… swim with them?"

"I wouldn't. Humans have used dolphins as their playthings, but they're not. Dolphins don't naturally swim with people. It's unnatural, really. Don't touch or pet them either, but you can enjoy them from a distance just fine."

Her eyes widen as she stares at me. "Will they be afraid of me?"

It's hard to imagine anyone or anything being afraid of Marialena.

I shake my head. "Maybe. It's not worth risking it. Better to just watch them from a distance."

"Oh my God," she whispers again. "No *way*."

"What?"

"Is my hard-ass husband sympathetic to dolphins?"

Am I? I shrug.

"Maybe."

"Maybe? Oh I love that! Ha!"

I didn't expect someone who grew up so wealthy and privileged to be so easily amused or excited, but everything seems to delight her. *Everything.*

I've hardly gotten to know the woman, but I'm starting to see why the staff fell for her so quickly. It's hard not to.

Remember your purpose.

I married her for a reason.

I can't forget who I am.

I can't forget why I married her.

I can't forget how much I hate the Rossis and how perfectly this worked out in my favor.

And I definitely can't let myself become enchanted with her.

I wonder if I can have a night, though. Just one night where I let her bewitch me and revel in her charms.

Just one night.

CHAPTER TWELVE

Marialena

I wish I could call my sister. I wish I could call my friend Sassy, or my brothers' wives. It seems selfish to keep the awesomeness of this place to myself, but something tells me if I start going on and on to anyone on the phone about this, Salvatore might not like it.

So far, I've seen the swell of smoke from the dragon's lair, I've heard the jangle of the treasure he hoards, and I've even been burnt by his fiery breath. But I know I haven't seen the full force of the fire-breathing dragon he most certainly is.

Mama always told me I was too impetuous, too "pie in the sky" for my own good, that my optimism would bite me in the ass. But I never understood why.

I won't lie and say the weight of what happened today doesn't bring me down. When I glance down at my hand and see the golden ring on my finger, I almost wince. This isn't a joyride or a date. I've taken vows of *forever* to a man I hardly know. A man who isn't afraid of violence, who craves dominating me, who has hard and fast expectations of my behavior.

But I've always known I'd end up with someone just like him. I told myself for a while I might escape the shackles of marriage, but I knew if I didn't, it would definitely be to a man like Salvatore.

He won't love me, I know that. We'll be together in name only, like everyone else in his family and half the people in mine. Yes, some of my siblings have managed to marry happily, but in the grand scheme of mob life, that's the exception to the rule. And if I let myself hope…

I remember what Romeo said. I remember his warning. Romeo said he went to jail for murdering his betrothed…

"Salvatore?"

"Yes?"

"Can I ask you a question?"

"You just did."

He might be a man to be feared, but he's honest, I'll give him that. I know it likely has to do with the fact that he literally doesn't fear anyone or the consequences, but it's something I hold onto.

"Did you kill a woman you were betrothed to?"

I'm not prepared for the complete lack of reaction from him. No blinks, no flaring of the nostrils, not even so much as a twitch of his fingers. "I did. She attempted to poison me, and we've already established that's a foolish thing to do."

I'm not sure what to make of that. "She tried to poison you?"

He nods. "Her family tried to take advantage of mine. I didn't allow it. When I caught her attempting to take my life, she left me no choice. Unfortunately for me, her family had a legal team that had a few connections."

I don't know what to think of his response. On the one hand, I'm grateful for his honesty. On the other…

How would Romeo handle it if someone he was engaged to attempted to take his life?

"We're almost there," he says, as if what we just discussed had no significance at all. If I were a normal person, I'd feel sickened by it all, but I'm not. I wonder if something inside me is broken.

The hotel on the island looks nothing like his home in Tampa. It towers high into the night, the lighting and landscaping like something out of a movie. I reach out and gently stroke the wide, violet blossoms of tall flowers that line the walkway leading to the hotel entrance. For some reason, Salvatore shakes his head, but he looks only bemused, not angry.

His men take our luggage, and uniformed guards flank our sides. If there are other people at this hotel, they've hidden themselves well.

"It's quiet here," I say. "Is anyone else here?"

"There'd better not be," he says with a scowl.

I blink. "You rented a whole private island, then?"

"I did."

"On short notice?"

"Yes."

He paid them well, then. Not a shocker.

"So we're alone."

"Well, no. There's staff."

Ah, right.

As we approach the entrance, the gleaming glass doors glide open for us. I stifle a squeal of delight when I see a dolphin-shaped water fountain in the lobby, spouting water high into the air. It's backlit with LED lights, making the whole display light up like constellations in a night sky.

My husband leads me in past the fountain.

Gah. Husband. I wonder how long it'll take to get used to that.

"Where to?" he asks the guard.

"This way, sir."

I swear I see the shadow of someone or something pass into a room to our far right, but when I look for confirmation from Salvatore, he isn't showing any signs of having seen anything. Huh. I chalk it up to my too-vivid imagination. He did say there was staff here. Maybe someone forgot the bubble bath or something.

The men bring our luggage into the room then silently leave. Salvatore thanks them, but they only respond with curt nods. Seems most of his men are well-trained and know that he wants to be alone right now.

Alone with *me*, that is.

My heart beats faster.

The room isn't anywhere near as large as my room in Tampa, but this one's well-appointed and luxurious. In the very center of the room's a large, circular bed.

"I've never seen a bed in the shape of a *circle* before," I squeal. "Oh my God. It's like the Poconos. Tell me, do we have a champagne glass-shaped jacuzzi, too?"

He quirks a brow at me. "Why don't you go see? I haven't been here before."

Everything's white and gold and gleaming, speaking of luxury and comfort. It smells clean and inviting, with soft hints of lavender and vanilla.

I push the door to the bathroom open.

"No flute-shaped jacuzzi," I yell over my shoulder, in case he wants an update. "But *mamma mia*, is there ever a jacuzzi!"

It's as big as a small swimming pool. I want to strip my clothes off and dive right in. Fill it with bubbles until they nearly spill over onto the floor and hit my chin. "Salvatore!" I shout.

"Yes?" I squeal when I hear him right behind me. I cover my mouth with my hand and stifle a giggle.

"Sorry," I whisper. "Didn't know you were that close. There's a *bidet* in here."

He looks to where I'm pointing. "So there is." He speaks with practiced patience, clearly not as invested in all this as I am.

I open the large mirrored cabinet over the sink and finger the paper-wrapped toiletries. I've been raised wealthy, and hardly deprived my entire childhood, but the raw excitement of the newness of it all thrills me. My pulse races with every luxuriant scent and detail, from the ridiculously plush towels that feel like clouds, to the washcloths with ribboned edges, to the light blue bottles of toiletries reminiscent of a spa.

"I want to take a bath," I breathe. "Oh my God, it looks amazing."

"You'll have time for that later."

I look up at him when his words fall heavily. I blink, processing what he's saying.

Later.

Now, we have other things to do.

Things like... consummate the marriage.

Give him my virginity.

Learn to obey him or suffer the consequences.

Easy peasy. *Eep.*

I turn to face him. I can't use the hunger excuse.

"I'm a little tired." *Lame.*

He's leaning against the doorframe casually, his large hands shoved in his pockets. I look away quickly. The pose, the look in his blue eyes, the way his suit hugs him to perfection, makes him look as if he stepped out of a magazine for men. One might even call him charming.

"You'll have plenty of time to sleep later."

Figures.

Yeah, I'm not ready for this part of the ceremony yet, but I also know I don't have much of a choice. Consummating an Italian mob wedding is at the very top of the rules list, as inflexible as the sun rising.

"Shouldn't there be… I dunno, wine involved with the next step?"

"The next step?" he asks, his voice as smooth as satin but eerily quiet.

"I… if you're… if it's time to…" My cheeks flush hot and the words get stuck in my throat.

"Fuck you?"

"Salvatore," I chide, clutching my throat. "You make it sound so…"

"Crude?" he supplies once again.

"Yes!" I am literally burning up.

"You're pretty when you blush," he says approvingly. "I thought I'd have to work a lot harder to get that color in your cheeks." Tipping his head further to the side, he eyes my ass. "And I can't wait to color *those* cheeks."

Oh, very clever, Mr. Capo. I swallow my outrage, quickly recognizing it has no place here.

"You'd like wine first?" he asks curiously.

"At least," I croak, then quickly wish I could take my words back when his eyes narrow dangerously.

"*At least?* Is there something else you'd rather use to take the edge off?"

Oops. I shake my head and wave my hand. "Oh, I dunno, a romantic stroll on the beach..."

"Liar. Thought I told you what would happen if you lie to me." I really am shit at lying.

I clamp my mouth shut. I really need to watch my damn mouth around him. What I wanted to say was that getting well and truly cross-faded with some wine and a joint would be ideal, but some guys—especially old-fashioned, head-of-the-house types—don't always look kindly upon things like weed.

And he's seriously looking for a reason to put me over his knee.

"Do you smoke?" he asks, disapproval rolling off him in waves. So much for covering that up.

Lying to him is a bad idea. I dive in for the truth. He can't get mad at what I've done *before* we met, can he?

I swallow hard. He can do anything he wants.

"Like regular old nicotine cigarettes, no. I've smoked weed, but not regularly and not recently." Good thing my cheeks are already flushed pink, or I'd start all over again. Last week isn't *recently*, I rationalize.

No, it's been longer than that. Several weeks, anyway, since my smoking partner's Mario and he's been traveling lots.

I wait for a sign of his anger, but his natural look is so stern, it's hard to discern a difference. "As Marialena Capo, you will smoke *nothing* from here on out—"

Goddamn it.

"—unless it's with *me* and I give it to you."

I nod my head but I'm still stuck on *Marialena Capo*.

Wait. What?

Unless he gives it to me... now that's interesting. Okay. Makes sense. He's a guy that won't even eat a cannoli he hasn't vetted, why would he let me source my own weed?

Great. Now I want a smoke.

"Got it. That's a fair compromise."

"Glad you agree," he says sarcastically, reminding me that he truly doesn't have to agree and doesn't care if I do. "Now. I'll order wine. Are you hungry?"

"For once in my life, no, but give me a minute."

Not only did I feast before we came here, but my nerves are galloping through me so hard and fast I couldn't eat now if I tried. I stifle a yawn, but he notices.

He nods. "Fair enough."

I jump when he pushes himself off the doorframe.

"You're skittish, like a little rabbit."

"Well I… never have been before but… you're kind of scary."

"Scary?" he repeats and holds his hands up in the air. "I'm on my best behavior."

"That doesn't quite help your case," I say honestly.

A casual shrug. Why does even that look sexy? "I wasn't trying to."

I don't realize I'm backing up as he advances on me until my back hits the porcelain vanity. My eyes graze over the stubble on his cheeks, the hard slash of his mouth in a perpetual frown, his tanned skin. I've seen him move with the grace and power of a tiger, but have only ever seen him fully dressed. On the cusp of being stark naked with him, curiosity pings me.

What's he look like under all that cumbersome clothing?

"We're alone now, sweetheart. We have a job to do. You're tired, and you want some wine, and I'll grant you both wine and a nap. But this will be on my terms now. Do we understand?"

Oh, we do. I nod.

"Good girl. Then strip."

Strip!

"Like… naked?"

A muscle tightens in his jaw. Uh oh. "You're trying my patience, Marialena."

I nod and swallow and stumble forward so I can do what he says. This is a normal thing, I tell myself.

He's my husband, I tell myself.

I keep myself in good shape and all that, and there is no reason he shouldn't like what he sees, I tell myself.

My hands still tremble on the buttons, and after I try to undress myself, I quickly realize it's a two-person job.

"I can't reach the buttons," I say on a whisper, to the floor.

"Turn around, then."

My knees tremble when I turn to face the vanity, which gives me the perfect view of a huge, oval-shaped mirror and my husband's hungry gaze.

Frowning, intent on doing his job, he begins at the very top.

"I don't know why wedding dresses have these ridiculous buttons," I chatter nervously. "I mean, is it a crime to put a damn zipper in?"

I draw in a breath when he straightens and meets my gaze in the mirror. "No cursing out of my wife's mouth."

My jaw drops. No cursing? Good Lord, how did I marry a mafia Puritan?

I swear to God he's making shit—*crap*—up now just to catch me off guard. Just to play with his authority. Just to undo me.

And is *damn* even really a swear? *Barely.*

"Not sure about you," he says in that husky, scary voice of his. "But I like the buttons. Adds a bit to the foreplay."

The first button slips open. The second. I'm amazed his large hands and thick fingers are so agile. When the third opens, the dress loosens at the top. I anchor my hands on the sink in front of me to keep myself steady when he lowers his mouth to my neck and kisses the skin he's bared. I draw in a sharp breath as his tongue follows the kiss, tracing a heated line down my spine while he continues to unfasten the buttons.

Oh, *God*, that tongue. That wicked, heated, sensual tongue of his. My eyelids flutter closed as he continues to undress me, kissing and licking and nipping his way down my spine until the dress is fully unbuttoned. I whimper when he gently folds the fabric down my shoulders and the dress pools at my feet.

"Fuck," he growls. Like most things in mob life, I suppose the cursing thing is a double standard. "You're gorgeous."

"Thank you," I whisper. For once I actually *feel* it. He demands honesty from me, and it seems he pays me the same courtesy. So when he tells me I'm gorgeous… I know he means it.

I stand in front of the mirror wearing nothing but a white satin thong and a matching satin bra, the pearly fabric vivid against my tanned olive skin. It's the kind of bra meant to seduce, not to support anything, so my breasts are nearly spilling out. My breasts look pretty damn good if I do say so myself. I'm not used to this kind of thing, but when the staff brought my clothes in to help me get changed, there they were.

I wonder if Salvatore picked them out. A part of me thinks he's too busy to care about such things. But another part of me…

"Do I get to undress you, too?" I ask. I hardly recognize my voice, all husky and sensual in the intimacy of this shared space.

"Do you want to?" he asks in my ear.

I swallow and nod. "I do. Uh, I definitely do."

"C'mere." I inhale sharply when he cups his hands under my ass and hauls me up. My legs instinctively wrap around his body—his solid, hard, very muscular body. My arms wrap around the strong column of his neck. I inhale his scent, at once virile and masculine. I try to breathe out my fear. It doesn't work.

Alright, then. I have to ride it.

I'm his now. There's no turning back. We either make this work or we don't.

I want to kiss him. I want to cup his face and kiss those full, pouty, angry lips of his. I like the way he responds when I kiss him, and for one brief flash in time, I feel like I'm not the one being conquered.

The staff's all evaporated as if they've become part of the woodwork, and for a brief moment it feels as if we don't just have this room to ourselves, or even the hotel to ourselves, but the entire *island.* And I know then that if I asked him for that, he'd give it to me. If I asked him…

I stifle a scream when I hear a sound right beside me. We aren't alone, and this time I'm not the only one who's noticed something awry.

Cursing, he lowers me to the floor and draws his weapon.

"Get behind me," he snaps. I quickly obey.

Both of us turn toward a small closet by the doorway. "Come out," Salvatore barks. "Show yourself." His weapon's at the ready. I hold my breath.

At first, there's no response, but as he steps toward the closet, I hear a plaintive cry.

"Don't shoot! Please, don't shoot!"

I gasp at the sound of the voice. It sounds like a child.

Salvatore curses under his breath but holds his weapon down. "Step. Out. *Now.*"

If that were me on the other side of him, I'd have peed my pants.

I peek around his shoulder as the closet door slides open and a small, thin boy dressed in ragged clothing and streaked with dirt shows his face. Salvatore reaches his meaty fist toward the closet and the boy flinches, but he only grabs a thick white robe and tosses it over my shoulder.

"Put it on," he growls at me. "Before I have to fucking kill him."

I'm more than happy to obey *that* command.

Salvatore doesn't waste a second. As soon as I finish tying the knot on the robe, he steps toward the closet, reaches in, and yanks the child out so he stands in the bright overhead lighting. I feel my eyes go wide.

He's got to be ten, maybe eleven years old. Obviously underfed and neglected, with gangly limbs and a gaunt expression, he's dressed in clothing that's too small and dirty with wear. His feet are bare, his hair ragged and long. His wide eyes are fixated on Salvatore's gun.

"I believe you can put your weapon away now, Salvatore," I say in a low voice, not wanting to startle the boy. My effort's fruitless, however, since the boy's already quaking just looking at my husband. I mean, he is terrifying. I don't blame him.

"I'll put my weapon away when I know who he is and why he's here." He does lower it, but only so he can reach his fist out and drag the boy toward him. With one angry shake, he rattles the boy's teeth together.

"Who are you?"

"My name's Jared!" the boy responds in a half-cry.

"Why the fuck are you here?"

"I—I hid when they vacated the island."

He gives him another shake. *"Why?"* My heartbeat thunders. He's going to hurt him, I know he will. My brothers or father would.

"I had no other place to go!" The boy sniffles and wipes at his nose.

"Please, Salvatore," I whisper. "We can talk about this rationally." It's one thing seeing him assault a full-grown adult who acted like an asshole. If he raises his hand to an innocent child—

"Stay out of this, Marialena," he snarls at me. I open my mouth to protest, unsure of what to do. If I push him harder, not only would I end up in some form of trouble, he'd likely dig in his heels and double down, proving to me he can do whatever the hell he wants. If he thinks he needs to teach this boy a lesson…

I put my hand silently on his shoulder but don't say anything. I watch his eyes close, as if he's trying to gather his composure. His nostrils flare as he inhales once, then exhales. The boy trembles in his grip.

"I almost—we almost—" He doesn't finish the sentence. I know. We were seconds away from being naked and fucking each other right here in this room, and the thought likely makes him want to break things. Can't say I'm super crazy about the thought myself.

"But we didn't," I whisper. "Let's find out why he's here," I say in a low voice. "And I know you'll do whatever you have to do to deal with him. He shouldn't be here and he's trespassing." I can't paint a picture of total innocence. That won't get us anywhere.

Salvatore's fist shakes as he drags the boy to the desk chair at the side of the room and forces him into a sitting position.

"Stay there," he orders, but I'd be utterly shocked if the boy so much as blinks his eyelids, never mind tries to escape. Salvatore's muttering under his breath, and I don't even want to hear what he says because I have no doubt he's spouting violent, angry things. "Marialena, go to the bathroom and shut the door."

I have no choice, I know this. I walk toward the bathroom, but before I enter it, I give him one last, pleading look, silently begging him not to hurt the child. He only narrows his eyes at me and stabs his finger at the door. I shut it harder than necessary and lock it just because I can, before I stick my tongue out at the door and simultaneously flip the door off.

Very brave, when the master of the castle isn't watching me. I roll my eyes at myself. I push my ear against the door, eavesdropping. If he hurts him, I am *so* out of here and interfering.

I can hear Salvatore peppering the boy with questions, but he doesn't have much more to say. He and his mother lived here at the hotel, but she took off last year and hasn't returned. He doesn't know why or where she is, or if she's coming back. The hotel staff has allowed him to hang around provided he stays out of trouble, and he does odd jobs for pay. No, no one's reported him to the police. No, no one took him with them when they vacated, but it's his fault because he was hiding from the hotel manager in one of the stockrooms and fell asleep. He didn't know we were coming until the ferry arrived, and he ran to this room to hide because it's the one people are least likely to use.

Fair enough. It all sounds plausible. But Salvatore needs to test everything, and doesn't take his story at face value. He calls one of his men to come retrieve the boy, and I hold my breath waiting for his orders. Will he hurt him? Call the police? Even my brothers might do any of those things.

"Feed him," he snaps. "Clean him up. For the love of fucking God, get him some clothes that fit, then get the name and contact information for the hotel manager."

A minute later, the door clicks and I hear him heave a loud sigh.

"You can stop eavesdropping and come out now," he shouts to me.

I open the door. I want to tell him I wasn't eavesdropping, but he's made it clear I shouldn't lie to him.

"Not going to tell me you weren't eavesdropping?" he says with a curious upturn of his brow. "Good girl."

I swallow and nod. "I was curious, but I didn't interfere when you told me not to."

"You had a few things to say," he says. He's leaning against the desk, still fully clothed, his arms crossed.

"I did, but can you blame me?"

He shrugs. "Not really."

A few silent beats pass.

"And what did you hear?" he asks.

"I heard you send him with one of your men," I say quietly. "Thank you for not hurting him."

He doesn't deny that he wanted to, or that he isn't the kind of man who would. "That was for you."

"I think he's just in the wrong place at the wrong time," I say softly. "I really do. It seemed accidental." I don't realize my hands are outstretched pleadingly, or that I've taken a step toward him until he reaches for my wrists and yanks me to him. I stumble straight into his chest, but don't let that stop me from saying everything I stifled when the boy was in here. "I don't think he was sent here by our enemies or anything."

"Me neither," he says softly, brushing a strand of hair behind my ear.

He doesn't?

"And I think people who hurt children are cruel," I say, pushing my luck. I watch his expression.

A shrug of his shoulders, but his words take me by surprise. "If you mean abuse, then yes, but there's a time and a place to discipline a child and not all discipline is abuse."

Of course he'd say that.

I take one more stab at reason. "You don't need to hurt a child to discipline them. *And* he isn't *your* child."

He grunts. "And he isn't yours to protect, either."

Oh, boy. I'm not sure if I'm too excited about raising kids with this man. We've got time to work on this, though.

I sigh. I won't convince him of anything, not now, so maybe that's another argument for another day, but I know for a fact I *will not* raise my children the way my parents raised me and my brothers and sister. We can and will break the cycle of abuse and neglect, just like my siblings have.

But I let it go. For now, our little stowaway has remained unscathed.

Maybe not. I don't let go of principles easily. "Discipline is one thing, *hurting a child* is another. Of all the people in the world, Salvatore, you and I should know that." He hasn't told me much about his upbringing, but I know he was hardly gently disciplined into mafia life.

He nods. "True." I watch his eyes grow distant, and I don't like the storm I see brewing in them. He's remembering things. Likely awful things. Painful things. I don't care if you're twenty or eighty, the pain of an abusive or dysfunctional childhood doesn't fade with time.

"You argue with me like I'm not a monster, Marialena," he says warily, eying me. "You act as if I'm a regular human, capable of reason and complacency."

"You're not?" I ask.

His thumb traces the side of my face. It makes me shiver.

"I'm a man used to getting his way. I've been crowned king and I've paid a steep, steep price for this crown." Bending his lips to my cheek, he gives me a brief kiss. "You're my only reward for what I've done. But make no mistake about who I am. What I do. If you're appealing to my conscience, you'll find yourself sorely disappointed."

Who hurt you? I want to ask. But I don't need to ask him. I already know the answer.

They all did.

I ask him the next logical question.

"What can I do to make it better?"

I watch those eyes of his grow hungry and predatory as he grips my ass. With one quick tug, he unfastens my robe. It falls to the floor. My nearly naked body leans against his clothed one.

"You were going to help me undress," he reminds me. "You asked my permission." He traces the line of my jaw with his index finger. "Why don't you start there?"

CHAPTER THIRTEEN

Marialena

I wonder if my inexperience will show.

I wonder if he likes that.

I wonder why I care, but I do.

I've fully prepared myself to close my eyes and think of England, to endure my duty by distracting myself. I can never love a man like Salvatore. I wonder, at times, if I could ever love *any* man after what I've seen and how I've been raised. I'd have been content to be single for the rest of my life rather than try to be someone I'm not.

But here I am, prepared to undress him, because I can't seem to keep my mouth shut and I apparently don't know what's good for me.

My hands shake as I reach for his suit coat. That has to come off first, I'm thinking. I lift one sleeve, give it a tug, and he helps me by shrugging so the jacket falls into my hands. The sheer weight of it surprises me, but I guess it makes sense. Layers and layers of fabric, and he's a big guy.

"Aren't you hot under that?" I ask. "I would be stifling."

"Why don't you help me take them off, then." Those blue, blue eyes of his grow molten.

"That's a good idea, sir," I say teasingly, but I'm only pretending to be brave. I'm scared as a little church mouse that once I undress him, he'll devour me. I'm not sure I'll survive. It's what men like him do. It's why people like me can't fall for them.

He could wrap me in his arms and there wouldn't be one speck of Marialena left showing, he's that much bigger than I am. I take a quick moment to admire the bulging breadth of his shoulders, the corded muscle visible even under his shirt, even the little vee of white where his shirt falls open. Somewhere along the line he lost his tie, which is fine by me because I know he'd only use it as one of his many tools anyway, and he doesn't need any more help.

Fingers still trembling, I reach for the buttons on his shirt.

"These look a bit easier than those ridiculous ones you had to work with," I mutter.

He only gives me a casual shrug. I'm stalling for time, of course, and trying to hide the way my hands shake when I get closer to seeing him unclothed.

One button. Two. Three. By the fourth, the shirt's looser, and I can see the tan skin above the white cotton T-shirt. On impulse, I lean in and brush my lips across the very top of the tee, where his naked skin shines like bronzed metal. If he has any reaction, he schools it well.

I return to unfastening the buttons. The fifth button, then the sixth come undone. The rest of his shirt is tucked into his pants. Now this is where things ought to get interesting.

I'm going to have a little.

I lower myself to my knees in front of him, peering intently at his belt buckle as if that's the only thing on my mind right now, and if he's thinking about other things, that's his dirty mind and not mine. I don't unbuckle at first, though.

I take a moment to breathe in deeply. To observe the tight ridge in his pants, the powerful stance of his legs spread apart. To watch the way his breath catches when I run my hands up the length of his clothed thighs. I kiss one thigh, then the other, and I know I'm really pushing the limits here, but I'm obsessed with the need to make him want me. We only have one "first time," and this is it.

His hardened length grows when I unbuckle his belt. I slide the tip of the leather through the metal buckle, then quickly tug it off. It slides through the loops like a charmed snake. I wait for him to ask for it, still aware that he threatened to take his belt to me once, but he only stands, stoic and silent, waiting for me to complete undressing him.

I curl the belt up slowly, almost methodically, and slide it onto the floor beside me.

Next, I reach for the fastening of his pants. My knuckles graze his flat stomach. I imagine what it would be like to have the heft and strength of his body over mine. To feel that immense power held at bay. I swallow hard. I let my fingers brush a little longer and a little further than necessary. I dip my fingers a little lower than I need to and pretend it's the button slipping through the buttonhole I'm focused on, not the way his erection strains against the silky texture of his pants.

The button pops undone. I look up at him from beneath lowered eyelashes. I almost stop breathing at the intensity in his eyes, the predatory, wolfish look of a half-starved animal.

If I hadn't seen humanity in him these past twenty-four hours, I'd run.

I slowly slide my tongue out of my mouth and lick the tip of the metal zipper. I grip it with my teeth, my eyes on his, and tug it down.

I savor the way his breath catches.

Slick arousal pools between my thighs. My breasts swell. My breathing slows, heavier and thick with the weight of sexual tension between us.

I don't know what it is about him—the way the blue of his eyes bore into me? The command in his tone and touch? Or maybe it's the vows that bind us together, that make us one despite neither of us wanting to make this choice. But I've never wanted sex with anyone like I do with Salvatore. Something tells me he'll rip me apart, but I don't care.

I want this. I want *him.*

This isn't love. There's nothing more than carnal attraction between us. But right now, that's good enough.

I tug down his pants and place my hands on his upper thighs. I feel the hard, thick muscle and coarse hair, the radiating heat of him burning my palms. Slowly, I drag my hands down the length of his legs, dragging his clothes with them. I bend my mouth to his fully covered erection and plant a tentative kiss.

His fingers stab into my hair, yanking my head back.

"I let you undress me," he says in a heated whisper. "Don't tease me, woman. Off with the clothes or I'll take you now."

Oh, what a big, scary threat.

I bite my cheek to keep from smiling and reach for his shoes. I unlace them, one after the other, my movements a bit more hurried than before.

I place the shoes beside him, and he steps out of his pants. I fold those, too, and place them next to his shoes, then rise to my feet. My head hits right around mid-chest for him.

"Let's get the rest of these clothes off," I whisper. I'm eager to see him bare-chested, though the sight of him in nothing but boxer briefs and a tee is something I could definitely get used to. "And what's the fun if I don't get to tease you a little?"

That earns me a good smack to the ass. I come up on my toes and grin at him.

"Marialena," he warns.

I finish unbuttoning his dress shirt then tug at the hem of his tee, drag it to his neck. I have a little fun before I take it off. With a quick flick of my wrist, I tug it over his face. Holding the tee in place I kiss his neck.

"That's it," he says, his voice muffled in fabric. He yanks the shirt off and grabs my wrists.

"Salvatore! I haven't even gotten to ogle your chest yet! I need to, like, gape a bit. Run my hands all over your muscles. I gave up a lot to come here, the least you can do—"

I'm up in the air and over his shoulder seconds before he gives me a sharp spank. I scissor my legs, kicking, and reach my hand out to his bicep.

"I can at least *feel* those guns."

"You'll feel those guns alright," he says, his voice touched with something I haven't heard before—amusement?

My pulse races because I know what comes after this, what happens next. I've tried to put it off with a little provocation, and we've had some distractions, but there's no more putting off the inevitable. The tangled web of emotion nearly chokes me. I didn't know it was possible to feel both aroused and excited and absolutely terrified at the very same time.

He makes short work of getting us to the enormous circular bed, then lays me down on my back, more gently than I anticipate.

"How about you ogle while I taste your pussy?" he suggests, those deep blue eyes darker now, stormy and focused.

Uh... not sure how I feel about that plan. I look down at the tiny layer of fabric that separates the bundle of nerves between my legs from his mouth and suddenly realize there's not a hell of a lot to stop him. But I'm caught up by the way his eyes rove over my body, the way he swallows, and the certain knowledge that he *likes* what he sees.

That's a good start, I reason.

"That seems like... week two kind of stuff," I say, my voice shaking. "Not *first night.*" What if he doesn't... like when he goes *down there*? I mean, I wouldn't. My mind races with the thought of what truly terrifies me.

He doesn't bother to reply to my futile protests, but only drags me to the edge of the bed and spreads my legs.

"By week two," he says in a husky whisper, the heat of his breath cascading down the tender inside of my legs like molten honey, "you'll know the feel of my tongue on your pussy. The feel of my cock stretching you wide. The heat and feel of me when I come inside you."

I stop breathing.

"By week two, you'll know the feel of my teeth, my mouth, my hands, and my cock. You'll know what it's like to be pinned down and fucked, taken from behind, and we'll start working on fucking you in every hole in your body."

Fuck.

Fuck.

Every hole in my body means....

I squeeze my eyes shut and will myself to breathe again. Maybe I married someone with, like...

compulsive sexual disorder. He's a sex fiend. A deviant. A *nymphomaniac.*

Who *does* that kind of thing?

I suddenly regret my virginity.

Maybe if I wasn't so new to all this I wouldn't be as petrified. I would know what I like by now. Maybe I wouldn't feel my hips jerk upward, needing more of him, at the slightest brisk breath of hot air.

I've talked to my sister and sisters-in-law, I've talked to my friends, I've even watched porn, but nothing prepares a person for what it's really like to *actually be in this position.*

I open my mouth to say something, to protest, to toss some witty quip at him to distract him, but no words come out.

I stop breathing again as he lowers his body over mine and braces himself on his forearms. Blue eyes pierce mine. My heart thunders.

"Watch me."

I nod, helpless to protest, to talk, to even take another breath.

I watch as he hooks his thick thumbs under my panties and drags the silky fabric down my legs.

"I mean it," he says warningly, his eyes meeting mine. "If you close your eyes or look away, I'll lift your legs right up off this bed to spank your ass the first time you do it. Do it again, and I'll fuck you before you're allowed to come. You only climax if you behave yourself."

I nod, opening my eyes as wide as I can. During his little speech he's managed to completely divest me of my panties.

Another hungry sweep of his eyes over my body tells me my fears were unwarranted. He *definitely* likes what he sees. Though his hands are as large as dinner plates, rough and calloused, he's surprisingly gentle as he spreads my legs apart. "Go limp, Marialena. Let me position you."

No idea what that means, but it's easy enough to do since I'm already boneless as he drags my ass to the edge of the bed and kneels in front of me. "One taste. Just one taste," he says, as if pacing himself. My eyes flutter closed, then I spring them open again when I remember his admonition. His eyes meet mine as he lowers his mouth between my legs and inhales. It's his eyes that flutter closed this time.

"Fuck me," he grates against my legs, before he drags his stubbled chin along the bare, sensitive skin of my inner thighs. I want to ask him *what,* but I still can't speak and I know he wants me quiet now. My pulse thunders when he bends his head to my bare pussy a second time. This time, I watch his eyes as his tongue parts my slit, just the very top. Now he's the one teasing me.

I cry out when he laps my swollen clit. I gasp when he drags his tongue slowly upward, his groans filling the room. My hips jerk and my breathing stops at the utter perfection of his tongue. I groan, needing *more.*

"You taste like fucking heaven," he whisper-growls. "Fucking *heaven.*"

I nod. I'll take his word for it. I need to feel that again.

"Fuck it," he says, shaking his head. "I wanted your bra off so I could taste your nipples before I ate you out, but there's no fucking way I can wait. Take it off. I want to see you bare while I eat you out."

I nod again, because I think I might cry if he stops doing what he's doing right now, then fumble with the clasp of my bra before it springs free. I whip it over my head. Still focused on me, he reaches for my nipples, drags his thumbs along the sensitive buds, then suckles my clit while he sends tingles of pleasure through my body.

It's too much. My eyes flutter closed under the onslaught of sensation, but quickly fly open again when he pauses with a growl of disapproval. *Shit.*

In one solid motion, he lifts my ankles, flips me over, and slaps my ass three times in rapid succession. I yelp at the flare of pain, but when he arranges me back in the position he had me in before, my clit throbs. The brief spanking's only made me wetter and more aroused than ever. When he laps at my clit again, I whimper with the increased sensation, as if all the blood in my body's centralized right here in this bundle of nerves he's licking with such perfection it's like he's reading my mind.

"Watch me," he whispers. "Remember what I said."

Obediently I watch him, even as my cheeks flush with embarrassment. I've never been so vulnerable, so bared, and it feels like the most intimate thing we could do. I tremble as he moves even closer to me, propping my legs up so he can reach me better, the tip of his tongue circling my clit. I groan, my cheeks hot as I'm helpless before him. My hips jerk. I'm on a rollercoaster and I'm climbing to the very top, ready to tumble over the edge.

Again, he licks me, again he squeezes and caresses my nipples. My entire body's enchanted and under his spell, from my pounding heart to my throbbing sex, to my swollen breasts. My mouth parts and my lips go dry.

"Come on my tongue, Marialena. Come for me. I want to taste your come on my mouth. Watch me."

A quick flick of my nipples, another sumptuous swipe of his tongue, and all feeling comes to an exhilarating explosion of sensation. It takes effort not to close my eyes, to maintain eye contact, but I do, even as the climax destroys me.

"Oh, God," I moan. He holds my hips down when I nearly fly off the bed at the power of my climax, still working my clit, still licking and laving and sucking and worshipping. He leaves my clit momentarily to plunge his tongue in my core, his own carnal moan of pleasure making me come even harder before he goes back to my clit and suckles again. It's so unexpected, so unapologetically dirty and carnal, a fresh wave of sensation washes over me, a second climax overtaking the first, this one harder, more powerful, infinitely sweeter than the first. Every nerve in my body screams in triumphal bliss.

He licks me until I can't take it anymore, until my hips jerk with an overwhelming amount of sensation, then gives me one parting lick before he moves his head away from me and kisses my still-pulsing pussy before kissing the inside of each of my thighs.

"That was the sexiest fucking thing I've ever seen," he grates in my ear as he lowers the heft of his body over mine and cradles me against him. "I will crave the taste of you until I can have you again. *Jesus.*"

I have a strange sensation of wanting to crawl onto him. I want to burrow on his chest. I want him to hold me so tightly it hurts. I want to share his bed. I want to listen to his heartbeat in his chest.

"Thank you?" I whisper tentatively. What do you say to a compliment like that?

I'm surprised to find there's a sheen of perspiration on my body. Oh, ew. I don't *sweat.*

"Can I take a quick shower before we, uh, continue?" I ask, embarrassed.

The way his brows draw together tells me that's a definite *no*.

"Why the fuck would you do that?"

"I'm all... sweaty, like I just played a round of tennis or something."

"And you'll get sweatier and soon you'll have my come leaking from your pussy onto your thighs. I don't give a shit about that. You'll fucking shower when we're done, woman."

Alrighty, then, Mr. Caveman.

I gasp when he takes my wrists in his hands and pushes them onto the bed. The loss of control and the spike of fear make my pulse race. I wonder if he'll kiss me, and then I wonder if I'll taste myself on him, and then I stop wondering things altogether as he parts my legs with his knee and I feel the massive, hardened length of him on my belly. He must've taken off those boxer briefs before he came up on the bed.

Oh, my.

Did he remember the part about me being a virgin?

I hold my breath when he whispers against my ear, "Try to relax as much as you can. It might hurt a little, and this isn't the way I'm going to hurt you."

Oh, so that's lovely. Glad he isn't even pretending he doesn't want to hurt me. Just not *sex* hurt, but his palm or belt can do that job.

Got it.

I draw in a breath.

Try to relax.

Both of my wrists are gathered in one hand as he guides his thick cock to my entrance. I feel the slickness between us, and now I know why he made me come first. I'm wet and pliant and as ready for his cock as ever.

I can't breathe for fear of what it will feel like when he glides into me. I'm glad he isn't making me look at him this time, because it's easier to focus on relaxing when I close my eyes and try to breathe.

"Relax, Marialena," he repeats, this time his tone harder.

The head of his cock throbs at my entrance. No condom. No birth control. Like most men like him, he wants to take me bare, and if children come as a result, so be it.

Slowly, he pushes further in me. I'm full and wet and my pussy clenches around him. Further. *Further.* I'm impossibly full, and it feels now like he's so far in me he's going to hit my lungs. I draw in a deep breath and remind myself that's not how anatomy works.

It hurts a little, a stinging sensation of stretching flesh that's never been stretched quite that far before, but I wouldn't say it's unbearable. It's a strangely good kind of hurt, the kind that feels right and natural.

The next thrust stretches me deeper. I gasp and my arms tighten around his neck. He's so big, I feel as if he's tearing me open, but as soon as I brace, he slows.

"Does that hurt?"

I nod. "A little." Now that he isn't pushing, it's not as bad, but when he does, it aches.

"Breathe with me," he whispers. I do. He takes in a deep breath, and I breathe with him, *in.* A little more of a thrust. *Out.* A little further in again until I feel him fully in me, stretching. A glimmer of pleasure sparks with the first feel of friction and the walls of my sex clenching around him.

"There it is. Good girl. Relax and breathe."

I close my eyes and breathe with him as he gently slides his cock past my barrier, deeper still, until he's fully submerged to the hilt. He stays like that for a moment, and I relish the sound of his own groans. "So tight, so wet, so fuckin' *perfect,*" he mutters. "Jesus, Marialena."

A shiver of pleasure washes over me, and a second when he slowly increases the tempo of his thrusts. The flash of pain melds to pleasure. Our bodies were meant for this, this coupling and sharing, this joined comfort and bliss. His sounds of pleasure only increase mine.

I'm lost to the weight of his body atop mine, the friction he builds between us, the pulsing need that's returned with a vengeance. I'm vaguely aware of the shadow of pain quickly fading with each perfect, blissful thrust.

"How are you doing?" he whispers.

I thread my fingers through his hair, suddenly craving the intimacy. Grateful that he cares.

"Ready to come again," I whisper. "Fuck me, Salvatore."

He smiles, holds me, and thrusts again. The first spasm of orgasm ignites me, and I begin to moan again. He lifts again, the next thrust softer but more intense. A third thrust, and I begin to climax, moaning and welcoming even the pain-laced feel of his cock. He gathers my wrists again, his lips brush my cheek, then his groan overtakes me when I feel the hot pulse of his release inside me. I'm on the cusp of screaming, my wrists pushed against the weight of his restraint, my body awash with pure, perfect, agonizing euphoria.

His hips jerk and I welcome the feel of him, the joining of the two of us in this shared ecstasy. I never knew it would be like this. How could I?

"Fuck me," he groans as his thrusts begin to slow. "Goddamn it, you're perfect."

His head drops to the pillow beside me. Our pants fill the otherwise silent room. He gently releases my wrists. My arms slide around him. We hold each other. This may be the only tender part of our marriage. Only time will tell. But if it is, I'll take it.

CHAPTER FOURTEEN

Salvatore

If I'd known sex with Marialena Rossi would be that fucking rewarding, I'd have gotten on a plane and found a way to make her mine years ago. I'd have fucking *seduced* her if that's what it took. Bribed Romeo with whatever I had in my possession, or better yet, stolen her and whisked her away where no one would ever find her.

I can't expect she'll ever love me, but I could've sought the comfort of her bed long before now.

Curled up next to me, her hair fans around her face almost like a halo, but I'm no fool. Marialena's no angel.

If anything, she's a little hellion, but she's *my* hellion. *All mine.*

"Why don't you go take a shower, and I'll order us some food." I don't want her to be alarmed that our sheets need changing. In some cultures and traditions I'd have had to show the telltale signs of her lost virginity with our sheets, but there's no one to prove anything to. I was the one that arranged this marriage.

"Alright," she says on a yawn. "Can you get something chocolate? I feel like good sex should be capped off with something chocolate."

"Of course." I give her a teasing smack to the ass that she sashays right at me as she heads to the bathroom.

Good sex.

I've never been so honored someone's called sex with me *good*.

I've honestly never really cared. I've only had sex because I wanted to, and I knew women would line up to be with me because of my money and status. They didn't care about who I was. Half of them were afraid of who I was. They wanted me for what I represented, no more, no less.

I shouldn't care that she thinks sex with me is good. It's her duty to me.

I can't allow myself to get attached to her, to allow any feelings to surface at all. I know why I married her. Marrying her is only a stepping stone at the epicenter of my life's purpose. We can't be truly joined as a couple that actually has feelings for each other, and if I forget that for one minute, I'm fucked.

One day, she might know who I truly am. And if and when she does, she'll despise me. Better not to even go there from the beginning.

I hear the rhythmic beating of the shower water in the bathroom, and a few seconds later something I never expected to hear—she's *singing.* Not softly humming a little tune but belting out a song I don't know. I feel the corners of my lips turn upward, and it feels so foreign for a few seconds, I'm not sure why.

Then I realize... I'm smiling.

I never smile, not this kind of smile anyway, the kind that melts away sadness and brings a flood of warmth to your chest.

She sings in the shower.

I guess some people might find that annoying. I find it adorable.

I never expected she'd be like this, beautiful and responsive, softhearted and witty. I told myself this was a marriage of convenience, arranged with a distinct purpose. I even told myself that lowering myself to the point of actually having feelings for the woman would be a huge mistake, but a man would have to be inhuman not to feel something for her.

I know now why the Rossis were so reluctant to let her go.

Who wouldn't be?

I shake myself out of my reverie and *focus.*

I pull the room service menu out and check over my options, pick up my phone and make a call.

"This just for the two of you, boss?"

"Yeah, we're hungry." I hang up the phone. I want to make sure I have what she likes. Sue me.

I stand and stretch, call for someone to come and change our bedding, and walk to the bathroom. It's unlocked. *Good girl.* If she'd locked me out, we'd have a problem.

She's still singing when I enter. I just fucked the woman, but damn if seeing her naked silhouette doesn't make me hard all over again.

"You need a shower?" she asks, sticking her head around the frosted glass door to the shower.

I shrug. "I'm naked, and housekeeping is changing our bed, so I thought I could while away my time in here."

"Oooh," she says, cringing. "Did we make a mess? Ugh, that's gross."

I shrug. "It's not bad."

"You don't have to, like, *show* anyone like in the Dark Ages, do you?"

I feel my lips turn upward again. "Nah, we're good."

She ducks her head back inside and lifts a razor, giving me a little show with her foot up on the side of the tub. It's a cute little foot, delicate with a pale pink polish on her toes. I want to kiss the top of each one of them.

"Good," she says, her voice echoing. "Because *hello*, that is so gross."

I'm not used to people not being timid around me. Cristiano and my mother are the only ones that aren't. I wonder briefly if I've made the right impression on her, but then I remember she's a Rossi. Those men are known for being hard-asses, and she practically confessed to her father's heavy hand and abuse already.

There are perks to marrying a mob girl.

"Do you travel a lot?" Her voice sounds like it's in a tunnel.

"All the time. I travel more often than I'm home."

"Ahh, that's too bad."

"Why?"

Her response demands that she put her leg down, stick her head out, and give me an *are you serious* look before she resumes shaving. "Hello, that house is *amazing*. The balcony, the pool, *the beach?* Are you even serious? It's like something people dream of. I really hope we get to spend *some* time there."

"We will." As soon as I make sure my mother's nowhere in sight. I could handle her, and will, but I don't want Marialena to have to deal with her.

"Don't worry about your mother!" she says, as if reading my mind. "I will win her over, you'll see."

She shouldn't even entertain that thought. It's dangerous as fuck.

"I'm not *worried* about my mother," I mutter. And no, she won't win anyone over. "I just hate sharing the living space with her."

"Then why do you?" The water shuts off. "I don't know exactly how your family functions, but in mine, Romeo doesn't do anything he doesn't want to."

"It was written into the fucking agreement," I mutter. I'm grateful for the distraction when I hear a knock at the door. "And that's our food."

I don't want to discourage her, but the only way Marialena will "win my mother over" is if Marialena has my babies, partakes in my mother's scathing harassment of anyone and everyone around her, matches her quip for quip on the bitch scale, and eats nothing but sprouts and boiled chicken like her. She has a certain type she'll associate with, a certain type she'll tolerate, and anyone less is beneath her.

In short, if she ever became the type that could win my mother over, I wouldn't like her anymore.

I leave the bathroom and pull on a pair of boxers so I can open the door and take our food. The large table on wheels is covered with a white tablecloth, a flameless candle at its center. Half a dozen silver domes cover hot dishes of food.

"Thank you."

I scan the hall on instinct, to make sure nothing and no one is out of place. It's so customary for me by now, I can't even exit my car or the bathroom without having to do a quick assessment. But now it isn't just me I'm having to watch out for. Knowing Marialena's in the room behind me, knowing that she's my wife and will eventually carry our babies… I wish I had my gun on me and I wasn't standing here in my boxers.

But everything's placid as can be.

I take the food and head back inside.

She stands in the doorway to the bathroom, her damp hair up in a towel like a turban. The color on her cheeks makes her look younger, her skin dewy and begging to be kissed.

In my head I know I shouldn't fall for her. At the same time, I'm not sure any man could see a woman like that and be immune. I wonder if this is why so many before me have taken mistresses.

"Penny for your thoughts?" she says with a curious smile.

"How about we eat?"

"Salvatore," she says, giving me a look like she wants to push but knows it's not wise. "Are you evading the truth?"

"Come here." I snap my fingers at a little stool by a circular table. "Sit your ass down and have something to eat." I let a little of the asshole show. Not only do I have to not fall for her, I have to make sure she doesn't make the mistake of having any feelings for *me*.

Her lips thin, but she obeys, walking over to where I point. She's barefoot, a plush white robe cinched around her waist.

I start taking off the silver tops to trays. I relish every little squeal of pleasure.

"Oh my God," she moans. "I *love* a good, authentic pizza. That looks like one you'd get in Rome. Is that mushroom risotto? And how did you know I love buffalo wings?"

What doesn't she love?

"I just got a sampling of everything."

"Everything?"

I shrug and scratch the back of my neck. "I mean, I'll eat, too."

Her peal of laughter makes me jump. What did I say that's funny?

"What?" I ask, not able to let this go. I take her by the arm and sit her down.

"You ordered enough food for ten. I'm not sure you and I alone will make a dent, but I'm willing to give it a go."

"I've got a big appetite."

She frowns. "If that boy is hungry…"

"My staff will feed him," I interrupt. I'm pissed we were disturbed and don't need to add the responsibility of a fucking child to my plate.

"Was there anything on that room service menu you *didn't* order?"

I nod. "Beet salad and quinoa. I hate them."

She sits, still dressed in her robe, across from me. "Of all the foods to dislike, you've chosen some good ones."

I grunt and sit down at the table, placing an empty dish in front of each of us. I give her a little serving of everything and the same to myself. We eat in silence for long minutes.

"Alright, I'm going to officially get fat as Mrs. Capo."

I wink at her. "I'll help you burn those calories."

She sticks her tongue out at me. "Sure you will."

"Watch it. We can do it with or without a sore ass. That's up to you."

She wraps her lips around a fried coconut shrimp, eats it in two large bites, then winks at me. "Again with the threats…"

I reach for an oblong plate I suspect is the one she requested and lift the lid without responding to her teasing. Yup. Sure enough, an assortment of decadent chocolate desserts sits atop fluted papers on the tray—a layered chocolate cake with thick icing, petit fours, chocolate-covered strawberries and cherries, a Nutella cheesecake, a mocha torte, and a chocolate lava cake dusted in powdered sugar.

"Oh my God," she breathes, reaching her fork out to stab one of them. I pull it out of her reach just in time.

"What did I say about behaving yourself?" I slide the platter away from her. "If you touch that without my permission, you'll be a very sorry girl."

"Salvatore," she says in a shocked whisper. "You *wouldn't*."

"Deny you dessert? Of course I would. I expect obedience from my wife. Submission. You took your vows, and I'll uphold them." Light glints off the top of the tray as if shining in front of her just to taunt her.

I cluck my tongue at her. "Now, are you going to taunt me and force my hand, or will you behave yourself?"

I manage to keep a straight face while she chews thoughtfully on another shrimp. "Denying me those desserts would be worse than a spanking."

"I can arrange both," I say casually, taking a bite of risotto.

"No doubt." The way her lips curve downward in a frown tells me I'm getting through. Part of me is teasing her because she's so cute when she doesn't get her way, but another part of me is totally serious. Things will go much better for her if she obeys me, and the sooner we establish that the better.

I decide it's time to test her a little. When she reaches for a slice of the pizza, I shake my head at her. "Not yet."

Watching me curiously, she removes her hand and lays it in her lap. I take a slice and eat it in front of her. Watching.

"Is it good?"

"Delicious. I'm hard to please when it comes to pizza, too."

"Why doesn't that surprise me? Let me guess. It has to be a good authentic Italian sauce, a crust that crisps well in a wood-burning oven, just the right amount of cheese, and few toppings. None of that meat lovers whatever or pineapple for you."

"Pineapple on pizza's a sacrilege."

"On that, we can agree."

"I thought you loved everything?"

"*Most* everything. But this is what I wonder. If I truly loved everything, would I really love *anything*?"

I swallow a bite of crust. "If a tree falls in a forest and no one is around to hear it, does it make a sound?"

"What came first, the chicken or the egg?" she quips.

My mind is still on what she said about love. She does love everything. But does she love every*one*?

I slide a slice of pizza onto her plate and let her feast. "You behaved yourself," I say with an approving nod. "You've earned your dessert."

This earns me a squeal when she claps her hands. "Oooh, my favorite part," she says in a breathy whisper. "Are you going to, like, feed it to me or something?"

"I've got a beautiful wife in a robe in front of me. What do you think?"

"I think you want me to strip," she says, her eyes on mine. Her voice drops to a seductive register. I swallow hard. "I think you want my hands in my lap. And I think you want to feed me that chocolate bite by bite and maybe do some other wicked things with it while we're at it."

My heart soars at her words, at the knowledge that she understands me, while at the same time, a warning bell clangs in my mind.

I don't know how I'll keep myself aloof and unattached from Marialena.

I don't know how I'll listen to her siren song and not crash my ship upon the rocks.

"And I think you're a fast learner, sweetheart."

CHAPTER FIFTEEN

Marialena

I wake from a troubling dream whose details fade the moment I wake. I'm tangled in sheets and painted with perspiration. I blink in the quiet, dark room and look around me. Why are the sheets tangled about me like this?

I look around. Salvatore isn't here.

It's the fourth day on the island. We've done nothing but have incredible sex, and lots of it, eaten so much delicious food it ought to be a crime, and walked on the beach in bare feet. It's been lazy and decadent and everything a honeymoon should be. I've wondered a few times if this is the only part of marriage to Salvatore I'll enjoy, but the eternal optimist in me can't help but hope. Still…

We go home tomorrow, and I wonder what life after this looks like. Salvatore seems restless, as if he can't allow himself to be idle for too long without a purpose. And I know the way mob life goes. There's always another war to fight, always another battle, always something lurking around the corner. Though he's nearly invincible and filthy rich, the payoff of it all is, he can hardly expend any time enjoying his wealth or privilege.

I wonder where he is. And again, I wonder how he'll be when the demands of his job and role take precedence over feeding me cheesecake and giving me orgasms.

Will he resume his position as acting Don and ignore me?

Will his mother throw a wrench into things and force us to find another place to live?

Will I be able to cut it as a newlywed?

My family's reached out to me intermittently, but Salvatore is a jealous lover. My responses have been brief. I hope they know that these days of being a newlywed don't allow for much time to text. I'm doing everything I can to learn what it means to be a member of the Capo family.

I miss my own family so badly, sometimes I have to excuse myself and have a quick cry. It helps. If Salvatore notices, he doesn't say anything.

Ack, of course he notices. He notices everything. It seems as if the power of observation is one of his many superpowers.

I'm glad he doesn't ask questions. He's been more doting than I expected, if I'm honest. I figured after consummating our marriage the first night, he'd probably leave me to the beach and sunbathing while he did his work, but it hasn't exactly been like that. He's spent way more time with me than I expected. We're actually getting to know each other.

I've seen glimpses of the scary man he can be. I've heard the low rumble of the monster's growl.

I overheard a conversation in Italian the night before last when he ordered someone questioned. "Use any means necessary. Yes, even that." My imagination had a hell of a time conjuring up images of "that." Then yesterday, when we were walking on the beach, I tripped. Salvatore quickly caught my elbow to steady me, but one of the guards flanking us caught me at the same time. I froze, knowing that none of his guards are allowed to touch me without a very good reason.

He excused himself from me. Escorted the guard, who looked as if he were being taken by the Grim Reaper himself, back to the hotel. I heard the guard pleading in Italian, begging forgiveness. Salvatore didn't reply. I haven't seen the guard since.

Still, if I'm really honest, all of those things are fairly consistent with how my brothers would behave.

And he hasn't *really* done anything to *me* that's too scary... yet.

I know the time will come. I know my brothers wouldn't fabricate things about someone just for the hell of it. So while I let myself enjoy the good parts—everything from our conversations to sex to meals together—I am not naïve enough to think this is all there is to Salvatore Capo.

I'm wide awake. We left one of the window shades half open, and outside I can see the vacant beach, one lone umbrella from earlier still keeping the sand beneath it cool. Beyond the beach, moonlight from the full moon glints as it reflects off the glacial blue of the water.

No footsteps.

I sit up and yawn, then look down at myself. I'm wearing nothing but one of Salvatore's faded Black Sabbath tees. He usually dresses professionally in a suit, like my brothers do, but he's got a small, well-worn wardrobe of casual clothes as well. Last night, he tugged this on me because I was cold. I like the smell of him on me.

I know it's dangerous to allow myself to grow sentimental and hopeful. I hope I don't regret it.

I grab a robe and sling it on, slide into my slippers and go looking.

It doesn't take long to realize he isn't in the suite. How did I not hear him slip out?

My heart thuds as I reach for the door. I haven't left this room without him since we got here, and I'm not entirely sure what he'd think about me doing it now.

He didn't say I *couldn't*. I don't *think*.

Noiselessly, I open the door. Other than his staff and the boy we found the first night who's remained under the watchful protection of staff until we go home, our hotel is vacant. It makes it easy to hear every word and conversation, though. So when I hear the deep register of Salvatore's voice nearby, I pause and listen.

I should turn around and go back to our room.

I shouldn't pry or step my foot in a place it's not welcome, but when I hear the higher-pitched voice of the stowaway we found, I freeze.

I don't care if I'm half dressed. I don't care if he'll get mad at me. I can deal with that. If he's being too harsh on a boy...

I slow my steps as I turn the corner. No need for me to make a big appearance. No need for him to even really know I was ever here.

Conveniently, they're meeting right outside the spa with a guest services doorway I can hide in.

Salvatore's passing in front of the seated boy. "What did I tell you would happen if you didn't stay out of trouble? The only reason you're even here is because my wife has a soft spot for children, and I happen to like her."

My heart does a little somersault. He likes me? It's a good start. But I don't like the tone of this…

"You said you'd hurt me," the boy says, his voice shaking. "And I was trying to stay out of trouble."

He said he'd hurt him? When?

Oh no he did not!

Salvatore crouches in front of him, and the boy flinches. What reason has Salvatore given him to? Has he hurt him already? A chill runs down my spine. I cringe. "You call setting fire to the kitchen napkins staying out of trouble?" When the boy doesn't answer, he reaches his hand out to him, and the boy flinches.

I've had enough.

"What's going on here?" I ask, wandering in and yawning as if I've just woken up and stumbled out of bed. I don't miss the way Salvatore's eyes narrow on me. He isn't falling for it.

"Get back in our room," he snaps. "*Now.*"

Goddammit. A direct order. I either do what he says, or I don't.

I know I risk getting in trouble with him. He's made it very, very clear what he expects of me, and I know I'm pushing it, but right now I don't care. Not when he's on the cusp of hurting a *child*.

"I will," I tell him, trying to appease him. "But it looks like you're going to hurt an innocent child, and I won't stand by and allow that to happen." My heart races as I say this because I know this is not going over well. I lift my arm to the boy. "Come here."

He quickly jerks out of Salvatore's grasp and runs to me.

"Is it true about setting things on fire?" I ask.

The boy, who's cleaned up since I last saw him, still has a rascally expression on his face which is not helped by a bucketload of freckles and an unruly cowlick.

"Well…" he begins, "I wouldn't say it was on *purpose…*"

I sigh. "You must not do something so dangerous again," I say. "If you do, you could—"

But the next second, the boy is torn from my grasp and shoved into Salvatore's guard's arms. "Take him away. Put him to bed. I'll deal with him tomorrow." The slash of his scowl and dangerous eyes turn on me. "I'll deal with *you* now."

Well that went well.

My cheeks flame with embarrassment as he drags me back to our room. The door slams. We don't say a word. I open my mouth to protest, but he tosses a palm into the air to stop me.

Okay, so, he needs a minute. Whatever.

"Robe. Off." He spits the words out as if they're poison. "Strip."

No *way*.

"You want sex *now?* No!" I'm so angry at him, I reach out to shove him, but he quickly grasps my wrists and twists my arms back. It doesn't hurt, but I can't get out of his grip either. I growl in frustration, so angry I could spit. I don't care if he punishes me. I don't care if he retaliates. He doesn't get to belittle me like that and then get all heavy-handed with me.

"Fine, then," he grates. "Have it your way."

Overpowering me is laughably easy for him. All he has to do is hold me in one of his arms that are as big as tree trunks and restrain me while he yanks the robe's belt with the other. I push and shove and protest, but it's useless. The robe falls to the floor like discarded wrapping paper, and there's nothing now that keeps me from him but the tee. I hardly process what's going on until I find myself over his lap, my legs restrained under one of his, my hands pinned to the small of my back.

"If you ever fucking saunter around like this in front of my men again, I will chain you to my bed naked for a fucking *week*," he snarls before his palm slams against my ass in the hardest spank he's ever given me. My legs flail and my back arches. It hurts so much I'm in shock, my mouth open in a frozen scream while he strikes me again. "You will dress in clothes." He punctuates every word with another hard spank. "You will never walk around half naked." Another searing spank followed by another, and another. The tee covers my ass but does nothing to shield me from the pain of his palm.

"Am. I. Clear?" Every word underscored by another hard spank.

"Yeeesss," I wail, submerged in pain and mortification. "Fine, yes, *yes!*"

"Good," he grinds out, satisfied with himself. "That was your punishment for walking around indecently. Now we'll address your disrespect in front of my men."

"Sal-va-*tor*-e!" I scream as he lifts the tee and bares my ass to him. Again, his palm falls heavily and again, he lectures the hell out of me.

"I've made it clear who I am and what I expect," he says, laying down one hard swat after another all over my ass and the tops of my thighs. I squirm and fight and try to get away, but his leg over mine pins me in place. I whimper and close my eyes as he continues. "You may *never* disrespect me like that. You come to me and you talk to me, but I have authority over you and my men and I will *not* have you undermining my authority."

On and on the spanking goes until my skin's aflame, on and on the lecture goes. "Do you understand me?"

"No!" I scream. I don't care what he does to me at this point. "I will not allow you to abuse a child, I don't care if you beat me or divorce me or leave me on the street!" I'm crying now, squirming on his lap. If I'm having children with this man, he needs to understand right now when and where I'll fight him.

That gives him plenty of reasons to continue spanking me, hard.

I keep pleading my case even though I don't really think it's working.

"You and I will have children together if it's meant to be, and I won't be with a man who abuses children!"

The barrage of hard slaps suddenly halts. "Excuse me?"

"You heard me," I say on a sob. "I won't agree to this. I won't agree to backing off." A fresh torrent of tears begins. I lived under the roof of a man just like him. While my mother couldn't stop my father, I won't do the same. "You're a monster and I hate you!"

"Is that right?" he asks in a slow, almost disbelieving tone. "You believe I was going to hurt the child, so you took it upon your altruistic self to save him?"

I don't respond, because there's a warning tone to his voice that gives me pause.

"And now you're blatantly defying me. You fully plan on coming between me and whoever I'm dealing with if it conflicts with your feminine sensibilities?" He delivers a hard spank that makes me squeal. "Answer me!"

"Yes!" I scream. "A thousand times *yes.*"

Silently, he moves his hands to his waist. He no longer holds my hands, but my legs are still under his, I'm still unable to move at all. I want to see what he's doing. I want this to end. I want to discuss this like two reasonable adults.

But it seems he has no such plans. I tip my head to the side just in time to see him snake his belt off his waist and double it in his fist.

"Salvatore!" I protest, pushing at him to get off his lap, but he's too strong, I'm too helpless in this position, and he's determined to teach me a lesson.

The first lash of the belt falls in silence. I gasp in protest, unable to breathe through the searing pain. My fingers clench into fists and I stifle a whimper when the second whistling lash lands.

"You. Listen. To. Me." Stripes of the belt land between each word. "I was not going to hurt him. He said that because I told him I would expect him to obey me, and apparently the last person he was expected to obey would treat discipline as an excuse to hurt him."

Oh.

I close my eyes as the belt falls again. And again. And again.

"I would not hurt a child."

"Yet you'd whip a woman?" I ask, my voice tremulous and broken.

"A fully grown woman under my authority, who promised to obey me, who actually *likes* being spanked? *Absolutely.*"

"I do not like this kind of spanking!"

It's like I flipped a switch. One second, he's thrashing me like I'm a bad schoolgirl, the next second, his voice drops. "That isn't true. You might not like the pain of it in the moment, but you *like* being overpowered."

"Not like this!" I insist.

He lifts the belt and I flinch, preparing for another hard spanking, but this time the leather caresses my skin like a kiss. The pain from a second ago somehow magnifies the sensation. I shiver, unable to stop my pounding heart. Almost cruelly, he spreads my legs by yanking them apart.

My pulse races. The cool, unyielding leather licks between my legs. My clit throbs.

Ugh, my traitorous, *traitorous* body.

"Tell me again you don't like being overpowered."

He's fucked me and made me climax so many times, maybe my body responds on its own by now to his overbearing ways. He's spanked me a few times but never used his belt, and other than a warning swat a few times, he's never actually punished me.

"Not like this," I say, but my voice melts into a moan when he strokes the leather between my legs. "I—I can't… I don't like when you treat me like a child."

A quick flick of his wrist sends searing pain to my pussy when the leather licks bare skin. Again, he whips me there, and again, until my pussy throbs and I'm parting my legs without thinking this through, dying for some relief to the pressure between my legs.

"I am hardly treating you like a child." His voice is thick with emotion and arousal as he alternates little flicks of his wrist on my pussy, my thighs, my ass, painting pain and pleasure all over the most sensitive parts of my body. "Am I?"

"*Mmmph,*" I say in response, unable to formulate words or express what I'm thinking. Well, no, he's being all sexy dominant husband on me now, but he did just punish me.

"I haven't changed any of my expectations for you, have I?"

I shake my head as my body combusts, heated and aroused with flickers of pain at the edges that only magnify everything I'm feeling.

"From the first day we met, I told you I'd expect you to obey. On the second day, you took vows to me and I made it clear I expected you to uphold those vows. Here we are, a week after we first met, and I've been nothing but consistent from day one."

Somewhere along the line, he lost the belt and now his huge, rough palm's stroking my fiery ass as he talks. Every touch of his fingers makes fire flicker between my legs. He caresses and strokes then spanks and kneads. The warring sensations make me half-crazy with need.

"Christ," he curses, when his fingers part my legs and he easily traces slick arousal through my folds. "You're sopping wet."

I want to deny it. I don't want to admit being punished like that arouses me, because that spanking fucking *hurt,* and if he gets any notion in his head about spanking turning me on like this, he'll spank me daily because he wants to, and I'm not so sure about that. I mean, there are other ways of getting laid without involving a session over his knee.

I gasp when he lifts me up, holds me against his chest, then stalks to the bed. It's an easy matter for him to place me over the edge so my belly hits the bed and my bare feet dig into the plush carpet on the floor. I reach my hands out on instinct and fist the bedspread just as he goes behind me and straddles me.

"I need to fuck you," he whispers in my ear. The rough rasp of his voice sends shivers skating down my spine. "Spread your legs."

I quickly obey. I drop my head to the bed, my cheek against the blanket. I heave in a breath and grasp the blanket harder. My knuckles turn white.

I tremble when his heavy hand falls to my neck and he presses me onto the bed. I can breathe, but I'm trapped under the weight of his hand. Bending his mouth toward me, he nips the tip of my ear, then drags his tongue over the stinging skin. My mouth falls open in a silent scream, unable to make a sound to combat the rapid pounding of my heart.

His teeth sink into my shoulder, my neck, as he tastes his way along my skin before he fucks me.

Is he committing me to memory?

Or does he want me docile and subservient?

And does it matter?

My mouth falls open when his thick thumbs find my ass, kneading the tender flesh before he dips his fingers lower and slides them through my slick arousal. I freeze, fearing he's going to take me like this.

"You said you were going to lead me up to that," I croak, half terrified and half electrified by the unknown of what he'll do to me next. And isn't that part of it, the attraction that pulls me to him, the not knowing what's coming next or what he's doing? The way he commands and overpowers me so I've lost all control, the very thing he demands above all. I never knew I was attracted to authority.

In fact, I thought I'd push against such treatment after the way I was raised.

But I don't. I don't at all. I crave his compelling, firm touch. I covet the sound of his voice washing over me with authority and conviction and heated awareness. I lust after his unyielding grip on my wrists, being conquered by him, the heft of his body atop mine. When he gives me that stern look, one brow raised as if to challenge me to defy him, my heart beats a little faster.

I thought I was immune to the power of seduction, but I was wrong. *So* wrong.

I close my eyes at the sound of his zipper, at the knowledge that he's going to take me whether I like it or not and oh *how I want that.* I lose myself to sensation.

The soft whoosh of his clothes sliding to the floor. The fierce grip of his hands on my naked skin. The heat of his naked flank pressed up against my throbbing ass. I hold my breath—*yes,* the feel of silk-covered steel when he slides his length to my core.

At the first thrust, I start breathing again. At the second, I moan with pleasure. By the third, I'm riding his erection, meeting him thrust for thrust, my climax building with every perfect, savage movement he makes inside me.

I ignore the fact that he was right. Whatever.

All that matters now is he doesn't leave me like this, all hot and bothered and craving the release only he can give me.

The weight of his body on top of mine increases as his mouth comes to my ear.

"Have you learned your lesson, Marialena? Or will I leave you needing more of me to help you know your place?"

Oh dear *God*, he wouldn't!

"Salvatore," I say pleadingly, putting all the power of persuasion in my voice. "Noooo."

"No what? No you haven't learned your lesson, or no, don't leave you on the cusp of climax?"

"Oh my God, don't leave me on the edge. Please!"

The steady rhythm of his thrusts comes to a sudden halt. "So you've learned your lesson?"

"Yes, yes, *yes!*"

"And that is…?"

He remains still inside me as my pussy begins to clench around him, the first spasm of climax washing over me but needing just a touch more of him to bring me over the edge.

"Don't interfere with what you do. Don't disrespect you. Don't walk around anyone but you unless all my lady bits are covered fully."

"Good girl," he says as he leans into another perfect thrust. "That's my girl. Who's the one who sees what's mine?"

"You!"

"Who's the one you obey, no matter what?"

"You! You, of course, *you!*"

"And who's the one that owns you?"

"*You.* You. It's you," I breathe as the power of my climax tears me apart.

CHAPTER SIXTEEN

Salvatore

"I don't give a fuck about who's there, what they said, or what we need to do next," I tell Cristiano over the phone. "What I care about is that I get paid, and now, so I don't have to take matters into my own hands. You get me?"

"Yeah, boss, of course I do," he says on the other end of the line. "I'm on it."

Marialena sits by the pool at our home in Tampa drinking a piña colada. She's wearing a thin, seafoam green bikini that barely covers her tits and ass. I can still see the red marks of my handprints at the tops of her thighs.

I blink. "Excuse me, what the *fuck* are you wearing?"

She looks down at the bikini. "Isn't it adorable? Found it on clearance when I did some shopping a few days ago."

I put down my phone and give her the full power of my glare. "You went *shopping*? Without telling me?"

We've been home a full week and have actually enjoyed this week while my mother's traveling and Cristiano's on his best behavior.

"Oh, a little shopping never hurt anyone," she says innocently, batting thick eyelashes at me. She almost gets away with anything she wants when she looks at me like that.

"Who did you take with you?" I have to know whose ass I'm gonna beat before I deal with *her*.

"Salvatore," she says in a gentle voice. "Relax. I shopped *online*. Surely that's not unacceptable."

I sit back down and mutter under my breath. I didn't even realize I was standing.

"You need to work on that, honey," she says gently.

"On what?"

She leans closer and places a delicate finger on the side of my face. "You have a vein throbbing in your temple. Eeeek!"

It's an easy matter to grab her around the waist and have her straddle me. "Maybe I need to work on *you*."

"What about me?" The demure look gets me every time.

"Always *baiting* me like that. Knowing full well what will happen yet doing it just the same."

"I can't help it," she whispers, draping her arms around my shoulders. "I get all hot and bothered when you get adorably grumpy. Well, *most* of the time. When you get mad at Cristiano, I just want to smack him."

I might love this woman. The realization hits me like a two-by-four.

"Are you okay?" she asks, as her forehead knits in concern. "You look like you just saw a ghost."

"Fine," I manage to lie. "I'm fine."

I can't be in love with her. Falling in love with her is the opposite of what I was supposed to do. It isn't why I married her.

"Back to Cristiano. Why did you say that?"

The serious look on her face gets my attention. "Because he deliberately undermines you then plays like he's a fool, when he knows *exactly* what he's doing. I don't trust him. I've met men like him before, and you know what men like him do?"

"What?" I love that she's concerned. I love that she understands the world I live in as well as I do. Maybe sometimes even better.

"They betray you, Salvatore. And they're worse than your most mortal enemies, because they earn your trust before they stab you in the back." She frowns. "You should just fire him already."

I sigh. "Trust me. I'd love to. It's damn complicated."

She heaves a sigh of her own. "Family dynamics always are. Let me guess, he's grandfathered in or something?"

"Or something. And to answer your question," I say, changing the subject, "there is no way in hell this is okay to wear. It's like a scrap of thread that fell off a cheap piece of fucking furniture."

The coquettish little smile she gives me wraps around my heart and squeezes.

"I have a surprise for you," I tell her. "What will you do for me to find out what it is?"

I watch her bite her lip and squirm on my lap, her eyes wide with curiosity.

"Anything," she says. I wrap my fingers around her hair and yank her head back, dragging her mouth to my ear.

"You're the prettiest goddamn little slut I've ever met, you know that?"

"Mmm. I love it when you talk dirty to me."

I know she does. I'm a fan myself. "You want to know what you can do to earn your surprise?"

"Wait, I have to *earn* a surprise?" she asks with an adorable little grin.

"Not really, but I don't want to miss my chance."

The pool area rings with her peal of laughter. "Of course you don't. How very *like* you. And I already told you I'd do anything you want. Surely you can come up with a few sordid and deviant things for me?"

I imagine her lips wrapped around my cock, her tongue laving the veined length of it. I imagine her moans of pleasure while I play with her nipples and she sucks me off until I come, hard, wrapping my fingers in her hair while I—

"Hello?"

No. No way. Un-fucking-believable. I feel my whole face contort into a frown.

Marialena's matching frown tells me she heard Cristiano, too.

"Hey, anyone home?" His oily voice rings across the patio.

"I'm here," I say on a stifled growl. "Pool area." I bend and grab a red and white stripped towel from a nearby table and drape it over her shoulders. If he ever saw her like this…

"Hey," he says, waving to me. "Wasn't going to come by until later, but your mom needed a ride from the airport."

Motherfucker. It only gets worse.

"Picked her up, she's getting settled now. Tonight you've got the big shindig? You've got—"

Marialena's wide eyes look at me. "What shindig?"

"Shut it, man," I tell him, shaking my head at him. "Don't give her any details. Yeah, that's tonight. Didn't know my mother was joining us."

He grins. "She wouldn't miss it for the world. Plus, it's her birthday next Tuesday, so...

Fuck. I forget her birthday every year.

"Right."

"Preparations are underway, let me go check on things while I'm here, sound good?"

I nod, my teeth clenched. Behind me, the telltale click of my mother's heels in the foyer warns me she's coming as well.

"Can we go back to the island?" Marialena whispers.

I turn to Cristiano and give him a few instructions. After his fuck up a few weeks ago, I sentenced him to menial labor in one of our retainment facilities. He wasn't a fan, but he got it done. Now I want him to finish up there so I can send him and my mother to secure a wine deal in Tuscany.

I smile at her, drag my fingers to the back of her neck, and pull her forehead to my mouth so I can give her a kiss. "Soon, baby. Soon."

Though she nods, her eyes look a little doubtful. "Can you give me a hint about the surprise?"

"Only because you're being a good girl." I play with her hair, the thick, dark brown length like silk in my fingers. I watch as I wrap it around my index finger. She smells like dew drops and misty rain, so clean and fresh. "The hint is, we have a party tonight. A big old party with punch and canapés and music. And I invited some people you may know to join us."

I don't expect the way she stares, open-mouthed, the look on her face incredulous but hopeful. "Salvatore..." she whispers. "Did you... do you mean to tell me..."

"Your brothers and sister will join us this evening, yes. That's exactly what I'm telling you."

Tears brim in her eyes so quickly, I feel a pang hit my heart. If I'd have known how much this meant to her...

I swipe my thumb under her eye to catch a stray tear.

"Baby," I whisper. "Are you crying?"

"Happy tears," she says, her voice cracking. "I can't believe you did this for me."

"You'll pay me back," I promise.

"With obedience, my undying devotion, or blow jobs?"

I lean in closer, feeling her skin, still hot from sunbathing. Inhaling her scent. "Yes."

The clack of heels grows louder.

"I can start now," she says, her eyes on mine. "If your mother catches us doing nasty things out by the pool, maybe she'll leave us alone."

"Ha. Ha." I gently push her off my lap and give her a teasing smack. "Towel on, do not show yourself to anyone, and go get some clothes on, too."

"I hear and obey. Can I help with anything? It gets tiresome doing nothing but sitting around looking pretty, you know."

I haven't given her any jobs yet because I've wanted to make her comfortable and I wanted to see how she'd behave.

But maybe it would be nice to have myself a First Lady, someone to make sure shit gets done…

"How are they getting here from the airport?" she asks. Tampa International is only about forty-five minutes from here. The clicking of heels is right outside this patio, but she pretends as if she doesn't hear it at all.

"Romeo rented a car."

She nods. "And when will they be here?"

"Around five. We'll have a quick dinner together before everyone else arrives at seven."

The sliding glass door opens and my mother strolls out, her chin in the air and head held high.

"Hello," she says with a chilling smile before she gives Marialena a once-over. Marialena looks at me, her hand on the edge of her towel, and I know she wants to shock her so badly. I give her one stern shake of my head. So help me, I don't care if her brothers are coming, if she—

Grinning at me, she winks, then turns to my mother, walks straight toward her, and tosses her arms up in the air. My mother shrinks back, cringing, but Marialena goes off full throttle. "How *are* you? What would you like me to call you, by the way? Agnesia? Mother? Or is Mom appropriate?"

She tosses her arms around my mother's rigid shoulders as if she's completely oblivious to the fact my mother's standing as still as a mannequin.

My mother shoots me a furious look, but I only smile and shrug. "My new wife's effusive," I say, which she actually isn't, but I like her style and I'm game for playing along with this. "Aren't you, sweetheart?"

My wife draws back and kisses my mother's cheek. My mother's eyes grow wide and she looks at me helplessly, but Marialena's heading my way now.

"He's making me wear this towel because apparently my bikini isn't *appropriate*," she says with a little pout. "What a shame to live on the Gulf of Mexico and have to wear a *housecoat*."

Next, she tosses her arms around me and gives me a loud kiss straight on the lips. "I'm going to get ready, honey bun. You need anything?"

"I'm good," I say, coughing to hide my laughter from my mother.

"Toodles!" She wags her fingers at me and saunters past my mother.

Mother looks at me, her mouth gaping. I grin at her and shove my hands in my pockets. "Lovely, isn't she?" I don't think I've ever, in recent history anyway, grinned at my mother.

She opens her mouth, then closes it. Her eyes follow the retreating figure of Marialena before she looks back at me. "She's—"

I lean in and give her a calculating stare. "If you say anything—literally *anything*—that's less than respectful and kind about my wife, I will toss you into that pool behind me. Got it?"

I stalk past her, ignoring her protests and sputtering. I kind of enjoy the thought of her looking like a drowned rat when our guests begin to arrive.

Kiss. My. Ass.

I join Marialena up in our bedroom to get ready, but instead end up predictably distracted. She finally manages to persuade me to get ready for the party after assuaging my need to have her in the shower. She said it would kill two birds with one stone—shower and sex—and she wasn't wrong.

"I'll leave you to it," I tell her, stepping out of the shower and reaching for a towel.

"To what?"

"Beautifying or whatever the fuck."

She grins. "Happy to beautify for you." I watch as she pulls out one dress after another, lying them out on the bed while I step into my usual pants and suit coat. First, a pretty white sheath dress, followed by a maxi dress in a sunny gold, the color of fall marigolds. A modest pink dress with an empire waist follows a silvery-white floral thing that hugs her waist and flares dramatically.

"They *all* look good. Why so nervous?"

"My family's coming," she says, as if that explains everything.

"I'm aware. You grew up with them. Why would it make you nervous to see them now?" I finish fastening my cuff links and turn to face her. She stands in nude-colored panties and a bra, her hands on her hips.

"I've... never seen them before as Mrs. Salvatore *Capo*," she says, her eyes suddenly watery. I give her a curious look, still trying to understand.

"You're an adorable Mrs. Salvatore Capo, and you fill your role well, Marialena." When she still looks uncertain and bites her lip, I call her to me with a crook of my finger. "Come here."

I watch her look at the dresses, her closet full of shoes, then back at me.

"You just fucked me in the shower," she says warily. "Are you already—"

"Come *here*."

I snap my fingers and point to the floor in front of me. She knows better than to delay obedience. If we weren't crunched for time…

When she reaches me, I drag her closer, my hands around her waist. "Listen up, sweetheart." I slide my finger under her chin, holding her gaze.

"What?" Her chin wobbles a little. Downstairs, the sound of doors opening and staff calling to one another echoes in the large rooms. I can see it in her eyes how nervous she is, how eager she is to please her family.

"When you took vows to me, you became a Capo," I begin, gentling my voice because the message I'm delivering is none too gentle and won't be easy for her to take. "You're no longer Marialena Rossi. What your family thinks about you is no longer relevant. The only person you should care about pleasing is *me*."

Her large, luminous eyes go even wider. "I know," she whispers. "I know, Salvatore." Gentle, warm fingers meet mine. "Yes, it's true, I want to prove I'm not just some silly girl who does whatever the hell she wants on a whim. I'm the youngest Rossi, and I haven't proven myself. So I won't deny there's a part of me that does want to show that I'm capable of filling this role that's been forced on me. You know I didn't choose this. I won't pretend otherwise. But now that I've vowed myself to you, I'll do everything in my power to make sure I uphold my vows."

My heart warms, expanding. I bend to kiss her and brush my lips across hers.

"But this is the first meeting of our families formally. It's the first time your mother will meet my family. And I want to make very, very sure that I make the right impression."

I kiss the apple of her cheek. "You're a good girl. I understand. Just know that it doesn't matter to me, any of it. If they approve. If my mother approves. In fact, a part of me feels you're doing something goddamn right if she doesn't."

"I like that. She's so high-strung and uptight, and it's easy to bait her."

"Maybe don't bait her *too* much."

"I'm not afraid of her."

Her lowered voice and twinkling eyes make her look like a little winged wood nymph, ready to fly away from me on dainty gossamer wings to cause mischief. I half imagine she'd fill that role quite nicely.

I catch myself with the whimsical thought, and almost want to shake myself. I don't think like this. I definitely don't ever think about things like fairies and wood nymphs and fanciful flights.

What the hell has this woman done to me?

I didn't think any woman ever had the power to change me.

I was wrong.

She does need instructions, and not because she needs to prove herself to me or anything like that, but because she needs to prove this to herself.

"Go downstairs. Check on the food. Do a taste test, make sure everything's hot and seasoned well and that there's enough of it. The last time we hosted a dinner, we ran out of salad plates and the coffee was cold."

I've cooked much of it and the rest has been cooked by my staff.

"On it!" she says, grinning at me. With her head held high, she marches to the door.

"Marialena!"

The sharp tone of my voice makes her freeze mid-step. Looking over her shoulder at me, she looks perplexed. "Yes?"

"Put some fucking clothes on." I stab my finger at the pile of dresses. "Silvery white."

It's the only one that puts me in mind of a nymph. I keep that detail to myself.

CHAPTER SEVENTEEN

Marialena

WHEN I LOOK into Salvatore's eyes, when I hear what he says… when I truly *listen* to him, I hear more than bravado and swagger. I see a man who lost his father at a very young age and is afraid of falling in love because he's steeled himself against it.

Yeah, so I like to play armchair psychologist. But a woman like me learns what makes people behave the way they do. When you strip away pretext or veneer and boil down what makes people vulnerable at their very core, we're really not much different from one another. Beauty and wealth, honor and prestige, they don't change who people are at their core. They don't change what people still crave and need to be human.

Humans need to be loved. Humans need to be needed. Humans need security and comfort.

Humans need each other.

Even the rich, capable ones that command a room or an army or a nation.

So when I see Salvatore, I don't see Don Capo, head of Tampa's elite and most feared. No.

I see a man who's caught in his role, trapped in a family that cares more about his power and money than the man behind those cerulean eyes of his. He doesn't have the companionship of his siblings like I have. He doesn't have the real love of a parent like I have. He has nothing but wealth and power, but that isn't enough to bring anyone happiness. Humans aren't solitary creatures.

I see the way he tries with me. I see the compromises he makes, the softening of his heart. And while I'm not sure what exactly brought him to a place where he's actually willing to bend, to subdue himself, to allow himself to no longer be a wild beast but *domesticated...* I like that I may have had a part in all that.

I won't let him down. I've meant every word of what I said. When I commit to something, I stick through it until the end.

But the question is… when will we have our end?

It's hard to imagine any mob couple lasting for decades, though I've known a few. They weren't like us, though. Never. Two born and raised mafia? We're testing the limits of our own human frailty.

Or are we?

Maybe I'm the only one who hopes for more than hot sex and the security of wealth. Maybe I'm the only one who wants more than she can touch and hold.

Or maybe I've finally done what my family's warned me about for years, and let my optimism make a fool of me.

I never hoped a man like Salvatore would love me... until I saw the man behind the curtain. I felt the whispered promises of hope begin to grow within me. Though I've never been one denied love because of the tight-knit family I grew up in, I spent a lifetime dealing with rejection from my father. The rest of us—my mother and siblings—were like flowers that grew through cracks in concrete. Never meant to thrive. Never meant to live. Defying the odds. But despite the oppression and abuse, we lifted our faces toward the sun.

We survived.

I'm the last remaining Rossi left to solidify our family's stronghold, and I knew, though I denied it sometimes, I wouldn't shirk my duty.

And I knew the day would come when my brothers would marry me off. It seems I knew even when I was a child that unconditional love was not in the cards for someone like me. I would only be loved if I met certain expectations, followed certain rules, and ultimately denied who I was above all.

So I came to our marriage knowing full well I had a role to play, no more, no less. I never actually expected he'd ever overcome his need for control and power because those were the conditions. I told myself I could accept it all as part of our dynamic. I'm a mob princess, after all. I know how it all works.

But I've seen glimmers of more. I've felt the hint of authenticity when he touches me, when he holds me. When we make love.

I don't know what this is yet, but I do know I'm not just checking off a box for him. There's a depth to our relationship that transcends just filling roles.

Before he leaves me to dress in the silvery-white floral dress, the feminine little number that cinches at the waist and flares dramatically halfway to my calves, he kisses me. It's not just any ordinary kiss. Someday, after years have passed and we've children between us, when we've kissed each other so many times we've lost count, he may learn how to give me a parting kiss on the cheek.

Suffice it to say, he hasn't learned that yet.

I stare into the mirror, breathless and pink-cheeked, my lips swollen and my pulse racing. *Damn*, Salvatore Capo knows how to kiss.

A gentle knock at the door tells me my staff has arrived to help me dress. At home, I didn't have staff to tend to me like this. I could have if I'd wanted to, but I never wanted someone to help me do the things I felt perfectly capable of. Here, I allow it, because I don't want to accidentally misstep, and it helps to have someone who essentially functions as a personal stylist. One might say it takes the guesswork out of things.

I glance at the time as Clarice, a twenty-something college grad with glasses on the tip of her nose and a wide grin, slides into the room.

"Oooh, I love that one. I *love* that dress," she squeals, clapping her hands. "It's so gorgeous!"

"I hope I don't spill marinara on it," I say with a frown. "Oh! That reminds me!" I glance at the time. "Can you get me ready in fifteen minutes?"

I need time to make sure I can oversee the food as he instructed before my family comes.

Clarice cringes. "If you've already washed your hair…"

"This morning!"

"Okay, alright, let's get a move on, lady." She claps her hands, and I half expect little mice with scissors and a bobbin of thread to come running in. "Let's get this done!"

Fifteen minutes later on the nose, I stand, sheathed in the nearly sheer fabric, my hair pinned up in an elegant up-do, impeccable makeup from mascara to highlighters to a lip stain she swears won't wear off when I drink, and death-defying stilettos Salvatore bought me as a gift when we left the island. Even in these, he's got half a head on me, but it does make me feel more powerful standing tall.

"You look amazing," Clarice says. "Stunning! Your husband will want to marry you all over again!"

I give her a quick hug to thank her, then glance at the time, grab my phone, and head to the kitchen. "Thank you!"

I listen for the sounds of Salvatore or his mother nearby, but I hear nothing. Now that we've been married for a little while, Salvatore's more comfortable leaving me on my own when he tends to business. As far as his mother, I just don't trust her. And after what he's told me about her… suffice it to say, it would be amazing if he managed to exile her out of the country when we have any children, because that woman is not coming within ten feet of her grandkids if I can help it.

I'm almost at the kitchen when I hear the low murmur of voices. One rises and one falls. I turn the corner to find Cristiano and Agnesia having a heated, whispered conversation. Cristiano gives me a lewd once-over.

"You look fabulous," he says. His compliment feels oily and slick.

I allow my voice to go cold and detached. "Thank you."

Agnesia walks away without a word.

Salvatore needs to ban these two and never let them near him again. One of them will betray him, if not both, and soon. They probably already have. While he doesn't trust them, he's led me to believe their relationships are complicated. *How* complicated are they?

Staff flits about here and there, cleaning, setting the table, dusting, while I head to the kitchen. A nervous excitement buzzes around the group of kitchen employees until I enter the room. I smile brightly and give them a little wave.

Pierre, the plump and pleasant head chef, smiles at me. He worked in some of Tampa's most elite kitchens before Salvatore roped him into coming here and working alongside him. Turns out it's not his first mob gig, and as a result he's one of the most trustworthy people Salvatore employs.

"I don't normally allow other people to cook in my kitchen when I'm present," he explained to me when we met. "But first, your husband does what he wants, so that was an easy answer. Second, he's a joy to cook with."

Joy to cook with, those were his exact words. Not sure I'd call Salvatore a joy about anything—okay, maybe a *few things*—but hey, if that works, it works.

"Mr. Capo's asked me to oversee tonight's food preparation." I give them a smile. "You know how he is." I wave my hand. "Do you have everything prepared yet?"

One of the older servers purses his lips at me. "Well, this is a first."

I bristle, my spine stiffening and give him a frosty look. I'm not a confrontational person usually, but my husband has expectations and I have a very specific role to play.

"Excuse me?"

He picks up a wooden spoon and gives the pot a hearty stir. "I said this is a first. It isn't often Mr. Capo micromanages the kitchen staff."

Oooh, no he does not.

I draw myself up to my full height, which is definitely assisted by the stilettos, and give him what I hope is a piercing look. I may be a pretty laid-back girl in general, but once again I remember I was raised by Tosca Rossi.

Jared passes behind me. When we were unable to locate his mother, I begged Salvatore to let him stay with us. He's been a huge help around here, and a comfort to me when Salvatore's busy. He winks at me and gives me a nod before he slips away unseen.

My voice takes on a sharp edge, though I keep my tone polite. "Mr. Capo asked his wife to ensure everything is prepared for his guests. Since his guests happen to be my family, I was more than happy to honor his request." I tilt my head to the side. "Is there a problem here?"

"No problem, no problem at all," Pierre says, glaring at his employee. "Of course, Mrs. Capo, you are more than welcome to try everything!"

I sample each food item in turn, from the antipasti to the primi, excellent cuts of steak, all the way through the menu until we get to the *formaggi e frutta*, a dessert platter of imported cheeses.

"It's perfect," I tell Pierre. "We're having a party of nine for dinner before tonight's main event, so let's ensure we have enough tableware as well. We had a bit of a shortage last time, and I want to make sure Mr. Capo's satisfied."

Pierre's associate mutters under his breath and I catch him rolling his eyes.

He's done.

"Your name?" I ask sweetly.

He gives me a sharp look. "Josiah."

"Josiah, I think it best you take the rest of the evening off." Maybe I'm overstepping. Maybe I'm losing my temper. But there's no way my husband would allow disrespect from his staff, so it thereby follows I am the one that will ensure his staff behaves the way he expects.

"Excuse me?" He looks as if he's about to throw a plate across the room.

Pierre steps in and takes Josiah by the elbow. "You heard her. Let's have a talk."

He curses under his breath. I wait until he leaves, then turn to see the shadows of onlookers in the doorway. My stomach plummets until I recognize my sister Rosa, looking gorgeous and stunning as ever, beside Romeo, whose eyes have gone a bit wide in surprise.

"Well, well, well," Rosa says with a smile. "Seems all our little sister needed was a ring on her finger, hmm?"

I squeal and launch myself at them, grabbing them both around the necks to squeeze the life out of them. "Oh my *God* did I miss you. I missed you so much! Salvatore just had me check on the food for tonight to make sure it's perfect and it so is." They kiss my cheeks, one after the other. I squeal again when I see Tavi, Orlando, and Mario standing behind them.

"Thank fuck," Orlando mutters. "Airplane food was nonexistent and none of them would let me eat at the airport."

"You'd ruin your appetite and we're not going to disrespect the Capos, Lando," Rosa says, rolling her eyes.

"Dude," Mario says under his breath. I grin at him. "This place is *epic*."

"You're the one who lives in a castle," I remind him.

"Ain't the same," he whispers. "You have the Gulf of Mexico out your window." He swivels to look at me. "You got a guest room?"

"I think there's like ten," I tell him.

"Mario!" Tavi elbows him. "Knock it off."

"What? We're family now. Capo can stay at The Castle or Tuscany any time he wants."

"Thank you. I'll keep that in mind." My pulse races when I hear the deep timbre of Salvatore's commanding tone. I quickly look over at him to see he's fully dressed for dinner, but although his tone is softer than normal, he's wearing his stern Don face.

"He means it," I tell Salvatore. "And I would very much take him up on that if I were you."

He reaches me, then gently slides his hand to the small of my back. Romeo's eyes follow the possessive gesture. Rosa's gaze widens ever so slightly. Is Salvatore pissing on me in front of his associates? "I'll have to keep that in mind, won't I?"

I nod and wink at him. He nods and winks back.

"Dinner's perfect," I say in a low voice. "But I have something to tell you."

I turn back to Rosa and Romeo. "Just a second, guys."

I pull Salvatore to a quiet nook in the room. "I did a taste test like you said, and everything is perfection. But one of your staff members gave me shit about everything."

I fill him in. I watch the dark storm cloud roll over his features, but he doesn't speak. "He had the nerve to disrespect my wife," Salvatore mutters. "And what was your response?"

Now I'm proud of my response.

"I told him he'd be taking the night off," I say. "I truly hope I didn't overstep, but he was being so rude—"

"My home is your home," Salvatore says. "My staff is your staff. My garden is your garden. Make yourself at home, Marialena, and if anyone in my company gives you a hard time, you come to get me. You got me?"

It sounds so magnanimous, as if he truly wants us to make this work. Then why does my heart beat so fast, as if waiting for the conditions? Maybe it's decades of living the lifestyle I have, seeing what I have, but I can't shake the nagging feeling I get that there's more to Salvatore than I've bargained for.

I nod and swallow the lump in my throat. "I got you."

I look to see Romeo has a look of surprise, but Rosa's face has gone soft and gentle. They share a look but don't say anything.

"Dude," Mario says, shaking his head. "This place is incredible. Give us a tour?"

Salvatore gives him one of his very rare smiles. "Of course. We have time before we eat."

I feel proud walking beside my husband, showing my family our home.

"You're welcome to visit," Salvatore offers. My heart swells. "Now that we're family."

I turn to see Agnesia standing in a doorway. She sees us coming. I expect she'll table her hatred for me for a little while anyway, and at least attempt pleasantries with my siblings. I wish my mother had been able to come. To be honest, I'm not quite sure she was invited.

But instead of doing the polite thing, Agnesia turns on her heel and stalks away. I look to Salvatore, but he only rolls his eyes at me.

"Let her stew," he says in a low voice. "She's losing control of everything around her and not handling it very well."

"You could say that again," I mutter under my breath.

By dinner and several bottles of wine later, we're all loosening up a bit. Mario is regaling us with tales of drag racing in Tuscany, and we segue pretty easily into a lively chat about the trouble we got into as children.

"I saved her ass a time or two," Mario says with a wink at me.

"And I saved yours a couple of hundred times or three."

Romeo chuckles and puts his wineglass down. "You could say that again."

"Surely not since you've become Don," Orlando says with a twinkle in his eye. "Right?"

"Definitely not," I agree.

"I thought we taught you not to lie, Lena," Tavi says with a smile and a wag of his head.

"Au contraire, mon frère, you taught me to lie with discretion and candor."

Salvatore smiles. "I approve."

No one misses the underlying thread of truth.

"Do you remember that time Mama caught you and Mario drinking by the quarry?" Rosa asks, shaking her head. I feel Salvatore stiffen beside me. It catches me off guard. I quickly turn to look at him, but his face remains impassive.

"Which time?" Mario mutters with a grimace, making everyone laugh.

"Lena was *young*," Rosa says. "She had, like, barely turned sixteen and you were trying to convince her to get a tattoo from your novice friend."

"Oh my God, I remember that!" I cover my mouth with my hands. "And we managed to convince her we were doing a recycling project with the Boy Scouts, and all the empties were part of the experiment?"

Mario guffaws. "How could I forget? Mama never went to the quarry. Not sure why she was even there that day."

Salvatore puts his wineglass down, picks up his knife and fork, and cuts a thin slice of steak. "Did you frequent the quarry?" he asks. "Seems a dangerous place for kids to go to hang out."

"That's maybe why we loved it," I say dryly.

"Did your father know?" His question falls heavily. The table lapses into silence. My heart beats faster, and I suddenly lose my appetite. I'm not sure what's happening here.

"He did," Romeo says, picking up his glass and holding it out to Salvatore. "May I have a refill?"

"Of course, brother," Salvatore says, but instead of reaching for the bottle, he nods his head at one of the staff. "Fill Mr. Rossi's glass, please."

Mr. Rossi.

It's the first time I've heard him address Romeo that way. Dread prickles my skin. I place my fork down as Salvatore gets to his feet.

"Salvatore," I say gently, trying to get his attention.

He looks my way and shakes his head. "Stay," he says, his voice low with authority. "Visit with your family." He turns and faces the rest. "Please excuse me, I have a quick matter to attend to. I'll join you all when the rest of the guests arrive this evening. My staff will show you to your rooms."

Without sparing me another look, he turns and stalks out of the room.

What just happened?

I open my mouth to ask, but Romeo catches my eye and gives me a quick shake of his head. He's right. We won't speak freely here if there are surveillance cameras and staff eavesdropping in every corner.

"So tell me," Rosa says, a teasing smile playing on her lips. "You pregnant yet?"

CHAPTER EIGHTEEN

Salvatore

MAYBE THEY'RE curious why I left so abruptly. I can't share my reasoning.

I berate myself halfway back to our bedroom because I know I made a mistake in letting myself have feelings for her at all.

The quarry. The fucking *quarry*. How could I have been so stupid?

My father was killed when I was in kindergarten. I remember coming home from school with my bodyguards, my Spiderman backpack swinging merrily. I remember the line of sleek cars by the front door. I remember my mother's fury and anger and that she never shed a tear. I remember I had to wear a suit that I hated to the funeral, and it was my first introduction to the responsibilities ahead of me.

I knew that my father was in New England, but I didn't know where. At the time, it might as well have been China, it was that far away.

No one was ever found to be guilty of his death. We never sought vengeance, and if I'm honest... I'm not sure I want to now.

I know what the laws of mob rule state. I know that I am responsible for avenging my father's death. But what if the person responsible for killing him is no longer here?

I have questions that need answers.

So I leave Marialena to her siblings. I hear their laughter and their jokes, and I'm glad for her that she has their companionship. But I'm also glad that I've severed the ties between her and them because the choices before me will be made that much easier.

She has mentioned her father. She's mentioned how he abused them, and of course it was no surprise to me because men like him treat anyone other than their peers as nothing but servants or lackeys. Beneath them. I know this well.

But I never asked her more about him. His history. His nicknames. His trademark moves... all facts that would've clued me in so much sooner.

I pace in our bedroom and look at the time on the clock. We only have two hours before the rest of our guests arrive.

I have questions for Cristiano, but I don't want to put a bug in his ear either. I need to have answers, though. I think about who is older than I am in my group, who would know the answers to my questions. My mother... *No.*

I call Federico. He answers on the first ring.

"Boss?"

"I need you to find the date of my father's death. Give me everything you've got."

"Yes, sir. It's in our records, won't take long. Will call you right back."

The seconds seem to pass by like the ticking of a time bomb. I pace with my hands in my pockets. What will this mean? If he corroborates what I suspect...

Finally, he calls me back.

"September, twenty-five years ago. We don't have the exact date because his body wasn't found until weeks later, remember? But there were witnesses that saw him at a nearby quarry."

A cold chill skates down my spine.

"Right." I pinch the bridge of my nose and close my eyes. Marialena probably would've been a toddler at most, three maybe. But Romeo... Romeo would've been a teenager. Romeo would've known things.

I'll have questions for him.

"Tell me again how he was killed."

"Knife up the back of the head, lacerations on his body..."

Our door opens.

"Salvatore? Are you okay?" Marialena walks in.

"Gotta go, man." I hang up the phone and face her. "I told you to stay with your family." I can't keep the ice out of my voice. I hate that she flinches.

I'd move heaven and earth to keep her here with me. No one, literally no one, has ever looked at me with concern in her eyes like that. She's worried, but she's also truly concerned about my well-being, and I swear to God she's the only one that ever has been.

I sit on the edge of the bed and crook my finger at her. "Come here."

My voice is husky, and if I didn't know any better, I would think it was affected by emotion. But I don't allow emotion to do that to me.

She walks to me with concern in her eyes. "Is it my family? Are you uncomfortable with them here?"

Uncomfortable? No, sweetheart. Trying to talk myself out of murdering your brother. Trying to figure out how I can salvage our marriage when I have to avenge my father's death.

"It's nothing," I lie. "I got a present for you."

A look of concern flits over her features before she smiles. "Okay. I'm glad it's nothing. They went to their rooms to get ready for tonight."

Good. Keep those fuckers away from me.

I take a long look at her. I know that she doesn't believe me, but we both are wise enough to know sometimes it's best to leave a sleeping snake well enough alone and not fucking poke it with sticks. Sometimes, it's better not to know things.

I open the side table and pull out the box of edibles. "I think tonight will go a lot better if we have a little bit of an edge."

She smiles at me. "You just want to fuck me high."

My voice is even deeper when I respond, "You're goddamn right about that." Sex with Marialena is the best thing I could've ever imagined. Sex with her uninhibited and high…

Right now, I have more reasons than that. I just can't tell her.

From what she says, she's a lightweight. I take out the small, sugarcoated candy shaped like a slice of lemon.

"Have one of these." She's not new to this, so her reaction will come quickly.

She sniffs the edible and sighs. "God, how I've missed that smell." She slides it into her mouth and smiles at me.

"Sit here." I take her onto my knee.

"Are you going to ask me what I want for Christmas?"

I smile at her and kiss her, tasting the sweet essence of her flavored like fine wine, imbibing her scent and thanking my lucky stars that I ended up with a woman like her. She opens her mouth to let me in. Our tongues tangle, and I swallow the sighs she releases. I slowly lower her backward as her mouth parts further. I bite her lip and kiss my way up her jaw to her cheek.

"I got all ready for the party," she says. "Hair, makeup, clothes… I'll have to do it all over again." But it's the feeblest of protests as she melts into me, her body malleable against mine.

"You have staff to help you get ready again."

"It will still take time…"

"We have time."

She doesn't protest but gives me a wicked grin. "Well then."

"Where did you go to smoke with Mario?" I ask, as if it's only curiosity.

She grins. "God, it's already kicking in. That's strong stuff. And it's been a while." She takes in a deep breath. "Okay, alright. Focus. You asked where we smoked. Sometimes we would go down by the ocean. The wind swallows up the smell, you know. We had a cliff overlooking the water in Cape Ann. You've seen it before by The Castle." I nod. Her hands roam up and down the length of my body as if memorizing me. I growl, my erection hardening as I pull her closer to me.

"If we were in Tuscany, we had various places hidden away in the vineyard, which is huge. But at home, after we were discovered near the cliffs by one of my father's men who tattled on us, we decided to go down to the quarry."

"The quarry." My pulse races. I kiss her neck and press my lips to her pulse. So vulnerable. So fragile. "You mentioned that at dinner."

"Yeah, nobody goes there because everyone believes it's haunted. Maybe it is. Lord knows my dad murdered enough people and brought their bodies to the quarry." She rolls her eyes, probably expecting that I'll go along with this as I've gone along with everything else. It's no surprise to someone in the mob that certain members murder each other. It's no surprise that they take lives and it's further no surprise that they have pet places to hide the bodies. What is the surprise is how casually she speaks of it.

I knead her breasts and tug down the top of her dress. Her nipples are delicious.

She gives me a grin. Her voice is a half moan as she says, "Oh, God. I *love* that. Yes, yes, *yes.*"

"Are you fucking orgasming?"

"Hard to tell when I'm high. It all feels like that."

Her breasts feel heavier, her nipples more sensitive. Her pussy is already throbbing, ready for my fingers, my cock, my tongue. And when she comes, she'll scream herself fucking hoarse.

Excellent.

I feel the effects of my own edible hit me. The edges of my anger blur a little. She quickly becomes the epicenter of my universe. Everything looks more vivid—her gorgeous body, those swollen lips that need attention, the swell of her breasts and dainty features.

"We don't have a quarry like that down here, but I can imagine it was a perfect place for your dad to hide people." She's too high now to give a concern about what we're talking about.

She only moans and giggles. "Yes, exactly. It was like an episode of *Stand by Me*, looking for a body. We always were."

She reaches for me. Electric arousal courses through me as she lightly brushes her thumb over the fabric of my undershirt.

"Did your dad have one of those signature moves?"

"Mhm. He was quite proud of himself, but it's gross. I don't want to talk about it. Not now, Salvatore," she says with a little frown. "Let's not talk about that now."

Her lips pull downward in a pout.

"You don't have to tell me if you don't want to," I say gently, hoping the lack of pressure brings the answers to light. I can find out in other ways as well. Romeo's just down the hall.

"It's just gross. He'd slice down the back of people's heads. We called it modern scalping and his friends called him The Skull." My blood runs cold. My skin feels prickly and suddenly too warm.

She wrinkles her nose. "Gross, right?"

My whole body tightens.

"Gross."

"Let's not talk about this anymore."

It's fine with me. I have my answers.

"Salvatore… I want you so fucking bad…"

I give her ass a quick slap to chastise her for the language, she knows better than that. Of course this only makes her moan, and her fingers run to my waist where she starts to unbuckle my belt.

"I wanna feel you spank me while I come," she whispers. She likes that when she's sober, never mind when she's high.

I kiss and bite her lips as I lift her dress. I drag her thong down and gently rub my thumb over her throbbing parts. She lets out a moan so seductive, my own parts throb.

"Take out my cock," I growl. I have a purpose, but I'm not inhuman. And I have a gorgeous woman eager to please me. A woman who's taken my name and wears my ring.

She slides my cock out, bends down, and runs her tongue over it before she slides it in her mouth. I groan out loud as I reach for my belt. While she kisses and licks me, I double the belt over and slap her thigh. It only makes her suck more eagerly. We keep up the spanking and blow job until I'm right on the edge.

"Wait."

I slide my cock back inside my pants, swing her out, and drag her over my knee. I reach into the bedside table and grab the hot pink sex toy I bought for this purpose. There are many options on it, and I know exactly what she needs. "Hold this between your legs." It vibrates in her hand.

She quickly obeys, her hands trembling. I'd bet half my kingdom she's already on the cusp of orgasm.

"Oh, God, Salvatore. I want you so bad."

That makes two of us.

I slap the belt down, hard. She can take it hard like this. A red stripe blooms across her ass as she slides the vibrator between her legs and presses it to her clit. Fuck, I love how dirty she is and how she eats up every damn thing I do to her.

"Oh, God," she moans, squirming as she nears climax. "Yes," she whispers. I slap the belt down and she jerks her hips, on the verge of climax. *"Yes!"*

Again and again I spank her as she moans, holding the vibrator between her legs until she tenses then screams her climax. On and on it goes as I hold her over my knee. Still climaxing, I pull her upright and onto my lap.

I pin her hands to her sides, lay her back on the bed and tug her panties down. Drape her legs over my neck and lick her slick pussy.

She gasps and tries to move away. "Ah, too soon, so sensitive," she whispers. I ease the strokes of my tongue until she's eager for more, on the verge of a second climax. I grasp her wrists and ravage her with my tongue until she screams my name and stabs my hair with her fingers, grasping for purchase. She comes so hard she lifts off the bed. I lazily lap her until she sinks back to the bed, then kneel over her and glide the head of my swollen cock between her legs.

"I want you in me," she says in a plea that's nearly a moan. "Please, Salvatore, I want your cock in me." I thrust into her, grateful she can take me like this now. With her arms around my neck she holds on tight and her beautiful legs wrap around me. Every thrust feels like a claiming, a punishment, a branding. I fuck her until my balls clench and my release spills inside her, marking her as mine. She moans into another orgasm, gasping for breath as we come together.

I hold her. Her heartbeat hammers against my chest. My senses are alert, as if the lines of my existence are painted in bright swaths of color, vivid and clear.

"Was that a fucking triple?"

She sags against my chest. "I maybe lost count. Holy *shit*. I don't know how I'll be able to go to this party. I... can't even walk. I don't know how you're still breathing." She gasps again. "I'm trying to remember how."

I hold her against me. I steal this one moment of peace with her before God knows what happens next. We can't go on like this, I know it.

"Let's do that again sometime," she says with a grin.

"We will."

It only takes a few minutes to clean up. She needs a little help getting ready for the party, but soon, she's all dolled up and as gorgeous as ever. Grinning at me, she looks as if she wants to dance. I half wonder why it took me this long to get her a damn edible.

"I think a little bit of my lipstick is on your collar, sir," she says with a giggle.

I look down. It's barely noticeable. "Well, would you look at that."

For some reason this makes her giggle. She damn near thinks it's hysterical.

Fully dressed and put back together, I look down at my phone and realize I have ten missed calls. Fuck.

I pick up my phone and scroll—my mom, Cristiano, a couple of my men, including Federico.

Federico's message gets straight to the point. "Got what you asked me for."

A part of me wishes I could leave well enough alone, but I know better than that.

I take Marialena's hand. I wonder what my next course of action is. She's answered what I needed to know. She's confirmed the truth.

I either shield her from what happens next or drag her straight through it.

"You okay?" she asks. "We just had like the most incredible sex ever and you look a little out of it. I feel like I could sleep for days, but I think we need to go play host and hostess, and I seriously hope they have some good desserts down there. I need—"

"Chocolate," I finish for her. "I can arrange that."

I evade the question. No, I'm not alright at all.

CHAPTER NINETEEN

Marialena

I'M NOT REALLY sure what's going on with Salvatore. One minute he's holding me, we're making love with such intensity I see stars, and the next, he's pulling away. I want to reach out to him and pull him back to me, hold him so he stays right here with me, so that I know nothing will change.

But I can't do that. If we are going to love each other—really, truly *love* each other—I need to be able to trust that he'll come back to me. I need to trust the authenticity of his feelings for me. I can't control him and fear the loss of his time or attention.

That's easier said than done, though, when you've seen what I have and experienced what I have.

"Okay, alright," I whisper to myself. "Get your shit together. You have a job to do, and you're no longer Marialena Rossi. You are Marialena Capo, and your husband is counting on you."

I meet up with my sister and brothers, and we head downstairs.

"Shit," Mario says to me under his breath. "Has he told you who's coming tonight?"

I shake my head, suddenly apprehensive. "Uh, no…? Who?"

"Literally *everyone*. I guess it's tradition down here for men like him to have a post-wedding party."

"Right," Romeo says. "Since most of the weddings are arranged, or a quick one like yours, they take the opportunity to spread it wide and clear that you're married now."

"Got it. So… give me names?"

I feel my eyes widen as I hear the names of our friends and enemies, associates and alliances, and names I've never heard before. "Castellanos… Campanelles… Regazzas…" And before he finishes, I see my cousin Sergio in the background.

"Montavios," I supply.

"Yup."

I look around the room to locate my husband, but before I can find him, he finds me. I feel his familiar warmth and his hand on the small of my back, his rough voice in my ear. "You look lovely," he whispers. "No one would know how you got that flush on your cheeks…"

"Salvatore," I hiss. "Behave yourself, please."

He nips my ear. My cheeks flush hot. "Not a chance."

My heart flutters at the way he literally just does not give a fuck. "Dance with me, Marialena," he says, handing his drink to a waitress as she passes.

I reach for him and let him twirl me onto the large expanse of a dance floor lit from above with a glittering crystal chandelier.

I follow his lead, as he dances one step ahead of me. I've been trained to dance like this, as it's part of the expectations for a woman like me. Rosa and I took lessons with Mama when we were little, then professional when we were older, so we could keep up with formal occasions just like this. It seems Salvatore has, as well.

I step back, then forward, away from him, then close again, as if our dance is a metaphor for the walk we'll take as husband and wife. His eyes on me are hungry and greedy, as if he doesn't want to waste a breath doing anything but looking at me. I melt a little.

With a quick flick of his wrist, I spin out, then back in again, tucked up against his chest. His fingers cup my jaw, the rough warmth erotic and possessive. I gasp as his mouth finds mine and he kisses me like we're long-lost lovers, like I'm the very oxygen he needs to breathe. I melt against him. He made me come so hard I saw stars not an hour ago, but when my lips part and welcome him in, a familiar flare of warmth and heat dances between my legs.

I blink when he pulls away, and my mind begins to play tricks on me.

Was that a farewell kiss?

Why would I even think something like that?

I want to hold him to me. I want to wrap my arms and legs around him like a barnacle stuck to his side. He'd never be able to extricate me. The image amuses me, and I mentally blame the residual effects of the edible.

"What's so funny?" he whispers in my ear.

"I was imagining you were a ship and I was a barnacle, and you couldn't pry me off."

I expect him to laugh or teasingly swat my ass or tug my hair, but he doesn't. I watch the light fade in his eyes as he lapses into the same melancholy brooding he did when we first met. I open my mouth to ask him what's wrong but can't bring myself to voice my concern. Instead, I lay my head on his shoulder.

"It's gorgeous in here tonight," I whisper. It is. Candlelight flickers on high tables, and large boughs of white flowers adorn every flat surface. At the entrance to the patio, the doors are wide open, and a string quartet plays music so beautiful it makes me want to cry. Couples dance and sway and mingle, and though none stare to avoid being rude, I know they're all watching us.

Normally, he'd flirt with me, tell me something like *it's not as gorgeous as you.* But he doesn't. It isn't just the need for attention or compliments that sets me on edge, it's his whole demeanor. Detached. Resigned. Angry.

"Salvatore," I say pleadingly. "Please, tell me what's bothering you?"

"It's nothing," he lies.

I sigh. "I'm not allowed to lie to you, yet you've done nothing but lie to me since this evening began."

I gasp as he holds me tighter, but he doesn't respond. He doesn't deny it, either, but I feel him stiffen when his gaze falls on someone who just came into the room.

"Here, sweetheart," he whispers. "Have a dance with your brother."

"Salvatore—"

But he's gone. Romeo's in his place.

"Something wrong?" Romeo asks, swinging me out onto the dance floor. It feels like he's taking on the role of father figure, and we're having our commemorative dance.

"He's... acting strange," I say, shaking my head. "I can't quite put my finger on it."

"He seems fine to me," Romeo responds, but he hasn't really known Salvatore all that long. While he seems "fine" to Romeo, it's because he isn't acting like a douchebag. There's far more to Salvatore than "fine" and "asshole."

"No," I tell him, shaking my head. "It started at dinner."

"Oh?" I've got Romeo's attention now.

"Yeah..." My voice trails off. When exactly did it start? I play back the conversation in my mind. "It was... someone mentioned the quarry."

Romeo keeps dancing, but I feel a slight stiffening in the way he holds me. "The quarry," he repeats. "Okay."

"And then... well, later, in our bedroom, he asked me a lot of questions about the quarry."

"Did he?" I have the distinct feeling Romeo knows more than he's letting on.

"Are you just going to keep repeating things to me?"

We swirl past Cristiano, who's watching me with a steely gaze.

"God, I hate him."

"Cristiano?"

"Yeah."

"Same. He's selfish and conniving, and it's surprising to me Capo still keeps him in his company," he says in a hushed voice. "But we have to respect your husband's decisions and not express criticism." He stands up taller. "Which is exactly why I'm listening and repeating things. I'm reserving judgment."

"Yeah, it was just... I dunno, odd. He asked me all about our father, and I told him how they used to call him 'The Skull,' and how his signature move was a modern-day scalping. It was like—"

I stop talking because Romeo has come to a halting stop.

"Did you discuss anything like... a timeline? Our ages?"

I shake my head. "No, but I told him how we'd hide down there and look for bodies, because—" I close my mouth. Now that I'm saying this out loud, I'm not so sure I was supposed to say that.

Did he get me high on purpose?

"I..." My voice trails off.

Romeo's face has gone ashen.

"What is it?" I ask in a whisper. "Romeo, please..."

But instead of answering he only tugs me into a corner of the room where Tavi and Orlando stand drinking amber liquid in crystal glasses.

"Y'alright, bro?" Orlando asks him.

"We need to have a word," he says, jerking his chin to the corner of the room. "We'll be back, Marialena."

"Hey, wait," I protest. "You can't just… go have a word about something that's a major concern to *me* and exclude me. What the hell?"

Romeo looks at me sadly and shakes his head. He opens his mouth to speak and then clamps it shut as if thinking better about it. "I love you, Marialena, and you'll always be my favorite little sister." A lump rises in my throat. "But you're Marialena Capo now. Your allegiance is to your husband."

Marialena Capo. I swallow a sob that rises in my chest at the enormity of this shift. It's not like I was unaware, but I'm still hit with the painful loss of the way my family would confide in each other.

What's happening? I hate that I don't know who to trust or where to look. I feel suddenly cast away from anyone that ever loved me, including my new husband. I blink back tears as a member of staff sidles up to me. "Another drink, miss?"

I shake my head no. It's time I sobered up.

"Hey, you okay?" I look up to see Rosa a few feet away, a glass of wine in hand and a look of concern on her face. "Marialena?"

The sympathetic sound of her voice makes me want to cry. It's easier to stay strong when I don't have someone nearby ready to catch me.

I look around for Salvatore, but he's nowhere to be found. I release a breath and jerk my head toward the patio. "Hey, wanna go for a walk? It's gorgeous out there. I saw actual *dolphins* the other day."

"Absolutely, let's do it. That white sand beach is like straight out of a resort catalog."

"Right?"

On my way out, I survey the food and accept a few thanks and well wishes, some from people I don't know and some from people I do. It takes us longer than I expect to make it to the exit, and when we finally do, I sag against the vacant doorway.

"Not easy being popular, is it?" Rosa asks teasingly.

I shake my head. "Not easy being known by everyone in the room, either."

People knew who I was when I was a Rossi, but I wasn't the most important person in the room half the time. So even though I didn't get privacy necessarily, I was often left to my own devices, and that was good enough. Now, though…

"It isn't easy, little sister," Rosa says softly. "I somehow got lucky."

"The *second* time around. Let's not sugarcoat the first, babe."

Her first husband cheated on her and beat her before my father found out. None of us knew that she was already in love with our very own Santo, a sworn member of the Rossi mob who came to live with us when he was a child. She's found her happily ever after, but only after much pain and heartache.

"True," she admits. "So what's going on?"

We look out at the water, as the waves lap on the crystal white shore.

"I don't really know. I can't put my finger on it. And if I even verbalize what's concerning me… I don't know, I think it sounds stupid?"

She takes a sip of wine before giving me a wry smile.

"Try me."

I look around us to make sure we're alone. And though we don't have total privacy, no one is near enough to hear us.

"I… feel like I have to put a wall up around my heart to protect myself from him. I feel like… if I drop my shield even for a moment, then I can't… I can't trust him not to break my heart."

"Of course," she says, nodding. "Understandable. I think half the women that marry men like we did hope to change them or reform them." She huffs out a mirthless breath. "But that's incredibly unlikely. The best that we can hope for is to be loved despite our circumstances, and for fidelity."

I nod and swallow the lump in my throat. "True."

"Be careful, love," Rosa says. She brushes a stray strand of hair behind my ear. When I look at her, I suddenly see the lines around her eyes. She's getting older. We all are.

"He just... shuts down," I say softly. "He... doesn't seem like he wants to hurt me, but at the same time, how could I not be hurt if he's telling me one thing but his actions don't jive with his words?"

She sighs. "Unfortunately, there's not much you can do. You're bound to him by vows and family obligation. You should *never* allow him to abuse you, and you should never allow yourself to be taken advantage of. You know if either of those things happen, you call Romeo. You call *any* of us."

"Right." My stomach plummets. "He doesn't, though, Rosa."

How can I tell her how much I love the way he is with me? All protective. When he talks to me, I feel like I'm the center of his world. When he looks at me, I know I am.

I can't tell Rosa any of this. I'm not sure what I can.

Maybe abusive or unfaithful men pull the wool over the eyes of their lovers. But Salvatore's the type not to hide who he is or what he does. He's never pretended to be a good man.

Mario and Tavi saunter out to see us, each with a drink in hand. "You did good, little sister," Mario says with a grin. "You did real good."

Tavi's less effusive than Mario, but his eyes still twinkle at me just the same. I open my mouth to respond when Mario's phone rings. He turns away from us and glances at the screen. "Gloria," he says with a wink. Gloria, his wife, works for us as one of the private investigators. My heart gives a little twinge. I miss *all* of them.

We look away to give him privacy, but when Mario stiffens we can't help but listen.

"Are you serious? Are you *sure,* babe? You can't make an accusation like that without... okay, okay. Yeah. I will."

He's white as a ghost as he bends his head toward me. "Stay very calm. No sudden movements. Gloria's sending me texts she wants me to look at with you. She says it's urgent, and she's asking Romeo to get our guards and our car now."

A cold chill runs down my spine. I look around for Salvatore, his cousin, my mother-in-law, but none are anywhere near here.

What?

I stare as his phone vibrates with messages from Gloria.

It takes me a second to realize what I'm seeing, and when I do, it takes all of my self-control to keep myself in check. "Oh, so cute," I say, pretending I'm seeing adorable puppies or one of my nieces or nephews in case anyone is spying on us.

A picture of the blonde woman I rescued in the shop fills the screen. She's sitting with Salvatore at a bar.

Mario swipes.

She's with Cristiano.

Agnesia.

He shakes his head.

Salvatore, pushing an envelope toward her and looking over his shoulder.

Those could mean anything. That could've happened before—

Another text from Gloria.

The picture with Capo happened one hour after Marialena "rescued" the blonde. The pictures with the others were the next day when they initiated her payout. Her name is Penny Marcioni. She's a well-known con artist hired by his family. Marialena was set up.

I look up at Mario and blink. His face is a mask, unreadable. His phone beeps again, and we both look down.

She's in grave danger. GET HER OUT OF THERE NOW.

My heart plummets. All of it was a lie. He set me up. I'm so naïve, I believed he actually loved me.

"Let me get my things," I whisper.

"We have no time, Marialena," Rosa whispers back. "We'll bring our car around. We have to leave *now*, before Romeo goes after him. God, he'll start a war…"

"Good," I say between clenched teeth. I hated Cristiano and Agnesia, now I hate the whole family, all of them, and their underhanded, conniving, betraying ways.

"Not good. You don't know what you're saying," she whispers. "Trust me, it's never good when two families war. Innocent people will die."

My throat tightens. Rosa sees the look on my face and hers falls as she drapes an arm around me.

"It'll be okay. Trust me. It hurts now, but it'll be okay." It worked out for her because she ended up with Santo in the end. But me? I thought I loved him. I gave my virginity to him. I gave my *heart* to him.

I nod and try to put on a brave face but can't stop the tears from falling. I swipe at them angrily. I have no time to cry. There will be time for that later.

Rosa takes my hand and tugs me along. I hold my head high, pretending that nothing's wrong. I smile at those we pass, doing everything in my power not to betray that I'm heartbroken, hurt, and angry.

"There," Rosa says, as a silver Mercedes swings in front. "Get in."

Behind us I hear the unmistakable sound of a gun being cocked and an oily voice. "Did you really think it would be that easy?"

CHAPTER TWENTY

Salvatore

I SHOULD BE with my wife. I should be walking around inside with my gorgeous woman on my arm, playing the part of newlywed Don while the music plays and my friends and enemies ply us with wine and gifts. Instead, I'm brooding in our theater, drinking whiskey while I ride the tail of a high.

Jesus.

I don't know what to do with the knowledge that my wife's family was responsible for my father's death. I want to kick Romeo's ass. I don't give a shit that he was a teen. But most of all, I'm mad at myself for not realizing the most obvious thing from the beginning.

I should've known.

How can I go on and pretend all is well when it isn't?

How can I be anything but a coward if I don't avenge my father's death?

Would anyone have any respect for me if they knew what I did?

So many questions. So many twists and turns. And for once in a really, really long time, I'm fucking sick of living this life of betrayal and angst, wealth and sin, lies and manipulation.

And Marialena. *God.*

I never planned on loving her. She was only supposed to be a means to an end, a pawn in the game we play daily. She would've been roped into a loveless marriage sooner or later, I reasoned. Why not to someone who would lavish her with wealth and not abuse her?

As if that makes anything fucking better.

God.

No matter how I roll the dice, I lose. I fucking lose. There's no winning any of this.

I finish off my drink and get to my feet when the door opens and two guards come in with Cristiano in their lead.

"You gotta get your ass out there," Cristiano says, his face a mask of concern. I don't trust him. I feel my spine stiffen immediately.

"Oh?" I don't like him telling me I "have to" do anything. "Why's that?"

"Because your pretty little wife's trying to run away," he says. "Lucky for you, she's left a trail of breadcrumbs."

What?

I grab his shirt front and yank him straight off the floor. "What the fuck are you talking about?"

"Dunno what her deal is, but they brought a car around and tried to get her out of here."

"Did you ward her off?"

"Of course I did," he says with a lewd grin. "Bring her in!" he yells over his shoulder. I drop him.

One of our guards brings Marialena in. Her hair's askew and her dress is torn. There's a smear of lipstick across her cheek, and one of her lips is swollen. I clench my fists in rage. I don't care what she did, I'll make whoever hurt her suffer before they die.

"Don't put me anywhere near him," she says, turning her face away from me. "Let me *go!*"

A cold detachment settles into my chest.

"Where do you think you're going?" I don't mean the question to come out as a snarl. I want to snatch her to me and lock her up, then find out whoever hurt her and punish them.

"Bring the others in," Cristiano says. They drag Mario and Romeo in next. They're cuffed and obviously furious.

"You played us, Capo," Romeo says.

I stare at him, trying to get a hold of my fury, trying to process the accusation. "What the hell are you talking about? You're the one who's trying to take my wife from me." I try to temper my rage. Something's not adding up here. The Rossis wouldn't have let me take her, wed her, fuck her, only to come and try to take her home again. Only a fool would do something so blatantly stupid, and Romeo Rossi is no fool.

"Sit them down. We'll talk in a minute," I tell my guard. I jerk my chin at Marialena. She won't look at me, silent tears falling down her cheeks.

My voice is deadly calm, almost a whisper. "First things first. Who tore her dress?" I ask.

Silence.

I pull out my gun and cock it, put it at Cristiano's temple. His buggy eyes narrow on me. "You wouldn't dare."

"Who. Fucking. Tore. Her. Dress?" I ask again.

One of the guards raises a shaky hand. "She tried to get away. Cristiano told me to restrain her. She wouldn't cooperate. When I did, the dress—"

He falls to the floor with a bullet between his eyes. Direct hit to the t-spot.

"I was merciful on him because he was following Cristiano's orders," I say coldly to the rest of them. "Who bloodied her lip? Tell me, or I'll line every one of you up and kill you execution style until I have an answer."

Another guard I don't know starts to cry. Fucking bastard. I wouldn't want him working for me knowing he'd fall apart like this anyway.

He's next. His body falls beside the first.

"Did anyone else lay a finger on her?"

Silence.

I look to Marialena. "Did anyone else touch you?"

"Other than your cousin?" she says coldly. "No."

Cristiano ducks, but he's too slow. The first punch knocks out teeth. The second leaves him winded and doubled over. The third has him on his knees vomiting blood.

There are grave consequences if I kill him, but God I wish I could.

Federico stands to the side, his gun poised. "Where are the rest of them? I want all the Rossis here, immediately."

"You won't get away with this," Romeo says. "Doesn't matter what you do to us. We already know what you did. We know how you set her up. You could kill every one of us here, and my family will hunt you down. I've already alerted the Montavios, and they're assembling now."

"You of all people should know no one levels accusations against me without suffering, Rossi. But if you're unconscious and unable to talk, you're no use to me, so I'll let this slide with a warning."

Marialena glares at me. "You set me up, Salvatore," she says, and her voice breaks. "How could you? How *could* you? I thought you were better than that."

"I have no idea what the fuck any of you are talking about." I pinch the bridge of my nose and ignore the stabbing pain in my temples. I feel as if my head will explode. Outside the room, I hear our guests arriving, cars parking, the distant sound of glasses clinking.

Her voice wavers. "You told us you were marrying Castellano's daughter. You took *me* as punishment because I interfered. That woman I rescued was not Erica Castellano, and you know it."

I don't speak at first. The Rossis may take this as an admission of my guilt, but I have no idea what she's talking about and need to hear the entire story before I piece together who's at fault here.

"Who told you that?"

"Don't tell him anything." Mario speaks up.

"To what end?" I ask him. "You're leveling an accusation against me that would start a war. You've tried to take my bride from me, another act of war. I'll do what I have to. So will you. But before we put half our families six feet under, I deserve some fucking answers."

"It's unlike you to play dumb," Marialena chides. I hate the way her eyes brim with tears, as if she's gutted that I betrayed her. It's getting harder and harder to hold my temper back. I want to hold her to me and shake her at the same time.

"Who. Told. You?"

"You have investigators," Romeo says. "And so do we."

I turn to Mario. "Your wife, then?" I know who they are. I know every one of their roles. The momentary widening of his eyes corroborates my suspicion though no one speaks.

"You leave my wife out of this!" Mario wrestles with the guard that holds him, and reaches for his gun with his cuffed hands.

I spit out my words, so angry at whoever's done this to us, my hand shakes on my weapon. I cock the pistol. "Drop your weapon and ask her where she got the information."

"We're not playing into this, Capo," Romeo says. "We know what your—"

"And I know your family was responsible for my father's death!" I turn to face him. "I have every right to demand you give Marialena to me based on that knowledge alone. You know I'm entitled to retribution. You know what I have to do."

Romeo's gaze registers nothing but cold calculation. He knew, then. "So that's why you set us all up. That's why you manipulated us. Why not state it up front? Why the convoluted games?"

"I don't play games, Rossi."

"But you do!" Marialena yells. Her voice trembles as she turns away. "You told me you loved me."

And I meant it. I fucking meant it.

Mario lunges at me. Someone shoots a gun. Someone else screams. I grab for Marialena, jerk her to me, and push her beneath me as Romeo attempts to do the same. We each have one of her hands as if we're trying to tear her in two.

"Let her go," I tell him. "She's mine."

"I'm no one's!" she screams, and wrenches her hand from Romeo. I reach for her, drag her over to me, and hold her to my chest. I restrain her with one arm and train my gun on the others.

"Mario's wife Gloria told you this. I'm assuming there are reasons for her accusations."

"You cannot talk your way out of this," Romeo growls at me. "You admitted yourself you wanted retribution for your father."

"I didn't know your father killed mine until today. If you give me a fucking chance to talk, you might learn something. All of you put your fucking weapons down and listen before we start a war we can't end." I don't want to kill them, not like this, with half-truths coming at us like wayward arrows.

"He's lying," Tavi says.

"Am I?" I ask him. "You're a detective now, too?"

"We have evidence that you were with the con artist who tricked Marialena."

"You keep saying that. I want proof."

"Wait."

Marialena's stopped struggling in my arms. "We can make accusations all day long." She has a strange look on her face. "Salvatore may be ruthless, but he's brutally honest. It isn't like him to lie."

"It makes sense, though," Mario says, glaring at me.

"I don't trust him," Orlando says.

Romeo takes a step toward me and I brandish my gun.

BOOM

A shot rings out. We all still. Marialena glares at all of us, her gun in hand. "I have *not* given up everything that ever had meaning to me just to lose it all." Steel laces her voice, her gorgeous eyes flitting from me to her siblings then back to me.

A knock sounds at the door. Silence reigns for seconds. Another tentative knock.

I steady my voice. "Who is it?"

"Jared, sir."

I open my mouth to tell him to go away, but before I do, Marialena speaks up. "We can't talk right now," she says firmly but gently. "You need to go away."

"It's urgent!"

Cursing, I drag her over to the door with me and turn the knob. Wide, terrified eyes look up and meet mine.

"Let me in," he whispers. "Please. I have to tell you something." He looks over his shoulder. "If they hear me, they'll kill me."

"Talk. It better be fucking important."

I ignore Marialena's look of reproach and Romeo's stance that tells me he's willing to throw down if I hurt the boy.

When he sees Cristiano unconscious on the ground in front of him, he takes a step back.

"What is it?" I demand.

"If he hears me…"

"Rossi, see if he's conscious."

Romeo kicks him. Cristiano doesn't move.

"Nope."

Jared speaks in a rush of words, his voice barely above a whisper. "I couldn't help but overhear," he says. "I was sent to the storeroom to get extra chairs for the guests. I overheard your mother and cousin talking."

I draw in a deep breath and release it. "Let's hear it."

"Your mother said the message she sent to the Rossis was received. She said they fell for it, you didn't know, and now they'd wait for everything to play out. I don't know the details, sir, but when I heard the fighting—" He looks from me to Marialena. "I don't want you two to hurt each other. I don't want anyone to get hurt."

Marialena reaches for him and gives him a huge hug before she turns around and levels her gaze at the rest of us. "Put your guns away and let's figure this out already before you dumbasses hurt each other."

CHAPTER

Salvatore

. . .

WE DECIDE to continue to play along for now. I want to see how my mother and cousin handle things when they believe I've fallen for what they did.

So I take Marialena by the arm and make a public display of marching her back to our room. I order her siblings to be brought along with us, restrained by my men. Cristiano's come to, following us with a scowl. Jared's been dismissed and kept safely with my guards until I deal with my cousin and mother.

Cristiano has had his weapon taken from him. He has no idea what we discussed or what role he plays in the next part of our plan.

For one brief moment, Marialena's eyes light up when she sees my mother. I can almost hear her thoughts. *Ah. Just the woman I want to see.*

That might be a first. But as soon as my mother turns the corner, Marialena's gone back to angry and resistant.

"Agnesia! Tell your son to let me go. He has no right to manhandle me like this!"

Not surprisingly, my mother looks pleased that my wife's not on good terms with me right now. "Salvatore, our guests are arriving," she says, unable to hide the pleasure in her voice. "Surely whatever it is your wife has done to displease you can wait?"

"They betrayed us, Mother."

I watch her closely and note the way she looks quickly to Cristiano. The quick look confirms my suspicion. I want to toss Marialena behind me and grab my mother and Cristiano instead, but I have to stick to the plan.

Marialena's words come back to me.

They betray you, Salvatore. And they're worse than your most mortal enemies, because they earn your trust before they stab you in the back.

"Did they?" With a sigh, my mother shakes her head. "I expect nothing less from the Rossis."

Marialena tightens in my grip.

"You tend to our guests," I tell her. "I'll deal with them privately."

"People will ask where your new wife is."

"Tell them she's not feeling well."

My mother nods quietly.

"Cristiano, clean yourself up and go with my mother." They leave as I take Marialena and the Rossis back to my room.

"Let them go."

Federico hesitates. "Boss…"

"Let them *go*. If I have to tell you again—"

Warily, Federico obeys, as do the others.

"All of you, sit down. No weapons unless it's necessary. None of you pulls a weapon on my family." I jerk my head toward Mario. "Get Gloria on the line." Then toward Federico. "And you let us hear the conversation with Cristiano and my mother."

Mario gets Gloria on Facetime. She answers immediately, sitting at a large desk surrounded by monitors. At first, she doesn't speak, but when she sees all of us, she addresses Mario.

"Mario, what's going on here?"

"We need to dig into the intel you gave us."

When she tips her head to the side curiously, he continues. "Where did you get the footage showing Capo with Penny Marcioni?"

"From the club."

Her fingers are already flying over a keyboard while the monitors behind her flash. "They allowed me access to their— *oh. Oh, shit.*"

"What, babe?" Mario's pacing.

"We were given this footage when I asked club security, and they were pretty easy to convince," she says with a sigh. "I should've known better. *God.* The time stamp's been tampered with. I didn't think to check it."

"What does that mean?" Mario asks.

"It means the footage was from a few days prior to the day she met Marialena," I supply. "I'd never met

Castellano's daughter. I was introduced to her as such. My mother and Cristiano arranged the marriage when I was away, and I knew it was the next logical step. As far as I knew, she escaped, and Marialena was to blame. I acted on that knowledge."

Romeo exchanges a look with his brothers.

"You don't have to believe me," I tell them. "We'll get to the bottom of this. We already know someone's fucked with the time stamp, making it look like I was corroborating with her. So no one sent this to you, Gloria?"

"I got an anonymous tip," she says on a sigh. "*Ugh.* I fucked this all up, I am so sorry."

The message my mother sent to the Rossis is sitting right in Gloria's goddamn inbox.

"It's not your fault," Mario says, glaring at me as if to challenge me to defy him. "Gloria, stand by," Mario instructs as Federico holds up his hand.

"Go."

He taps a button on a small speaker and my mother and Cristiano's voices fill the small room. Cristiano has no idea we put a small microphone on him when he was still unconscious. The plan is for him to be alone with my mother to see if they'll give us anything to go on.

"As of right now, he believes Marialena interfered with his wedding with Erica Castellano. He believes he's justified in taking her, but he's pissed because he knows the Rossis killed his father."

"Right. Perfect. Rossi will see the footage soon and know that Salvatore tricked them, only he doesn't know the Rossis believe that yet. Rossi may be holding back his trump card. Now we have the Rossis and Salvatore convinced each betrayed the other."

The voices become jumbled, and it's hard to hear them.

"—kill each other, we win."

Romeo and I meet each other's eyes as their underhanded plan unfolds before us.

"They wanted me to marry you," I tell Marialena. "Wanted our family wed to the Rossis. I wanted that, too." I blow out a breath. Romeo looks at his brothers. "I didn't know your family was responsible for my father's death. Did you, Romeo? Nothing but the truth, brother."

"Not until tonight. Yes, I knew my father killed someone back in the quarry. We never identified who it was. I was a kid. My only concern was that my father didn't get caught, because I knew he'd be put away."

"They wanted you to think I set you up. They wanted to cause a war between us." I shake my head.

"Why?" Romeo asks.

"Because his cousin wants the throne," Marialena says through clenched teeth. "They knew it would be a lot easier to get rid of Salvatore if they could blame *you*. If the two of you fought each other because of revenge. Him, because our family was responsible for his father's death. You, because he set you up." She shakes her head and gives me a sidelong look. "What should we do about that, husband?"

I love when she calls me *husband*.

"We go out. We confront each other. We get them close enough to believe we're going to do exactly what they wanted us to." I scowl. "Then you'll let me handle the rest."

Romeo nods. "And in the end?"

"Let's get to the end first."

CHAPTER

Marialena

I KNEW he couldn't trust them, but I had no idea they would stoop so far, so *low*. I should know better, though. These are the lives we lead. These are the roles we play. Betrayal and revenge are our sun and moon, orchestrating our days and lives.

Me, though? If I had my way? Loyalty and love will *always* prevail. And I will work hard to see that through.

When I took vows to Salvatore, I didn't do so blindly. I knew exactly what I was getting into, exactly what I committed to. I know I'm a hopeless romantic, and only wish this time my romanticism doesn't lead me – or all of us – astray.

I'm frozen in place when Salvatore's blue eyes pierce mine. I read pain in his eyes and want to touch him. My own heart squeezes in sympathy. Gently, I lay my finger on his shoulder.

"What is it?" I whisper, unwilling to share a private moment with my family all around us.

"I don't want to do this publicly."

For one moment, so brief I almost miss it, the ruthless Don is gone, and in his place I see a man, once a boy, broken by his family's conditional love and selfish ways.

"Of course not," I say, my voice trembling with emotion. "Let's take this to the theater. Our guests are suitably entertained for the moment, I'm sure." Staff has continued to ply our guests with food and drink. I give Salvatore a wink. "We'll be fashionably late is all. I *will* get to that dessert table, Salvatore."

His heated gaze makes my heart beat a little faster. "I'll see to it."

I watch him take out his cell phone and call Cristiano.

"Meet me in the theater and bring my mother. We have to deal with the Rossis, and I want both of you present."

"On my way."

Even from where I'm standing, I can hear the glee in Cristiano's voice.

He thinks he's won.

The dark recesses of the theater seem a suitable place for a confrontation. Salvatore flicks on the lights just as his mother and Cristiano enter.

"What's happened, son?" Agnesia asks.

"Shut the door, please." Cristiano shuts it with a bang.

The deep etches along Salvatore's forehead look carved from stone as he scowls. "Rossi knew all along that his father killed mine."

"So that's why we're here, then?" Romeo asks. "Seems to me there's been more than one act of betrayal, Capo."

Agnesia's eyes actually *light up.* I want to slap her. Who could do such a thing to her own flesh and blood? My family may be crazy, but they are loyal to the core.

"What the fuck are you talking about?" Salvatore growls. He cocks his gun. I'd think he was a good actor, but he isn't acting. I know exactly why he's so angry.

"You never planned on marrying into the Castellano family, did you?" I didn't know Romeo was such a good actor. My heart hammers, waiting for the first gunshot, the first show of blood. Someone's going down, and soon. "You set my sister up and made her out to be the one at fault." Romeo faces Salvatore, his own gun drawn.

"Stop, both of you!" I say, turning to Agnesia. "Do something!"

She only shakes her head. "I can't," she says sorrowfully. "This is between the two of them."

"Oh, is it?" I clench my fists by my sides as Cristiano's recorded voice fills the small theater, amplified by state-of-the-art speakers.

"He believes Marialena interfered with his wedding with Erica Castellano..."

Cristiano reaches for his weapon before he realizes he has none. He freezes when he feels the cold metal of Mario's gun at his temple.

Agnesia's voice joins Cristiano's. *"Now we have the Rossis and Salvatore convinced each betrayed the other. If they kill each other, we win."*

Their conversation reverberates through the theater, surround sound making their voices sound ominous.

I note the very second Agnesia realizes the gig is up and we all know the truth. The aloof façade fades as her eyes widen with fear.

"He made me do it, Salvatore!" Agnesia says, pointing a shaking finger at Cristiano.

"Is that right?" I shiver at the coldness in Salvatore's tone. "Do tell."

"You *bitch*." Cristiano's eyes shoot daggers at her. "We had a deal. A promise!"

Salvatore raises his hand to strike Cristiano. Agnesia takes her chance and lunges at *me*. I'm taken so off guard I don't expect it. Though she's slight, she's vicious. I fall to the floor with a cry and throw my hands up to deflect a blow. A shot rings out. She falls beside me heavily, shot straight through the heart. I blink, shocked to see Mario's gun pointed at her. A slim knife falls from her fingers.

Cristiano takes the opportunity to try to run. Salvatore trips him. He falls beside Agnesia, grabs her knife, and swings himself toward me. I reach for my gun, but it's too late. Salvatore's already thrown himself on top of me. Cristiano stabs his chest.

"Salvatore! No!"

Romeo steps toward us, gun raised, and in seconds puts three bullets through Cristiano's head. With cold calculation, he turns to Agnesia and finishes the job.

The weight of Salvatore's body on mine terrifies me. My hands are stained with red.

"Somebody help!" I scream, but the theater is sound-proofed and nobody hears me. I push myself to my feet and run to the door. I yank it open and scream for the staff. "Come quickly! Salvatore's been hurt!"

Hurt trying to save me because *of course*.

"I'm fine," he groans, rolling over. "Jesus, woman, relax." He gives me a faint grin. "Get the damn doc to wrap me up so we don't miss the dessert table."

"Salvatore," I breathe, tears blurring my vision. My throat feels clogged. I gingerly move his jacket and yank open the buttons of his shirt to find the knife has only grazed his skin. "Ugh. Men! Honest to God!"

Salvatore shakes his head. "God, Cristiano was a fucking pussy to the end."

I laugh through tears. "That he was."

Salvatore's men pour into the room and take in the scene. "Get me a doc, and get rid of these bodies. These two betrayed me. I have evidence I'll share later. The Rossis are innocent." He repeats what he's said as his men look on. Within minutes, everyone's run to do his bidding. As Don, he owes no one an explanation, but if I know him, he'll tell them everything.

I'm not surprised they have a house doctor like we do, who quickly tends Salvatore's wounds and doesn't even look at the dead bodies on the floor.

Federico brings him another set of clothes. I help him change.

"Rossi."

Romeo kneels on one knee beside him.

Salvatore extends his hand. "I think it's safe to say we're even, brother."

Romeo shakes his head. "I'm sorry you caught the worst of it," he says with a sigh. "But yeah, man. Let's call this a draw."

I swipe at my eyes that *will* water despite my greatest efforts. "I love both of you crazy idiots."

My husband's pale and a bit shaky but he hides it well.

"Are you sure you're okay?" I ask him as I help him change into clean clothing.

"Of course," he says with an eye roll. "I've cut myself worse shaving."

I watch his strong, masculine fingers fastening his cuff link and reach for his hand. I kiss his palm, then each of his fingers, one by one.

"We can make this work, Salvatore. I know we can." I close my eyes to stop myself from crying. We've had enough drama for one evening already.

I watch as Salvatore stills, his fingers still grazing the gilded edge of his cuff link. "C'mere," he says in a husky voice, drawing me to him. I brace myself so

I don't press against his injured side, but it's useless as he crushes me against him, his fingers tangled in my hair.

"You *will* persist in mussing up my hair and makeup, won't you?" I tsk under my breath. "Men!"

"Oh, I could do better than that," he whispers in my ear. "How about I present my wife to the masses with a 'freshly fucked' look?"

I bite my lip and pretend to think about it for a minute. "Hmm. Well… Salvatore!"

I squeal when he pinches my ass.

"Later, baby. Later. And yes, Marialena. We absolutely can and will make this work. With two stubborn-as-fuck people like me and you, we can make *anything* work."

I listen to the steady beat of his heart and sigh. "I'm sorry about your mother," I say softly. Even though she betrayed him, she was still his mother. "When my father died, I felt relief at first," I admit. "It was the end of an era of tyranny, bullying and abuse. And yet… I don't know. I guess I couldn't help but mourn, not really him, but what could've been. What should've been. You know?"

"I do," he says warmly. "I do know. And I guess eventually I'll deal with that, but for now, we have people waiting to see us and we have a show to put on. Are you ready?"

"I will be, as soon as I can put my lipstick back on for like the twelfth time," I mutter. "Hey!" I yelp when he cracks his hand across my ass. "You've been looking for a chance to do that, haven't you?"

"Mhm."

I mutter under my breath as I reapply my lipstick, but I'm at peace. My family waits for us outside this room. We've formed an alliance with them, and I no longer feel as if I have to choose sides. And after they've gone, I'll take my place here, with Salvatore, and face our new life together.

"Very impressive, husband," I tell him, looking at his reflection in the mirror. "You don't look like you took a knife for your wife at all."

"Dammit, don't I? Maybe you should put a Band-Aid on my cheek or something."

I turn and plant a kiss on his cheek. "How's that?"

His low growl rumbles straight through me. "Get out there and get some chocolate cake before I lose my mind and ravish you right here, right now."

"You say that like it would be a bad thing."

I take his hand. We walk, side by side, out of our bedroom to where our guests, my family, and the rest of our lives wait for us.

EPILOGUE
MARIALENA

Six months later

I STAND on the cliff that overlooks the rolling waters below The Castle and breathe in the familiar salt air. The air here feels different from the air outside our residence in Tampa. It's cooler, more pungent, and when the wind whips over the water, it bites my cheeks.

"So that's where you used to hide." Salvatore's deep voice rumbles in my ear as his hands span my waist. He jerks his chin at the perfect little dip below the line of visibility, where Mario and I used to hide to smoke.

"Yup. If you stand at the Pavilion outside The Castle, you can't see anything below the edge here," I explain.

"Isn't that convenient," he says with a knowing twinkle in his eye. When I first met him, I would never have believed that a man like him was capable of having a *twinkle* in his eye, but he so does.

"Salvatore," I say, drawing out each syllable. I know exactly what that look means. "Nonna's party's in ten minutes. You know that!"

Nonna's eightieth birthday only comes once, and this is a special one. It's the first time all her grandchildren are married, and the first time Salvatore and I have come to visit The Castle as a married couple. After several months of business, travel, and events where he proudly showed me off as his new wife, we finally made it back up to New England.

"Like I need more than ten minutes?" he says, as his hands tighten on my waist. I know that insistent touch all too well. Before I know what he's doing, he's got me by the hand and we're walking down the all-too-familiar steps that lead to my hiding spot.

"Mario could find us," I say, but my protests are growing weaker.

"Mario and Gloria went into town with Orlando to get the pastries. You knew that." His voice takes on a stern edge that makes my body heat deliciously. "Do I need to punish you for trying to deceive me?"

My skirt's hiked up around my waist and he's doing all sorts of wicked things to me. "No," I pant. "I'm an angel, you know that."

"You were an angel this morning," he says, his voice warm with approval. My cheeks flush hot at the memory. "That I know. But now..."

I spread my legs and grind against him. "Now I'm your little slut," I supply.

The wicked chuckle he gives me tells me he very much appreciates this response and approves. "That's right."

The fact that someone could find us sounds like such a silly notion now as my need for him thwarts all rationale. My head drops to his shoulder. I moan. My eyes flutter closed as the hint of a breeze kisses my skin, a wave crashes on the shore, and the first spasm of pleasure crests over me. "Shh," he whispers in my ear. "We wouldn't want anyone to hear you."

My reply is a garbled mess of words. I slump against him, spent.

"Hey! Marialena! Salvatore! Where are you?"

I quickly right myself and glare at him, but the wicked glint in his eye tells me he's anything but repentant. My body, still thrumming and heated, tells me it doesn't regret anything either.

"What, baby?" he whispers as he pats my belly. "Do you think they forgot about the fact you're pregnant?"

I shake my head and wag my finger at him because I'm not really sure how to come back from that.

"We're here!" I shout, just as Rosa looks over the edge.

"Ah, should've known. Of course you'd show your husband your favorite hiding spot. Careful, Lena, Mario may never forgive you." She grins. "Nonna's already hit the wine hard and is ready to party, you don't want to miss this."

Salvatore takes me by the hand, and we follow Rosa back to The Castle. Romeo's had spotlights installed, so The Castle's lit up like a thing of beauty, majestic and timeless. I imagine I'm a fairy-tale princess. My eyes grow a little misty.

"You alright?" Salvatore asks, as I brush the back of my hand across my eyes.

"Eh, pregnancy hormones," I say with a laugh. My heart is full. I love having the man that I love here, in my home, where I first learned the meaning of the word love.

"I love you," I say tremulously.

He gives my hand a little squeeze. "And I love you."

Uproarious laughter greets us when we enter the dining room. Romeo and Nonna are dancing to a lively tune piped in through overhead speakers. He can hardly keep up with her. With her ruddy cheeks and bright eyes, she's shed decades here in this dining room.

"I feel like I'm in Italy," Salvatore says. "A tune from the old country."

"Here, drink this," Mario says, plying him with a tall glass of wine. "Then you'll really feel as if you're there. You can drink two, one for you and one for Lena."

"Hey! That's not fair. Ugh, someone should've reminded me pregnant women can't drink wine."

"We all have to make sacrifices," Salvatore says with a look of utter martyrdom as he takes both glasses of wine.

Nonna sees us and smiles, her eyes a bit glassy. *"Chi si volta, e chi si gira, sempre a casa va finire!"*

I smile at her. "Always, nonna." I may travel the world and marry, have children and move away, but I will always, always have a home here at The Castle, with Nonna and my mother, my siblings and little nieces and nephews.

"Ah," Romeo says, nodding at us. "But don't forget, *Tra Moglie e Marito Non Mettere il Dito,* Nonna." *Never interfere between a husband and his wife.*

"She isn't interfering, Romeo, only reminding me that I will always have a place here with all of you."

"La famiglia e tutto," Salvatore agrees a bit gruffly, but I can tell by the way he squeezes my hand that he has no hard feelings. Though we have family, our loyalty now lies with a small, nuclear family of our own. Nonna grins at him, releases Romeo, then reaches for Salvatore's hand.

"I can't!" he protests, holding up two wineglasses to show his occupied hands.

Nonna shakes her head and tips her hand up like she's holding a phantom glass.

"Drink up, husband," I tell him with a laugh. With a grin, he drains his glasses, hands the empties to me, then joins Nonna on the dance floor. Nonna loves him because he trusts her food and the enormous platefuls he eats rival my brothers.

In the past few months, we've ceremoniously buried his cousin and mother, and he's appointed new leaders. My brothers told me they were vetted to within an inch of their lives, and I'm not surprised. They said this with no small measure of approval, though. Even though I'm a Capo now, they like to know I'm safe.

Salvatore rewarded Jared for his bravery and help, and when we couldn't locate any of his family, Salvatore begrudgingly agreed to let Jared stay. He softens Salvatore a little, even more than I do, and I know it'll only give him good practice. Both of us, really.

Much to Salvatore's exasperation, I had all of his bulletproof vests upgraded to deflect blades as well, because much to my chagrin, though bulletproof vests can deflect bullets, they can't deflect *blades* unless specifically designed to do so. Who knew? I argued that if I can't buy shoes without protection, he can't buy vests without, either. He finally agreed.

Mama exits the kitchen, laden with trays of dessert. "Come, everyone. Mangia! Even you, Salvatore. I brought your favorite."

I eye Mama. Is the decadent cake, Salvatore's favorite *bacio* with chocolate and hazelnut mousse, a peace offering?

"Grazie, Tosca," he says, giving me a secretive wink.

"Wait, I thought you got that for me?" Santo says to Mama. "You know I love that cake."

"Hands off my cake, buddy," Salvatore yells over Nonna's shoulder.

"Wait, I thought that was *my* cake," Mario says.

"You said you got it for me!" Tavi shrugs off his jacket and starts to roll up his sleeves.

"Ah, boys, you are not getting into a fight over dessert," I begin, as Romeo clears his throat.

"But *I* was the one that asked for the *bacio*."

Oh, God. They are *not* getting into a fight over this. "No one touches my cake," Salvatore says, ignoring me entirely.

"You guys. Hey! Hello!"

"Let them eat cake," Rosa says as she sips her wine. "He has to fight over food once in a while, Marialena, or he'll never really be one of us, will he?"

"Boys. Boys!" Mama says as the double doors to the dining room open and several members of staff follow her, bearing large platters with several more cakes. Mama beams. "I got one for each of you. See?"

Romeo releases Mario from the headlock he discreetly put him in, and Salvatore resumes his dance with Nonna. Tavi grunts, and Santo kisses both of Mama's cheeks. "We won't each need a cake, now, Mama," he says. "Really, that was unnecessary."

Rosa shrugs beside me. "Not so sure about that."

I exhale. Phew. So no one will be fist-fighting over cake today.

"Ahh, drinking our wine, eating our desserts, and dancing with Nonna?" Mario says softly, so only I hear. "Your husband knows how to convince our family to love him. The only question is, has he convinced *you*?"

"Oh, he has," I say with a smile. "Nonna!" I raise my voice loud enough for everyone to hear. "I have an announcement."

Nonna finally lets Salvatore go. I hold my hands out to him. Bending toward me, he kisses each of my cheeks before leading me to the dance floor.

Mama looks at me as Salvatore swings me out in front of him. "Yes?" she asks. "Well, don't leave us in suspense, for goodness' sake."

I pat my belly. "*Stiamo avendo due gemelli!*"

"Twins?" Mama gasps.

Cheers erupt all around us. Nonna's making loud proclamations and blessings on our *bambini*, Romeo opens another bottle of wine, and Mama's eyes shine.

I bask in the warmth of Salvatore's embrace as we navigate the dance floor, my brothers argue over the last of the pastries, and my sister and Vittoria start compiling a list of baby names.

"I love you," I whisper in Salvatore's ear. "And thank you."

"For what, beautiful?"

We dance, the lights ahead flickering like a chandelier in a ballroom. "For everything," I whisper, my throat tight. "Stupid pregnancy hormones."

I blink, one lone tear rolling down my cheek.

"Thank *you*," he says.

"For what?" I wink.

"For proving me wrong."

"Did I?"

"Of course." He twirls me out, then tugs me back to his chest in time to the music. "I thought marriage was only business and love was for fools."

"Ahh. The classic, age-old bachelor's tale, then. So you're thanking me for not leaving you a bachelor?"

"I'm thanking you for making me the happiest man alive."

We dance, encircled in one another's arms. Two families, united. Two hearts, entwined. One future, together.

BONUS EPILOGUE
FROM THE AUTHOR

Thank you for reading Oath of Submission!

I hope you've enjoyed this book!

Would you like to read a free bonus epilogue?

Who wants to see more?!

Get yours here: BONUS EPILOGUE

PREVIEW
STOLEN PROPERTY

Book 1 of the new *"Masters of Corsica"* series

Chapter 1

Fabien

Her name is Nicolette.

Gray-green eyes as soft as velvet.

Rosy red cheeks and a heart-shaped mouth that—

"Fabien."

I look up at my mother from my steak, fork and knife poised in each hand.

"Are you listening at all?"

I'm not used to eating with other people. This is the first time I've come back to my childhood home in three months.

"He's doing it again," Thayer mutters.

I work alone, I work long hours, and I work in quiet, unless I need to call in back-up.

Except when I come home.

Today, though, my mind is a million miles away because of the security footage I saw before I joined them for dinner. They think I'm focused on work.

I'm not interested in eating. I'm interested in the woman with the delicate but proud features, and an abundance of dark curls that grace her shoulders. The woman with eyes both intelligent and strong but curious and compelling enough to make me wonder... how easily would she submit to me?

The woman I'll buy.

"Fabien. Please. This matters. Did you hear a word I said?"

"I heard a few," I say in protest. "Something about... wine, and appetizers, and a live band for Antoine's wedding."

"What's on your mind?" Maman asks curiously.

I will own Nicolette.

I've already sent a message to Gwen to cancel Nicolette's clients for the rest of the night.

I definitely can't tell her that. I won't tell anyone. I don't need anyone to stand in my way because I will have this woman no matter the cost.

"Crunching the numbers?" Thayer asks. "Where are we profit-wise?"

"Boys, if you're talking about what I think you are..." Maman begins with a wince.

"Twelve million."

"Compared to last year's numbers, the tight business we run in Corsica is booming, thanks to an influx of tourists," Thayer says.

"It's about damn time. Given that it's one of many businesses we run, we're in a good place. And if your plan to expand works, we could double our profit in two years' time. The plan's contingent on many factors, though."

"Slipping under the radar?" Thayer supplies.

The ancient buildings and cobblestoned streets of Corsica, under the shadow of majestic mountains, aren't the only things that are outdated. Hard to imagine the laws still prohibit paid prostitution. Brothel-keeping and pimping carry the heaviest sentences of all.

Goddamn Puritans.

Why people think sex should be so carefully guarded remains a complete enigma to me. Sex, like food, is meant to be consumed, and healthy humans hunger for it. If we're honest, my job, then, as the owner and proprietor of *Maison de la Vallée Cachée,* the most high-end gentlemen's club in Corsica, means I'm basically no different than a restaurant owner.

"Fabien. We lost you again."

Maman releases a belabored sigh and pinches the bridge of her nose. I watch as she places her knife and fork down so she can give me a look best saved for an errant child. "Fabien." She repeats my name, this time pouring a wealth of guilt into each syllable. "You're the eldest. You should know better," she chides. "Tell him, please."

I take a large bite of steak and grind it with my teeth. Maman's the only person on the planet I allow to admonish me without recourse.

"She wants you to get a date," Thayer says. "No bouncing around the wedding venue like a damn ball in a pinball machine."

I don't bother to hide my look of disgust. "Really? That's the best you can come up with?"

His eyes snap to my mother, then back to me. "In polite company, of course."

"Of course." I look back to Maman. The woman has the patience of a saint and a spine of steel, a lethal combination in our circle. Tonight, I notice bags under her eyes I haven't seen before. I wonder if she's sleeping well. She hasn't, not since my father died. Five years is a long time to go without sleep.

I don't *date.* I take what I want.

I want Nicolette.

I will own her.

"I don't want anyone to *talk,* Fabien," she explains. "I'm just so tired of people talking."

"Why do you care?" I shrug, take another bite of steak, and chew and swallow before I continue. "People talk no matter what you do. No matter what any of us do. And if anyone talks about *you,* they'll answer to me."

"And me," Thayer chimes in.

"Yes, yes," Maman replies. "I've no doubt that my sons will defend my honor to the death, and I thank you. Where's Lyam? He said he'd be here."

"Haven't seen him," Thayer says, cutting his steak methodically into neat little squares before he eats.

Maman sighs. "Boys, there's more to it."

"Is there?" I continue to eat my dinner, but I'm already mentally on my way to Corsica, tonight.

She goes on about her sister's bragging about her son's engagements and marriages and the insidious implication that the three of us will never marry.

"Why do you care what Marguerite thinks about us?" Thayer replies. Of the three of us, Thayer most resembles my mother. They share the same dark blue eyes, olive complexion, and thick, wavy black hair. But as alike as they are physically, they couldn't be more different personality-wise. Thayer's known as *Le Sauvage,* The Savage, a nickname he's earned by being one of the most ruthless in our number. My mother, on the other hand, was never cut out for our lifestyle. She's far too tender.

"You shouldn't give it another thought. We don't."

"I *know,*" she continues, barely hiding a grimace. "And that's part of the problem, isn't it?" Shaking her head, she looks heavenward. "Why? Why couldn't you have given me *one daughter*? Just one?"

"Touché, Maman," Thayer says.

"I ask so little of you," she continues. "All I want is for you to bring dates. That's it."

"When's the wedding?" I ask. I don't give a shit about details like that.

Maman looks pained. "This weekend."

"Ahhh." Thayer says with a smile. "You don't want them talking about our business in Corsica. Admit it, that's what you're worried about."

Maman flushes, the color adorning her high cheekbones as if she just came in from a winter storm.

"Ah ah," Thayer chides. "You just completely gave yourself away."

"And what if I do? Is it a crime to ask your sons to attend a family wedding with dates to keep the loose lips from yammering on and on?"

We do love to tease her.

"It's not a problem, Maman," I finally say, when I really do fear she's taking us too seriously. "I'll make sure Lyam and Thayer get dates. I'll get one of my own."

Thayer's eyes narrow on me, but the quirk of his lips warns me ahead of time. "Planning a trip to Corsica, then?"

I look at him sharply.

"Thayer!" Maman's eyes widen comically. "He wouldn't!"

Of course I'm going to Corsica.

"Fabien," Maman says reproachfully. "You wouldn't… couldn't… hire one of *them* to accompany you? Would you?"

"Not hire an escort for the evening? Why the hell not?"

Someone who doesn't expect anything more than a paycheck? Done. Of course I'm going to Corsica.

My phone rings.

I look at the unknown number on my phone, and stare. Nobody but my family has this number. I answer on the second ring.

"Yes."

"Monsieur Gerard. Just who I was hoping to talk to."

I turn away from my mother and face Thayer. "Who is this?" I jerk my chin at Thayer who leaps from his chair and runs to the office. From there he can easily tap a phone call if I can keep them on the phone long enough.

"We know about your group in Corsica. We know who you're working with. And we know where your brother is."

Ice pulses through my veins.

Fuck.

Behind me I can hear Maman's worried questions. "Who is it? Fabian, who is it? Where is Lyam?"

"I asked who this is," I say, in a deadly whisper.

Nobody threatens my family. Nobody comes after us without serious consequences.

"In two nights, the talisman of Napoleon will arrive at the club. The Lyon family will take it into their possession. If you want your brother back, you will take it from them. It will be brought to The Underground. Your cousin Milo is head of security. Get what you can from him. You will come in disguise. You will obtain this talisman. And you will bring it to Les Bains de Caldane by sunrise the next morning."

The call disconnects.

Maman is on her feet ringing her hand. "Was it about your brother? Where is Lyam?" She's been through enough with us to suspect something's awry.

"I don't know," I tell her honestly. "But I'll do whatever I can."

"Fabien—"

"Don't try to stop me."

Thayer comes into the room and shakes his head. "The call was too short and expertly blocked."

"Of course." I blow out a breath. The girl with the velvet eyes will be my ticket into The Underground. "I'm going to Corsica."

READ MORE…

USA Today bestselling author Jane Henry pens stern but loving alpha heroes, feisty heroines, and emotion-driven happily-ever-afters. She writes what she loves to read: kink with a tender touch. Jane is a hopeless romantic who lives on the East Coast with a houseful of children and her very own Prince Charming.

You can find Jane here:

Jane Henry's Newsletter

Jane Henry's Facebook Reader Group

Jane's Website

- bookbub.com/profile/jane-henry
- facebook.com/janehenryromance
- instagram.com/janehenryauthor
- amazon.com/Jane-Henry/e/B01BYAQYYK
- tiktok.com/@janehenryauthor

Made in the USA
Columbia, SC
27 April 2023